Slap Shot Scandal

USA TODAY BESTSELLING AUTHOR

KARA KENDRICK

You miss 100% of the shots you don't take.

WAYNE GRETZKY

Editing: Nicole McCurdy/Emerald Edits & Beth Hale/Magnolia Author Services
Cover Photography: Cadwallader Photography, LLC
Cover Design: Emily Wittig Designs

For the eldest daughter people pleasers —
Sometimes you have to choose you.
Do it.

CHAPTER 1
WESTON

Big Boss: Meeting at HQ at 8 AM. Don't
be late

R ed-hot panic surges through me as I stare at the
message on the screen. Is this about getting beat
in the second round of the playoffs? We barely
scraped through to five games. But surely that's no reason
to call an emergency team meeting.

Scrubbing my hand over my jaw, I tap out a quick
message to my triplet brothers, Bennett and Callum.

Weston: You clowns awake?

A nanosecond passes before Callum responds.

Goalie boy: Barely. What the fuck is the
meeting about, Cap?

Weston: No idea

> Goalie boy: Bro, what good are you?

It doesn't take long for Bennett to jump in.

> Puck bunny: I've been asking him that for years. You're slow on the uptake, Cal
>
> Goalie boy: Shut the fuck up, Bennett. YOU know what it's about, smart guy?
>
> Puck bunny: No. But this time it doesn't involve me. Thank fuck

So my brothers are as in the dark as I am. At least neither of them seems to be involved. Thank god for small favors. Not that Callum gets into trouble, but every once in a while Bennett manages to drag him into the mix.

After all, Bennett earned the nickname Puck Bunny. He loves the ladies as much as they love him. With that predilection comes trouble—with the media, other players, rival teams. Hell, even the women themselves. I've had to bail him out more than a few times. And not to pat myself on the back, but if I wasn't team captain, he'd likely be in a helluva lot more trouble.

> Weston: No ideas then?
>
> Goalie boy: Nope
>
> Puck bunny: Nada

My gut twists into a tight knot as I kick out of the sheets and lumber over to the wall of windows overlooking the Manhattan skyline. The first weak rays of light spill into my bedroom, the sky a milky gray. The muted tone perfectly matches my mood.

What in the hell is this gonna be about?
I bet Coach knows.

> Weston: Hey Coach. Know what the
> meeting's about this AM?

I wait for the three swirling dots to appear, like they always do. But nothing happens. Uncharacteristic for Coach not to text back immediately. He's faster on the draw than Callum, his cell practically glued to his hand when we're not on the ice.

A few minutes pass and all I get back is radio silence.

Well, fuck. Coach probably doesn't even know.

Rolling my shoulders up and back to relieve the tension lodged between the blades, I hit the shower to get ready for the mystery meeting.

Thirty minutes later, I drive past a line of media vans, reporters milling about on the sidewalk in front of the arena. Normally, a few paparazzi hang out, hoping for a shot. But today, this place is a circus. Odd, considering we're out of the playoffs.

A few hawk-eyed photographers recognize my car, bright flashes of light popping and reflecting off the windshield. Instinctively, I duck my head and pull my ball cap lower to hide my face. I'd rather not be on the front page this morning, especially after losing in the playoffs.

What the hell's going on? Why is the media here during off-season?

I gratefully roll down the street to the side entrance of the arena's parking garage, happy to avoid the press. Swiping my key card, the gate lifts and I idle through to my personal parking spot.

CAPTAIN.

The title still sends a thrill shooting through me. Tangible evidence of hours sacrificed on the ice for the team and the game.

If only we'd had a better season. One that ended with a heavy-ass cup held high above my head.

We'll get 'em next season, I know it.

I throw my Porsche into park and hustle through the metal doors, half-jogging down the concrete hallway. One I've traversed many times before.

Somehow, this time feels different—and not in a good way.

My morning coffee rolls around my empty stomach like battery acid. I regret the split-second decision to bypass the meal plan egg frittatas. Seems like a big mistake right about now.

Rounding the corner toward the conference rooms, I run straight into a petite blonde, her attention locked on the phone in her hand.

"Oof." She collides with my chest, bouncing back slightly and wobbling on her sky-high heels.

I reach out and grab her by the elbow, steadying her. "I got you."

"Oh my gosh, I'm so sorry." She awkwardly pats at my chest, her delicate hand gliding over the cotton of my T-shirt. She's a tiny thing, her head barely clearing my pecs.

"I wasn't watching where I was going, I've never been here before…" The apples of her cheeks turn pink as she gazes up at me through thick lashes, hazel eyes locked on mine.

"It's fine. No biggie." She's so close to me I catch the sweet scent of shampoo drifting up from her long golden hair, her breath warm on my skin. An electric zing shoots through me right below her palm.

She bites at the corner of her glossy lip, and my eyes dart to the spot before I tear them away. I've never had any sort of HR complaint about me and I'm not about to start today.

"You lost?" I tip my head, trying to place her. She's definitely not on staff. Or at least she doesn't work directly with players. Not wearing that tight pink dress perfectly molded to her curves and heels. Clearly not a trainer or nutritionist.

"No. I'm in the right place. Main conference room, right?" She glances to the right, hooking her thumb at the open door, the room buzzing with people.

"Yeah. That's where the meeting is."

"Okay, great. Thanks. And sorry again about running into you." A blush creeps up her neck, almost matching the bright pink shade of her dress.

I rake a hand through my hair, trying to ignore the sudden acceleration of my heart rate. Has to be from racing to the meeting.

"Cap, what's up?" One of the trainers smacks me on the back as he passes by.

The woman's cell buzzes in her hand and she flashes me a quick smile, then scurries away, her heels clicking loudly as she moves down the hallway.

"Dude, any idea what this meeting's about?" Vic, one of the veteran players, mutters as I swing into the conference room.

I shrug. "None."

But obviously it's a big fucking deal, considering every seat in the room's filled with personnel of all types. Players, athletic trainers, assistant coaches, equipment managers, the community relations coordinator.

Everyone but Coach.

What the fuck?

I glance at my watch. 7:55. Maybe he's running late.

Callum waves me over to the corner and I stalk in his direction.

"What's up?" I shoot my brother a sideways glance, taking the spot on the wall next to him. Dark shadows ring his eyes. No doubt he's as haunted by the shitty playoff run as me.

"No idea. You see Bennett out there?"

I shake my head. "No. He'll be late. Always is."

Folding my arms over my chest, I lean back and wait along with everyone else. Chatter in the room amplifies as the seconds tick by, my nerves thrumming. Callum's quiet —per the usual—and I don't mind a bit.

Bennett strolls in at 7:59, acting like he's out for a Sunday freaking stroll. He shoots us a wave as he strides in our direction, joining us in the corner.

"Hey, boys. Any word on why we're here?" Bennett leans back, propping his foot on the wall.

"No. Was the media still swarming?" I fiddle with my fitness tracker ring and stare at the door, anxiety thrumming through my veins.

"Oh yeah. Every major news station's out there."

"Even Meg the hottie from Channel 9?" Callum elbows Bennett and he jabs him right back, grinning.

"Yeah. Even her."

"Was that awkward? Since you're a one-and-done kinda guy?" Callum teases and Bennett shoots him the bird.

"No. Because I shaded my face with my hands and sprinted past her shouting 'No comment.'"

"Of course you did." Callum and I laugh. Of all the

guys on the team, Bennett's got the worst reputation when it comes to dating.

Suddenly, the room falls silent and I jerk my head up. The team owner, Max Prince, strides in wearing his typical dark suit, even at this early hour. He's flanked by his assistant, Naomi, and the sexy blonde I just collided with in the hallway.

Bennett leans over and whispers, "Who's Malibu Barbie?"

Callum snickers and I shrug, every inch of my body tense.

The sea of people parts as Max enters, and he takes his spot at the head of the conference table. He doesn't sit, though.

"Thank you for coming on such short notice." Max's eyes dart around the room, making eye contact with a chosen few, including me. "I apologize for the early morning, but I wanted you to hear the news directly from me. Coach Evans is gone. Terminated as of last night."

A collective gasp rises from the room, side conversations breaking out.

What the hell? Coach was fired?

Max holds up a palm. "Before everyone begins asking the inevitable questions—Coach Evans acted inappropriately, in a manner not befitting a coach of this team. Therefore, I was forced to take action. A new coach will be appointed shortly. And we're mixing things up a bit next season."

What the fuck does that mean?

Bennett raises his hand. Of course he fucking does.

"Yes, Bennett?" Max points a finger at him.

"What do you mean, 'mixing things up?'" He air quotes Max's phrase.

Max presses his lips together, his gaze shifting toward the blonde. "Harbor, care to chime in here?"

The mystery blonde gives a shy wave and steps forward. "Hi, everyone. I'm Harbor Hayes, the team's PR consultant."

PR consultant? What's going on here?

The back of my neck prickles, senses on high alert. We've never interacted directly with a PR consultant before.

"I'm super enthused to be meeting with you all this morning. As Mr. Prince said, big changes are in the works. I'm here to help you make the most of these changes and polish your image."

Polish our image? What the hell?

Now it's my turn to raise my hand.

"Excuse me—what do you mean by 'polish our image'? What's wrong with our current image?"

Harbor smooths her hair over her shoulder, her gaze flicking to Max. He gives her a barely perceptible nod and she takes a deep breath, her chest rising and falling.

"There's been an incident—" She locks her wide eyes directly on mine. "And it's not great. Publicity wise."

Is she talking about the loss in the playoffs? Because all of this seems extreme.

"What are we talking about here? Sure, we lost in game five, but it happens to teams every year." I fold my arms across my chest, leveling my gaze on her.

She swallows hard, straightening her shoulders. "We're not talking about the playoffs. You're going to hear it eventually, so I'll tell you all now. Coach Evans had, um, sexual relations with Mrs. Prince. He's also currently under league investigation for illicit gambling involving the team."

Another gasp from the room and more side conversations break out.

I can't believe this. *Coach was banging the owner's wife? And worse—may have been betting on his own team?*

Mind spinning, I glance at Prince and his clenched fists, the stony gaze. Dude's usually uptight, but he seems more stressed than normal. Guess now I know why.

Harbor waves her hand through the air, silencing the chatter. "As upsetting as all this is, we need to come together as a team right now. Close the gates and shut down the rumor mill."

Max nods, agreeing with her plan. Then he steps forward.

"The performance in the playoffs, plus the gambling investigation, has sponsors nervous. To cut losses, I'm relocating the team. We're moving the franchise to Florida, effective this upcoming season. It will be a fresh start for this team. Everyone will be given a moving stipend and off-season practice with the new coach begins in one month."

Damn.

This keeps getting better. *Florida?* Great for Spring Break, but moving an entire professional hockey team there?

"Oh, hell no." Vic shoves upright from his spot on the wall. "I'm not moving to Florida! I got kids here."

Murmurs break out around the table and Max waves his hand through the air.

"Enough! You're free to make your own decisions. You'll break your contract, making you a free agent. But that's your choice. I'll need it all in writing by the end of the weekend."

More mumbling and grumbling rolls around the room. Harbor leans over, whispering in Max's ear.

"The team will reimburse everyone for the move, plus provide relocation assistance to secure new living arrangements. I ask that you not speak to the media at this time. Ms. Hayes will be the spokesperson for this team. Only the two of us will address the press. We'll hold the official press conference announcing the relocation in forty-eight hours. Until then, I expect complete media silence from everyone in this room. Additionally, Ms. Hayes will be spearheading a team rebranding campaign, helping rehab our image."

Rehab? Nothing's wrong with the team's image, outside of Mrs. Prince fucking around and Coach maybe making a few bets.

"Right. I have a few PR strategies up my sleeve, percolating, and I'm excited to be on board!" Harbor flashes a bright smile around the room, and I grimace.

I don't like this one little bit.

Not the new coach. The relocation. Not the rebranding, the bogus PR campaign. And I sure as hell don't like the sprightly blonde, flipping her hair and shining bright as the North fucking star up there.

"Thanks for coming!" Harbor waves like a damn theme park greeter, and I roll my eyes so hard the sockets hurt.

"What in the actual fuck?" Bennett grumbles, pushing off the wall. "Evans screwed Prince's wife? When? Where?"

"Really, Benny? That's what you're hung up on?" Callum elbows Bennett. "Not the fact that Coach may have thrown the playoffs? Or that we're all moving to Florida and getting a new coach? You're over here thinking about the lewd and lascivious acts of Mrs. Prince and Coach Evans?"

"Hell, yeah, I am. That was the interesting part of the story." Bennett runs his fingers through his hair. "Wes, you didn't know anything about this? I thought you and Coach were tight."

So did I.

I pinch the bridge of my nose, trying to dull the sudden throbbing in my head. Change always knocks me sideways and this is a shit ton all at once.

"No. I knew nothing." I take a deep breath, people already filing out of the room. Harbor and Max field questions and shake hands as players shuffle by.

Simmering anger bubbles up inside me. *Why didn't Max call me? I'm the captain of this team. He should have at least given me the courtesy heads-up, so I'd be prepared.*

Squaring my shoulders, I march over to Max and Harbor. Max is deep in conversation with the team doctor, leaving me alone with PR Barbie.

Who, upsettingly, is far more gorgeous up close. And she smells good too, like some kind of exotic fruit.

"Hello, I'm Harbor. You're Weston Steele, right? I ran into you this morning. Sorry I didn't properly introduce myself." She thrusts her hand in my direction and I give her open palm a withering stare, leaving her hanging.

"Yes, I'm Weston. The team captain and forward."

She retracts her hand, the bright smile faltering slightly. "How can I help you, Weston?"

"I don't think you can. You know nothing about this team, and probably less about hockey. How you're going to be an asset I have no idea."

"I assure you I have everything under control and it will all be fine. Better than fine. Eventually. This team's going to come out on the other side of this scandal stronger than ever."

"Maybe. Although I don't believe we have an image problem."

Harbor clears her throat, her cheeks staining a bright pink. "Um, trust me, we do. The story hasn't broken yet. But when it does, you'll be happy to be out of here."

A pit yawns open in my gut, but I forge ahead. "I doubt someone like you can claw us out of trouble." I rake a cold, assessing gaze up and down her body. She can't be more than a few years out of college. Under more favorable circumstances, I'd consider her attractive, with high cheekbones and glossy, full lips. But right now I'm just pissed off.

I lock eyes with her. "Like you know anything about hockey."

Straightening her shoulders, she doesn't break my gaze. "I appreciate that you're upset right now, probably knocked off-kilter a little."

I cross my arms over my chest and frown, swallowing hard. "You have no idea how I feel right now. I've given my all to this game. This team. This city. And now your big plan is to up and leave?"

"Trust me, Weston. It will be for the best."

"Ms. Hayes, with all due respect, I doubt *you* know what's best. For me or this team."

She lifts her chin, matching my glare. And damn if it doesn't spark something low in my gut. That blaze in her eyes? It should piss me off. Instead, I'm standing here thinking about how I can stoke it.

Not fucking ideal.

I spin on my heel and stalk toward the door.

"My dad was a hockey coach for twenty years."

I freeze.

"He always said a team that can't protect each other on the ice is defeated before the puck drops. You have a choice here, Weston. Protect the team or be defeated. You choose, Captain."

Gone is the soft-spoken, slightly shy woman from the hallway. Her tone's sharp, icy even. Hot anger ripples through me, pricking at my scalp and burning my neck.

Dammit.

She has a good fucking point.

But I'll never admit that.

Instead, I stalk out of the room without looking back. Pissed off that she's absolutely correct in her assessment— and she's already under my skin.

CHAPTER 2
HARBOR

All things considered, the emergency team meeting went about as well as could be expected. I figured most of the players would be shocked and upset, especially considering they just lost their coach in the scandal.

I hadn't counted on the team captain being all rage and jawline. He's very good-looking. Tall, dark, and handsome —also extremely pissed off. I'm going to have to thaw that frosty demeanor stat, though, because I need him on my side for this rebrand to be successful.

And it *needs* to be successful. If I kill this campaign, I'll be well on my way to being a force in the sports PR world. On my own terms, working for myself as a freelance consultant. This could be my big break, the one that catapults my career.

I kick off my heels as soon as I walk through the door of my tiny apartment and hurry over to the kitchen table. Setting up my laptop for the rescheduled meeting with Mr. Prince and the team, I ignore the churning in my stomach from my jangly nerves and all the leftover adrenaline from the world's longest day. This is the final meeting with the team to review the new campaign and negotiate the terms of my contract. If everything goes to plan, I'll seal the deal and land the biggest client of my career.

I'm sliding into a chair when a text pops up on the screen.

Dad: Florida? What the hell?

Oh shit. How'd he find out about this already? I haven't told anyone—not even my sister, Piper—and we've purposefully kept absolute silence on the media front.

I stare out the window and debate how to respond. I don't have time to get into it with him right now—Mr. Prince will be joining the call any second and I need to focus on getting the job before I worry about traversing the fallout with my father.

Harbor: It's a great opportunity

Dad: Some piss-ass town in the swamp
state? How, exactly, is that a great
opportunity, Harbor? I can get you a call
with F1 today

Frowning at the screen, my stomach twists into a tight knot. Of course he's critical of a potential relocation. He never wanted me to work in sports, period. Let alone hockey, his one true love.

Harbor: Thanks, but no

Short, to the point. The less ammo I give him, the better.

No sense reiterating that I want—no, *need*—to succeed on my own. Not take whatever golden ticket the great Coach Doug Hayes manages to score for his daughter. We've had that argument roughly one kazillion times over the last decade. He just doesn't understand and now's not the time to try to change his mind.

> Dad: This is a terrible fucking idea, Harbor

Wow, I appreciate the support.
Ring, ring.

Plastering a wide smile on my face, I accept the video call and forget about my dad for now. Mr. Prince pops up, along with the GM, and several key sponsors.

"Hello, Harbor. The gang's all here." Prince chuckles at his joke, and I keep smiling.

"Evening, gentlemen. Let me pull my slides up for you." I open the document as another text pings in the corner.

> Dad: Let me make a few calls. I'll get back to you ASAP. DON'T SIGN ANYTHING

I audibly groan, and Prince raises a brow. Coughing, I attempt to cover up my moan.

"Please refer to slide one. That's the overview of the rebrand." I begin walking everyone through the slides, going over the reasons for the relocation and the myriad of benefits to sponsors.

> Dad: Got you an interview tomorrow at 10
> AM EST with Los Angeles

I bite the inside of my cheek and hit the X on the text box, closing the message and concentrating on my pitch.

"We're going to focus on charity and community. *Hockey with Heart* will be the campaign slogan and we can use that on merchandise, really integrate it into all of our marketing efforts." I highlight the words on the slide with my mouse as the sponsors nod in agreement. They're into the pitch.

> Dad: The PR girl for the basketball team's
> going on maternity leave. You can take
> her position. She probably won't come
> back anyway

Good grief. My dad's an HR nightmare. And there's probably a 100% chance she's coming back—has he seen the housing costs in L.A.?

"Harbor, the deck is great, we love all the fresh ideas for the team." Mr. Prince nods enthusiastically and my chest lightens a touch.

"Thanks, Mr. Prince. I'm enthused about the opportunity for growth and believe the team and the organization can add real value to the community. That's important to me, and I know it's tantamount to your beliefs as well." I smile and try to throw as much enthusiasm into my voice as possible.

> Dad: If you want to play with the big boys,
> you need to be in a major city. Not some
> backwater pit stop

> Dad: You're a Hayes. Hayes = Greatness

Dad: With a fucking capital G, Harbor

The messages flash on my screen in quick succession, each one a sharp stab to the gut. I clasp my shaking hands together in my lap and pretend to be fine, happy even. Inside, though, I'm seething.

My dad's such a fucking asshole.

Smoothing my hair over my shoulder, I answer each and every question thrown at me flawlessly and shove away the simmering anger.

Dad: I raised you better than this

It's always about him.

Every. Single. Time.

Well, not today.

"We're prepared to offer you a one-year contract, with full relocation coverage, plus health and benefits. Double what we previously offered because we see the value in your plan." Prince leans toward the camera, giving me a close-up of his salt-and-pepper hair, the deep etches on his forehead.

Excitement fizzes through my veins, taking the place of the rage. I do love a good win. Plus, I've watched more game footage than half the players in the league. I understand this sport in my bones. If anyone can make this rebrand work, it's me.

"Yes."

Finally, something Dad can't criticize.

The offer's amazing, my best contract ever. Yet, even as I think the words, I know it's not true. My dad always finds something to critique.

Always.

"Yes? Fantastic. I'll have legal shoot the contract over tonight. One last thing—is Coach Hayes on board with you making the move? Wouldn't want the greatest coach of all time to be pissed at me for stealing his little girl from the big city." Mr. Prince chuckles, and I swallow down a grimace.

I nod, fidgeting with the stack of bracelets on my wrist. Now's not the time to hash my twisted family dynamics out with Mr. Prince. Especially when he's dealing with his own messy situation with a soon-to-be ex-wife.

"He's generally supportive." That's the best I can do without straight-up lying.

"Well, then, welcome to the team, Ms. Hayes. And please tell your father I say hello. We'd love for him to attend our opening game!" Prince shoots me one last grin, then disconnects and my screen goes dark.

Literally zero chance of my dad showing up for the season opener, judging by his latest text:

Dad: You're a damn winner. Start acting
like one

Folding my arms on the table, I bang my head against my forearm, once, twice, three times. Why can't my father let me live my own freaking life? He doesn't bother Piper like this, butting in and telling her how to run her social media business.

No, just me, for some perverse reason.

My therapist's calm, low voice echoes in my head: *Why do you let him get to you?*

I'm a grown-ass woman with several years of work with Dr. Martina under my belt. Apparently, it's not working though. Because I still have daddy issues. A consummate people-pleaser, and for some reason, pleasing Dad's always been the thing.

Guess I love a good challenge.

Because if there's one thing I know for certain it's that Coach Doug Hayes is never satisfied.

Ever.

His team won the Cup three years in a row. The first team to achieve the coveted three-peat. Year four they lost in Game 7. He had players watching footage of that one game all off-season, analyzing every single thing they did wrong.

Never satisfied.

So why the hell am I still trying?

Staring at the litany of messages, I debate how to respond. He's going to hear about the contract soon—it's best if the news comes from me. But I don't have a phone call in me right now, every bone in my body aching from exhaustion.

I tap out a text.

> Harbor: Thanks for the interview offer, but I took the job
>
> Harbor: Huge contract with benefits. Best deal I've landed

Holding my breath, I watch the swirling dots as my dad types his response. Nausea rolls over me and I feel like I'm going to throw up. I should be excited, happy, celebrating the win. Instead, I'm sitting here sweating, my stomach in knots.

> Dad: WHY THE FUCK DID YOU DO THAT?

Dad: I told you not to sign anything

Dad: I'll call my lawyer. We can get you
out of this

Oh, for fuck's sake.

> Harbor: No, Dad. This is happening and
> it's going to be great
>
> Harbor: I'm going to make this team into
> the next big thing

Dad: Right, Harbor. And hell's freezing
over tomorrow

Tears prick at the corners of my eyes. God, why is he always such a dick? I should cut him off, but my mother would never forgive me. Not to mention my sister.

No, I won't cut him off.

I'll do better than that.

I'm going to prove him wrong.

The Coastal Crushers are going to be big. Huge. The next great US hockey team. They'll win the championship. And when they do, when *I* make it happen, he can finally shut the hell up and let me live my life.

CHAPTER 3
WESTON

A tension headache's dogged me all damn day. The persistent throbbing started the second the bubbly PR consultant—with the too-bright smile and unshakable confidence—began dismantling everything I knew about my team's future at the emergency meeting. Try as I might, I can't shake the dull ache behind my eyes, or the knot of anxiety tightening in my gut.

I've cycled through all the usual methods—hit the team gym for a workout, then the sauna. Refueled at the juice bar, but the kale and pineapple smoothie did nothing to calm my stomach. I visited the trainer for a massage.

Pound, pound, pound.

Headache still fucking there.

I went to the meditation room and sat in the dark.

My worst idea yet because sitting in the quiet room alone, my mind flew straight to the scandal.

I can't believe Coach would do this to us.

To me.

Clips from the season ran through my head, a highlight reel of Coach Evans with the team.

Did he really throw the playoffs?

In the heat of the moment, I didn't consider anything other than wobbly stick skills coupled with shitty luck. But now, in retrospect…

Maybe he did. I mean, it's not out of the realm of possibility. Callum rarely lets the puck slip through. Yet somehow, Chicago scored multiple goals on us in the last game of the series, the one that ended our season.

Bennett spent more time than usual in the penalty box throughout the playoffs, giving the other team the massive advantage of an extra player on the ice.

Vic missed an easy goal. The veteran *never* misses.

And now here I am. Standing in the living room of my airy penthouse apartment overlooking the twinkling skyline, getting ready to say goodbye.

To my home, the city I love. To a team I thought I knew.

All to move to a new place and rebuild the team from the ground up because the coach I trusted and respected fucked Prince's wife and maybe bet against us. His players, the guys he called family.

I rake my hand through my hair, a harsh exhale fogging the glass window.

This whole thing sucks.

Knock, knock.

Only two people besides me have access to the penthouse via elevator keycards. I lumber over to the door and crack it open.

Callum and Bennett, and they're carrying a wobbly tower of moving supplies.

Guess shit's about to get real.

"Hey. Where'd you get all this stuff?" I swing the door open wide, and the two of them lumber in.

"Grabbed all I could carry from headquarters. Big stack of shit in the conference room. Figured I should scoop some before it's gone." Bennett drops the pile unceremoniously in the middle of the floor.

Throb, throb, throb.

I hate clutter even more than change.

"Figured you'd want some boxes. To pack up your meager belongings." Bennett straightens up, waving his hand at my admittedly minimalist living space.

"Just how I like it," I grumble, kicking at the cardboard with my toe.

"Should only take you about ten minutes to pack up your shit. You own more than one set of towels, bro?" Bennett teases.

"Yeah. I have two. Both white."

"Of course they are."

"That way you can bleach them. Get them extra clean." Callum elbows Bennett and my brothers break into laughter.

"Shut the hell up, you two. Are neither of you bothered by all of this?" I scowl down at the moving supplies. "A new coach, a new city, a new team name? How about being bossed around by the PR lady? That feel good to you?"

"Malibu Barbie? I have no issue with her bossing me around. Bet she'd be good in the bedroom, with that take-charge attitude." Bennett's lips tip into a smirk and the pounding in my head intensifies.

A vision of Harbor in lacy black lingerie dances through my mind and every muscle in my body tenses.

"Shut the hell up about Harbor." The words come out harsher than intended, my jaw clenching so tight I could crack a molar.

And not because he's wrong.

Because he noticed what I noticed—and I fucking hate that.

No one should be looking at her like that, anyway. Least of all me, as the captain. She works for the team now.

"Oh, Harbor now, is it? First name basis already, Cap?" Bennett's smirk turns into a full-fledged grin and my fists automatically ball, ready to punch that smug look off his face.

Instead, I roll my shoulders back, shooting Bennett a cold glare even as heat creeps up my neck.

"It's her name, isn't it? And why is it always sex with you? Are you ever *not* thinking about getting into someone's panties?" I ask.

"Typically, no. Unless we're talking about Prissy. I'm zero percent interested in her panties."

Prissy—short for Priscilla—is our gold-digging stepmom. She swooped in approximately three minutes after our mother passed away when we were thirteen and has tormented us ever since. We collectively loathe her.

I've always been tight with my brothers, but after Mom died and Prissy moved in, our bond grew stronger than ever. Three against one, and Prissy loses every single time. That really pisses her off.

Leaving for college felt like more of an escape—at least for me. As the "oldest" and most responsible triplet, I shouldered a lot of the emotional burden after our mom died. Getting away from the haunting memories, the deep freeze that was our home, was ultimately a relief.

Judging by our father's lack of communication, it doesn't seem like our dad misses us much. Sure, we all get the occasional text, the obligatory birthday call, but that's it. The bare minimum of parenting from our only remaining parent.

Whatever.

I'm a grown man now. I don't need his validation, love, or approval.

"The only man interested in Prissy's panties is our father, I can assure you." Callum frowns, crashing down onto my couch and kicking out his long, muscular legs.

It's not that Prissy's an unattractive woman. But her attitude's a real turn-off. The only person Prissy loves is Prissy. And maybe—maybe—our dad. Verdict's still out on that one.

More likely she's infatuated with his large bank account and celebrity, being a retired pro hockey player.

"Did anyone tell Dad about the move?" Callum raises his eyes to mine, then Bennett's.

I shrug. "No. Figured we're under a gag order."

"Right. Prince told us not to talk." Bennett's brows scrunch together, like he's thinking hard.

"I'm sure we could tell Dad. It's not like he's going to talk to the press or anything," Callum says.

"But what about Little Miss Priss? She's got a big ass mouth." Bennett makes a lewd gesture and my stomach turns.

"Bro. I don't even want to think about Prissy's mouth, okay? You guys want something to drink?" I grab a glass from a lacquered cabinet above the built-in bar.

Normally, I'm not a drinker. Especially during the season. But today I'm making an exception. Given it's off-season and I'm in the middle of a personal and professional crisis.

The strong, smoky scent of bourbon wafts up from the bottle as I pour.

"Here you go, boys." I hand Callum and Bennett their drinks, then take a long, slow sip of mine. The liquid burns as it slides down my throat, but at least I'm distracted from the throbbing in my temple.

"You think Coach actually threw the playoffs, Wes?" Callum peers at me over the rim of his glass, the city lights glowing around his hulking outline.

I huff out a heavy sigh. "I don't know. I'd really love to say 'no.' But the more I play back our games, the less sure I am. Of everything."

Understatement of the fucking year.

I've been reeling since this morning, ever since I bumped into Harbor in the hallway. My face burns remembering the way she gazed up at me through those long, dark lashes, the light pink flush of her cheeks as she apologized for mowing me down.

Before I knew who she was or heard her plans for the PR nightmare she was about to unleash on my team.

Bennett scrapes a hand over his face and crashes down next to Callum on the couch.

"Damn, this sucks. I can't believe Coach would do us like that." He gazes blankly across the room.

"Did you see the memo on housing that went out this afternoon?" Callum swirls the dark liquor round and round in his glass, tension etched on his face.

"You're cute. You think I read memos?" Bennett leans back and gets comfy, stretching out beside Callum. Callum pushes his thigh away and Bennett grins.

"I figured you didn't." Callum shoots him a sideways glare. "I'm not even sure you can read, bro."

"Hey. I can. I just choose not to bother. Because I have the two of you to keep me updated. What'd the memo say?"

"That housing will be limited. Short notice, smaller town and population, blah, blah, blah. Listed a few of the sites to check out. Management strongly encourages rental sharing," Callum says.

"Damn. How small is this place?" Bennett downs the rest of his drink in one large gulp. Maybe reality's finally sinking in.

"Small. Driftwood Cove's an old Florida beach town. Some minor league team was going to move there a few years ago but then bailed last second. That's the only reason they have a rink." I learned that little tidbit during my afternoon research session, after I gave up on the idea of ditching my headache.

"Super." Bennett slams his empty glass down on the coffee table, frown lines furrowing his brow.

"Not sure why Prince chose the place. Maybe he has some kind of business deal in the works, who knows? A pro hockey team could bring in a lot of money for the town. It makes sense on their end." I scoop up the three empty glasses and pour us all a refill.

"So, are we rooming together again, boys? Like the good old days?" Bennett asks, his tone more lighthearted than I feel.

"Sure." Callum puffs out his cheeks, blows out a breath.

I shrug, knowing I'm probably going to regret this decision. "I guess. But I want the biggest bedroom. Since I'm the captain. And you have to promise to keep the communal areas clean. No half-eaten, soggy cereal bowls left on the table or dirty socks strewn about."

"Chill, bro." Bennett holds up his palms, acting all innocent. "I would never."

"Uh-huh." I roll my eyes, remembering the last time I lived with Bennett back in college. It wasn't pretty.

"And you—" Bennett points at me. "You have to promise to abide by the tried-and-true ribbon signal."

Callum guffaws at this. "What makes you think you're going to get any action in Florida?"

Bennett shoots Callum an affronted look, one brow raised. "Have you met me? Of course I'm scoring down there."

I shake my head. "Women aren't going to be throwing themselves at you, Puck Bunny."

"Always underestimating me. I'm sure the ladies will be interested. Opens up a whole new dating pool for me."

"Always the optimist, Puck Bunny." Callum smacks his knee and Bennett grins.

"I try to stay positive."

Buzz, buzz.

My cell vibrates on the kitchen island, and dread rolls through me as I stare at the phone.

After a long pause, I check my messages.

Unknown number: Hi, this is Harbor Hayes, the PR consultant.

Like I know more than one Harbor.

Unknown number: Mr. Prince requested a meeting tomorrow morning, just the three of us, to loop you into the plans

Super. Now I have to meet with Malibu Barbie and pretend to play nice in front of Prince.

Throb, throb, throb.

Head pounding and palms sweating, I tap out a response.

> Weston: Fine. Where and when?

> Unknown number: 8 AM, headquarters

> Weston: I'll be there

Even if I won't like it.

I dig deep, restraining myself from typing out that last part. Just to be on the safe side, though, I toss my cell back onto the counter.

"What's wrong, Cap?" Callum's low voice jolts me back to reality. "Is that Prince?"

I press my lips together, my pulse kicking up a notch, muscles tight with agitation.

It's strictly aggravation with the situation. This has nothing to do with Harbor and those wide, hazel eyes she leveled at me in the conference room.

"No. It's Harbor. Apparently, Prince wants to meet with the two of us tomorrow."

"Oh, sounds important and official." Bennett draws out the words, mocking.

"Fuck off, Benny. And I'll report back as soon as I know anything."

Bennett salutes me and Callum nods, every bit of tension still very much alive and well in my body, my muscles.

Whatever Prince and Harbor have planned for tomorrow, I'll need to keep my guard up—eyes on the Cup, not the beautiful PR professional with a talent for making my blood run hot.

She's a walking complication.

And complications like that? They're always the hardest to resist.

CHAPTER 4
HARBOR

'm thirty minutes early for the strategy meeting, but I've already been awake for hours. I barely slept last night, between stressing over moving logistics, replaying the text exchange with my father, and freaking out about being in the same room as Weston Steele again.

Possibly sitting next to him, heat shimmering off those broad shoulders. Jaw tense, with a slight shadow of stubble. His deep blue eyes glaring at me, searing me all the way to my soul.

Stop, Harbor. Get it together.

I cannot—will not—get involved with the grumpy hockey star.

Personally, at least. Bad enough I have to deal with him professionally.

Besides, Weston Steele made it abundantly clear that he hates me. From my PR campaign to my sunshiney disposition. The man's a walking, talking, seething block of ice.

Adding to my anxiety is my father's voice echoing in my head: *You're not championship material, Harbor.*

Well, today I get to prove that wrong. I understand what separates dynasty-winning hockey teams from one-season wonders, and Weston Steele's about to learn that Hayes-level strategic thinking runs in the family.

I toss the manila file folder onto the conference table and sink down into a chair facing the door. The wall clock ticks loudly in the quiet space, *tick, tick, tick.*

Slow and rhythmic. Eyelids heavy, I lean back into the comfy seat, the conference room fading away.

"Prince paying you to sleep on the job?" A growly voice jolts me out of my trance.

Startled, I pop up, almost falling out of the rolling chair.

"I wasn't sleeping." I grip the edge of the seat for balance, heart pounding as I stare up at Weston. He pins his deep blue eyes on mine—even bluer against the navy of his fitted T-shirt—and it's like I'm stuck in his forcefield. Paralyzed by his granite jawline, shadowed with a days' worth of dark stubble. His hair's still damp from his morning shower and his fresh, clean scent fills the room. He's scowling, his lips set in a tight line. If he wasn't so surly, I'd probably think he was sexy.

"I was thinking. I do my best work with my eyes closed." I open the folder and grab a pen, pretending to jot down an idea.

"Uh-huh." He pulls out the chair directly opposite mine, sinking down like a lithe, grouchy tiger.

Dammit.

The last thing I want to do is stare at his stupidly gorgeous face scowling at me, yet here I am. Doing exactly that.

Noticing his high cheekbones, the curve of his lips, the straight nose with a scar across the bridge. The tiny crinkles around his eyes, actual physical evidence the man does have an emotion other than pissed AF.

My pulse races faster and heat floods through me, palms sweaty as we face off.

"So—what's the 'big plan'?" He places heavy sarcasm on the words and the low simmer in my belly bubbles to anger.

Taking a deep breath, I work hard to keep my composure. One of us needs to be professional here. Guess it's going to be me.

"Listen, I think we may have gotten off on the wrong foot. I understand you're upset about the relocation, and I get it. Honestly, I'm not thrilled about moving either. But I do believe it's the best thing for the team."

"I don't." He sits back, folding his arms across his broad chest. Muscular arms, complete with sexy man veins popping on his forearms. My belly flip-flops and my mouth goes dry.

Why does this man have such an effect on me? He's the last person on the planet I want to be talking to right now. Well, besides my father.

I swallow with effort and forge ahead.

"Here's the outline. Read it over and then tell me you disagree." I pull the five-page plan from the folder and shove it across the table at him, our fingertips brushing as he takes the paper.

Fuck me.

A ripple of electricity zings from my fingers all the way up my arm. A hot bolt of desire I definitely should not be feeling. Not now, not ever.

His grip tightens on the paper, those forearm muscles tensing slightly.

Am I imagining things or did his breathing pick up for a quick second?

Ducking his head, he studies the carefully crafted words I've spent the last twenty-four hours perfecting.

Tick, tick, tick.

I glance at my phone, but in reality I'm gauging his reaction, watching for micro cues. A lifted brow, a furrow. Any sign in either direction.

But the man's infuriatingly neutral.

Fucker.

Without a word, he slides the paper back across the table at me.

"You read the whole thing already?" My voice tips up in disbelief.

"Yeah, I did. The plan sucks."

Just like Dad.

The instant dismissal, the condescending tone. I've heard this exact same energy from my father a thousand times. *"You don't understand hockey culture, Harbs. What it takes to win."*

Well, I do know what builds dynasty-level team loyalty and a rabid fanbase. Time to show Captain Steele how three-peat energy is built.

"What, specifically, are you opposed to?"

"The whole damn thing. The move. Changing the team name. Your transparent attempts to ingratiate us with the community through mandatory charity events." He lifts his fingers one by one, ticking off every idea.

"You're opposed to charity events?"

"No. But I am if they're fake."

"Who says they'll be fake? All I'm asking is for everyone to make an effort, be a good citizen. Not a huge lift."

"Hmph," he grunts, shaking his head. "I don't like it. I don't think the people of Driftwood Cove will like it. They're not dumb—they'll see right through that plan."

"You have any better ideas, Mr. Smart Guy?" I fire back, folding my arms across my chest now and matching his defensive posture.

"No. But it's not my job to have the ideas. It's yours." He points at me and now I'm good and pissed.

"My point exactly, Mr. Steele. Let me do my job and you do yours. As team captain, you're expected to help sell the plan to your teammates."

"But I don't like the plan."

"Do you like every play the coach calls?" I fire back.

He stiffens, jaw ticking. "No, I don't. But that's different."

I jut out my chin. "It's actually not. Consider me the PR coach. This is *my* field of expertise. And I know what I'm doing. I bailed a professional tennis player out of a total crisis last year during the biggest tournament of her career. Also managed to keep a basketball star out of jail, then polished up his image after the skirmish with law enforcement."

Championship-level crisis management. The kind of work that separates the pros from the amateurs. Dad taught me that champions perform under pressure—and that's exactly what I do.

"Trust me—I know what I'm doing."

"Great, good for you. But those are two individuals, not a whole damn team."

I grit my teeth, acting way calmer than I feel. "I've worked with teams before too. Besides, the same principles apply."

Weston drums his fingers on the table and I relax a bit.

Maybe I made my point and he's going to go along with the plan. That would be a huge load off my extremely tense shoulders.

"I don't understand why we can't hire a new coach and stay in the city."

Dammit.

No such luck.

I heave out an exasperated sigh and glance up at the ceiling, debating how much to divulge. I figure Mr. Prince will tell him all the details anyway, since he wants him at the press conference. It wouldn't do for Weston to be caught off guard.

"The team needs to make a move. For self-preservation. If we stay here, we'll be ripped to shreds by the press. Your coach is under investigation. That's a huge deal and sponsors are freaking out about losing their investments. Add the sex scandal in there, and it's going to be a bloodbath. The media is already having a field day with this, and the details haven't leaked yet. Only vague rumors about a possible team shake-up and the news that Coach Evans is gone."

My cell buzzes on the table, the loud vibration echoing off the walls. I snatch it up, glancing at the screen.

"And so it begins…" I hold the phone out so Weston can read the blaring headline.

Coach Evans scores with team owner Prince's wife

"Shit." He scrubs a large hand over his jaw, eyes darkening. "I can't believe he'd really do that to us." His voice so low the words are barely audible, and for a moment there's a crack in his composure. For the first time since we met, he's not full of confident swagger. His shoulders slump slightly and I feel badly for him, for the team. Coach

Evans betrayed all of them and the sting's etched on Weston's face.

"I'm sorry, I know this sucks for you too." My hand trembles and I almost reach out to him, but he recovers quickly, defenses snapping back into place.

"How'd they get that photo?" He snarls at the full-color photo of Coach Evans and Mandi Prince kissing outside the arena. "Aren't you supposed to kill things like that?"

"They already had the photos, before I was hired. Coach Evans and Mrs. Prince got sloppy. But that's all history now. My job is immediate damage control, followed by a rebuild and growth plan. I've got this. You just have to trust me."

Nostrils flaring, he levels stormy blue eyes on mine. My breath hitches and my belly rolls as we stare across the table at one another.

"You're going to have to earn that trust, Ms. Hayes. That's not a party favor I hand out."

Earn it.

God, he sounds just like my father.

Prove you belong here. Show me you're championship material.

I should have seen this coming. The second I landed this job, I did a deep-dive on the team, researching every player, the coaches, the administration. I know about Weston's childhood, his brothers, his hockey star father, the death of his mom. His stats in college and the pros. Hell, I even know what he eats for breakfast.

Reading about his background, of course he's going to have trust issues. Especially in light of his coach's recent betrayal. However, I underestimated how deep those issues run.

"Sorry I'm late." Mr. Prince bursts into the room,

swiping at his brow and breaking the icy tension between me and Weston. "The media's swarming out there. Did you two discuss the plan, the rebrand?" Prince glances at both of us, his lips tight.

"Yes, I went over the plan with Mr. Steele. Here's a print-out for you, complete with timeline." I whip out Prince's copy and he grabs the paper, then collapses into the seat next to Weston.

"Wow, this is great." Prince scans the plan, his salt-and-pepper head bobbing. "The charity component, 'Hockey with Heart,' the potential for merch. Very clever."

Weston rolls his eyes, shaking his head slightly. "You don't think that's—I don't know—too gimmicky?"

"Not at all. The slogan's catchy and positions us as the team that cares." Prince rubs his chin, considering the catchphrase. "We could use it in all our social media. It's a great hashtag."

"I agree. I'm already thinking about merch options with the slogan. And we could have it stitched on the jerseys, right on the sleeve. A pink heart and a hockey stick."

"Very cute. Exactly the vibe a competitive professional hockey team wants."

Weston's sarcastic tone rankles me, but I don't take the bait. Not in front of Prince. He's the big boss, the guy I need to impress right now. I can tackle Weston later.

"It's the vibe you're going to need. With rumors circulating about Coach Evans—the gambling and the affair—" I cut my gaze at Prince, his frown deepening. I wonder if he's even begun processing the fallout of all of this or if he's focusing on work to avoid dealing with his emotions. "You need a softer touch. Something more community-focused, to draw the attention away from those two issues."

Weston puffs out a breath, both palms spread flat on the table. Scars criss-cross his middle knuckle and I wonder if he got the mark on the ice or in a fistfight with one of his brothers.

"It's too soft. What's the team mascot gonna be, a freaking teddy bear?" Weston scowls at me.

"I was kicking around a seahorse, actually."

"Aw, hell no. We're professional hockey players, Ms. Hayes, not some youth rec league. We play against the Sabers, the Bolts. We can't be the Fighting Seahorses!" He throws his hands up in exasperation and Prince grimaces.

Professional hockey players. Like I don't know what that fucking looks like. I've been around pro hockey since before I could walk. I know exactly what intimidates opponents, what the fans love.

"What about barracuda?" I counter quickly. "They're predators, fast and aggressive." I swish my hand side-to-side through the air, mimicking a quick swimming motion. His expression shifts and my chest lightens.

"That's…" His voice loses its edge as he considers the idea. "No, doesn't work. This is hockey, not marine biology." He folds his arms across his pecs and I press my lips together, aggravated.

"I see we have a lot of movement to get on the same page here. Unfortunately, Weston, we don't have much time. A press conference is set for this afternoon. I'm going to need you to be aboard the plan one thousand percent. And, as the team captain, I'm counting on you to sell it to the rest of the boys. We don't need to work out all the logistics—we can keep putting our heads together on the finer details, like the new mascot—but I am pushing the

'Hockey with Heart' slogan through. I really like that and see a lot of potential there. Well done, Harbor." Prince grins at me and Weston scowls, more pissed off than ever.

Cheeks flaming, I flash Prince a tight smile, doing my best to ignore the daggers Weston's shooting in my direction.

"Thank you, Mr. Prince. I love all the possibilities the tagline offers. Do you want me to build out a slideshow presentation to present to the team? Running it by you first, of course."

"Sure. Visuals always work well, thank you. Shortlist mascots as well."

"Great..." Weston murmurs, and Prince's forehead creases.

"Weston, why don't you and Harbor spend some time heads-down on this together? Since you didn't love the seahorse idea." He chuckles, a deep, throaty laugh, and a hot flush creeps up my neck.

Spend even more time alone with the man? Seems like a terrible idea.

"Oh, I'm sure Ms. Hayes is too busy with her visuals and uniform design ideas." Weston levels his icy stare at me and I square my shoulders, sitting up straighter.

"I have time. The mascot is a critical component for the new team branding. Happy to brainstorm with you, Captain." I fold my hands together and smile sweetly at him, fully comprehending what game we're playing here.

Weston narrows his eyes slightly. We're opponents now, but we still have to produce results.

This should be fun.

"Fantastic. The two of you working together will make a real powerhouse. Alrighty..." Prince shoves away from the table, standing. "I'm meeting with the GM, then we're setting up interviews for the coaching position. Meet back here at two PM for the debrief before the press conference."

With a quick wave, he stalks out of the conference room, leaving me solo with the seething team captain.

As soon as we're alone, Weston leans forward, palms flat on the table. Locking icy blue eyes with me, a shiver rolls down my spine.

"Just so we're clear, Ms. Hayes—" His voice drops to a low, deep rumble. "I'll play nice in the sandbox with you. For now, for Prince's sake. But don't expect me to follow along with your every little move. This is still my team." Something dangerous and electric flickers in his deep blue eyes, goosebumps rising on my arms. "And I'm not giving up control without a fight."

Control.

Championship teams require absolute trust and unified vision.

Exact quote from Coach Doug Hayes.

But this time, I'm not backing down. I've got the expertise and the strategic mind to prove it.

I match his posture, tilting forward until we're separated by mere inches of charged air.

"Then I guess we'll both be fighting." I stare him down, the tension shifting between us into something I can't quite place—and definitely shouldn't explore.

For the sake of my career. And also my heart.

CHAPTER 5
WESTON

Harbor Hayes is one of the most infuriating women I've ever met.

No, strike that. She's one of the most infuriating *people* I've ever met. Man or woman, she's got everyone beat.

She's peppy and optimistic and energetic and annoyingly attractive. The way she flips her golden hair over her shoulder, full of confidence. The subtle movement shouldn't affect me, but I've had a hard-on half the damn morning. Sitting next to her in the small conference room, the sweet scent of her shampoo winding around me every time she moves.

Not ideal, considering I'm supposed to be hating her. Her and her relocation plan, which we're unveiling to the media in the next fifteen minutes.

I'm used to facing reporters, answering pointed questions about the game. But today's press conference is different—and so much worse.

The questions won't be about moves we made on the ice, plays that didn't go as planned.

No, the questions coming my way will be personal. About my coach and how he betrayed his team.

Did I know anything? How do I feel about it? What does this mean for the team's future?

Questions I'd honestly rather not answer. But as Harbor pointed out, evasion sometimes isn't the best strategy.

"You okay?" Harbor cuts her eyes at me, tiny flecks of gold sprinkled in the field of mossy green and brown.

I nod, swallowing hard over the lump in my throat. The muffled chatter of reporters drifts into the empty hallway where we're awaiting our cue.

"I'm fine." I force out the words, my voice gruff and scratchy.

"Here, have some water." She whips a plastic bottle from her oversized bag and offers it to me.

I don't fight her on it, gladly accepting the beverage. Unscrewing the lid, I take a few long sips.

"Thanks." I tip my chin at her, my gut swirling with nerves.

"You're going to do great. Just remember what we practiced and stick to the script."

The tension headache from yesterday comes roaring back, the persistent throbbing at the base of my neck growing stronger by the second.

"Okay." I shove a hand in my pocket and try to ignore the wave of queasiness rolling through me.

You can do this, Steele. You're a professional hockey player. This is nothing compared to facing a rival on the ice.

"Weston…" Harbor's delicate fingers flutter to the navy tie currently choking me out, and she steps in front of me, adjusting the knot. I take a quick breath, inhaling her sweet scent, fruity with a hint of vanilla. The pressure in my head eases and my gut calms down, my focus on her.

"You've got this. If anyone asks a question you're not comfortable answering, tap the notepad and I'll step in, okay? We're a team out there." She gazes up at me through thick, dark lashes and my pulse accelerates.

So much for calming down.

"You two ready?" Prince comes from behind, slapping me on the back and bringing me crashing back to shitty reality.

Harbor drops her hand quickly, blushing. "Yes, sir. Ready to go. I was just briefing Mr. Steele one last time."

"Great. Let's go." Prince shoves through the door into the bustling media room and marches straight to the podium. The sound amplifies as Harbor and I follow close behind.

Cameras click and reporters start shouting questions at us before we even make it to the microphone.

"Is it true Evans is gone?"

"What about the infidelity rumors?"

"What's the future of the team?"

Flash, flash, flash.

Bright pops of white blur my vision as people shout their questions, each voice growing louder in an effort to be heard. I stand slightly behind Prince, Harbor next to me, letting the team owner field the first set of questions.

He taps the microphone, adjusting it before he speaks.

"Good afternoon."

A murmur rises from the crowd and he holds up his hand, silencing the room. "I want to thank everyone for showing up today. As you may have heard, the head coach, Sean Evans, has been terminated. We're in the process of interviewing a replacement."

"Is it true he had sex with your wife?" a reporter from Channel 6 shouts, and the crowd erupts.

Prince's jaw ticks, his fist balling on the podium. "I'm not answering personal questions. Evans no longer works for the team. After a season that didn't end as we hoped— with a win in the playoffs—we're moving in a different direction."

"What can you tell us about the gambling allegations?" another reporter shouts, and Prince's knuckles turn white.

"The league is in charge of all investigations. I'm not at liberty to comment on the matter. Next."

A dark-haired reporter stands. "Rumors are swirling that several key investors are dropping their sponsorships, not wanting to be involved with a scandal. What impact will this have on the team? Are you worried?"

Prince blanches at this question, and I'm glad it's him dealing with this set of inquiries and not me.

"This team is financially sound and remains a good investment for sponsors. Many of our partners stand with us, committed to the great sport of hockey and our joint charitable endeavors. I thank each and every one of them for their support and look forward to an even brighter future as we continue working together next season."

Damn. Great answer, enough to silence the reporters for a full minute

"Mr. Prince, is it true the team's leaving New York?" Meg, Bennett's hottie from Channel 9, hops up.

"The team is relocating for the upcoming season, yes." Prince nods, his mouth set in a thin, tight line. "We've enjoyed our time playing in this great city. But we're moving in a new direction and that includes a change of venue. The team will be heading down to Florida next season."

At this announcement, the room breaks into a frenzy of questions and comments. Harbor steps forward, whispering in Prince's ear. He nods and moves away from the podium, and Harbor motions for me to take his place.

I follow her direction as she lowers the microphone and addresses the crowd.

"We're here today to unveil the new team name and location. Joining us is a man I'm sure you all recognize, team captain Weston Steele." A loud echo of applause vibrates the wooden podium as I nod and wave at the sea of reporters. "Mr. Steele."

Harbor steps to the side, slightly behind me, but still close enough I feel her body heat. Our arms almost touching, her presence is comforting, grounding me in this surreal moment.

"Good afternoon." I adjust the microphone, screechy feedback jolting the crowd into silence.

Eager hands shoot up and Harbor points at the closest one, a reporter I vaguely recognize from past press conferences.

"Mr. Steele, what does the team think about the relocation? And do you know where in Florida you're going?"

The question sits heavy on my conscience as I stare out into the crowd. When I took the position as team captain, I never imagined myself here, standing at this podium and lying straight into the camera.

I square my shoulders, doing my best to project confidence. Harbor and I practiced answering this question, but right now I can't remember the exact words.

I wing it and lie. "The team's excited for new opportunities, yeah."

"So you're totally sold on Florida? After playing your entire career here in New York?"

Heat flames my face and my mouth goes dry. I curl my fingers around the edges of the podium. "I'll always have a place in my heart for New York, starting my career here. But looking ahead, the franchise's future is Driftwood Cove, Florida."

I barely manage to get the words out, every fiber in my body resistant to this move.

Another collective gasp, and the chatter starts up again. Harbor selects a new reporter waving her hand high in the air.

"After years in a big city, the team's moving to a town no one's heard of. How do you feel about that, Weston?" The reporter shoots me a pointed gaze and my gut churns.

I fucking hate the idea.

But I can't very well say that in a room filled with press. I pause for a second, then swallow and look the woman dead in the eye.

"It will be an adjustment, but we're looking forward to building a strong hockey-loving community there."

The reporter doesn't let up. "Seems like a transparent play to get the team out of the city. Did you or your brothers, any other players, know about the allegations against Coach Evans?"

My jaw tenses, heat flashing through me. "I'm not free to comment on that at this time."

"So you did know something then?" She presses the issue.

"No, I did not." Anger leaks into my tone as I glare at the reporter, my hands shaking with rage. I pray the cameras don't catch the tremor as my carefully constructed mask of calm threatens to slip.

Harbor steps forward, nudging me over as she takes the mic. "As Mr. Prince and Mr. Steele have both said, they're not free to comment while the league investigates. Next question."

Skillfully, she steers the conversation away from Evans and the gambling allegations and cool relief washes over me as she talks. She's in her element, professional and poised. Not timid or reserved, she handles the savage reporters like a damn lion tamer. Meanwhile, I'm over here sweating through my dress shirt, thankful I opted for the jacket. At least it hides the sweat stains.

A grudging admiration for her finesse hits me out of nowhere, catching me off guard. For a split second, I forget to be annoyed, forget to resist—her or the plan.

Then the realization hits me straight in the chest.

I may be captain of this team, but right now?

I need her.

Admitting that, even to myself, makes me feel more exposed than taking the ice without pads.

"Weston, can you comment on the new team name?"

I take a quick breath, pausing. Glancing over at Harbor, she tips her head slightly, giving me the go-ahead.

Lucky me.

"Sure. The team name is the Coastal Crushers."

Loud murmurs fill the room as the media digests the new name, discussing amongst themselves.

"Do you have a mascot yet?" a man shouts from the back, smirking.

Asshole.

"Not yet."

"Maybe the Terrible Turtles?" He snickers and I grit my teeth, struggling to keep my composure. It's bad enough we lost the playoffs, then our coach. Now some dickhead from the press is gonna sit here and mock me and the team straight to my face?

I've had about all I can handle for one day.

Harbor must sense my worsening mood. Her soft, smooth arm brushes mine as she steps up to the podium and gratitude surges through me as she lowers the microphone again.

"Thanks for the suggestion, Kent. I'll take it under advisement. Are there any other serious questions?" She scans the room, waiting. No one else dares raise their hand or offer any other stupid mascot ideas. "No? Okay then. Thanks for coming. Have a great rest of the day."

Harbor clicks the microphone off, then spins on her heel and exits the room briskly, her ass swaying side to side. I follow behind her, trying hard not to stare at the perfect globes in front of me.

It's really fucking difficult.

We shove out into the hall, Prince right behind, and Harbor closes the door on the media with a definitive snap.

"Nice work, you two." Prince tips his chin at us, unbuttoning his jacket and relaxing a bit. "That went about as well as could be expected. Thanks for shutting down the gambling speculation, Harbor. Legal will be sending a memo out with details, but it goes without saying that the only thing anyone should say about the matter is 'No comment.'"

"Understood." I wipe my palms on my thighs and take a deep breath, my heart rate finally coming back into the normal range.

"I know it's been a full day and there's packing to do. Table the mascot discussion for the plane ride on Friday."

"Plane ride on Friday?" I frown at Prince.

"Yes. Both of you should fly with me down to Florida

on the jet. You can work on the way there. The sooner I get this team out of the city, the better."

Prince nods as if he's settled the matter, then strides off, not waiting for a response from either of us. Harbor and I stand in the hallway, the low din of the press floating through the door, an awkward silence stretching between us.

"You did well out there, Weston." Harbor breaks the tension, tucking a stray hair behind her ear.

"Thanks. I appreciate the assist."

"Sure, no problem."

We lock eyes for a long second and my stomach does a weird swoopy thing. *Must be my nervous system regulating after the adrenaline surge from the press conference...*

"What do you think about the Fighting Terrapins?" She tilts her head, long, blond hair flowing over her shoulder.

"No. No turtle. Fighting or otherwise."

She laughs, a light, melodic sound floating on the air, and there's that same swoopy sensation again.

Steele, get it together.

"Fine. With you as captain, maybe I should lean more toward a crab." Her full lips tip up into a smirk, then she spins on her heels and struts away. Leaving me standing in the hallway, speechless and staring at her perfect ass.

CHAPTER 6
HARBOR

The last few days have been a whirlwind of packing and planning. All my belongings are boxed up and headed down to Florida on a moving van. With any luck, I should have my stuff in the next week or so. In the meantime, I'll be living straight out of the carry-on I'm wheeling behind me down the black tarmac toward the team's private jet.

My stomach swirls the closer I get to the plane—and, let's be honest—Weston Steele. I saw the softer side of the grumpy captain the day of the press conference. Turns out he's not growly all the time and may even possess a sense of humor.

Who knew?

But I need to keep my focus strictly professional. My entire career rests on the success of this rebrand. Still, I can't ignore the racing of my heart when he levels those deep blue eyes on mine, the flutter in my belly.

The man's maddeningly attractive, even with the piss-poor attitude.

It's just my luck that the first time I spark with anyone in ages, the man happens to be the grumpy team captain. Unthinkable to go there. Like, beyond off-limits.

I can't even remember the last time I went on a date. Everyone I meet is through my job, and I need to keep my image squeaky clean when it comes to my clients.

Especially the gorgeous male ones.

My focus is on the work, not the players. It's difficult enough being a woman in the male-dominated sports industry, everyone constantly second-guessing my knowledge and authority. Any whisper of impropriety is basically the kiss of death to my career.

To be safe, once the details of the new campaign are worked out, I won't spend so much time with Weston. I'm confident I can keep my distance and stay strictly surface level with him. No problem.

A flight attendant takes my bag at the bottom of the stairway, and I climb the metal stairs up to the plane. A light wind whips my hair around my shoulders as I step into the cabin. Unlike a typical commercial flight, the jet's calm and quiet. Soft music plays over the sound system and the cool air smells fresh and slightly minty.

"Harbor, glad you could make it." Mr. Prince waves from his seat at the front of the plane. The general manager's sitting beside him sipping a Perrier. Two other men I vaguely recognize sit across from them in a two-by-two seat configuration, with a small table between them.

"Thanks for having me."

"I'm looking forward to seeing the final strategy and all the details this week." He smiles at me, takes a sip of his drink.

I better get Weston on board sooner rather than later. I'm running out of time.

Winners don't make excuses, Harbor. They create results. My dad's voice echoes in my head.

Well, I'm about to deliver championship-level results— if I can get the team captain to stop fighting me at every turn.

"You bet!" I force confident enthusiasm into my voice, returning the smile.

Prince resumes his conversation with the GM, and I glance around at my seating options. There's a sofa-like lounger at the rear. Not very conducive to business, especially while wrangling my laptop. The middle section of the plane has the more traditional seats, although these are much wider and plusher. I slide into one of the two open seats on the right and peer out the window at the city skyline. A twinge of sadness pings through me. I don't know when—or if—I'll be back in the city again. Although I moved around a lot as a kid, I've been in Manhattan for several years. Since I graduated from college, my longest stint anywhere.

I'm going to miss this place. All the hustle, the grit and determination. The bright lights and the constant break-neck pace.

There's no place like NYC, that's for sure.

"Anyone sitting here, Hurricane?" Weston's deep, gruff voice interrupts my pity party.

"No."

Dammit.

My voice comes out all weird and breathy, my stupid heart pounding a mile a minute. I should protest the slightly derogatory nickname, but I'm distracted by the strip of abs peeking out from beneath his T-shirt as he tosses his duffel into the overhead bin. I try not to stare.

Try even harder to ignore the delicious scent drifting from his skin, cedar and man, as he sinks down beside me.

He's so tall and broad, his body takes up every inch of the extra wide seat, our arms brushing on the armrest.

"Sorry," I murmur, easing away from him. As if there's anywhere to escape. I'm sandwiched between the window and this hulk of a man for the next few hours.

"It's fine." He shifts in the seat, stretching out his long legs. I can't help but notice how tiny I am next to him, practically half his size.

Good thing you're keeping this strictly professional. You probably can't handle him anyway, if the palm - penis size thing's really true.

My cheeks heat as I stare at his massive hands resting on the thighs of his dark joggers.

"You have any more good mascot ideas?" He interrupts my dirty thoughts and I clear my throat.

"I'm assuming Coastal Crabs isn't going to work for you?"

"No, definitely not. Don't think anyone on the team wants to be associated with crabs. For obvious reasons."

I'm sure I turn bright red, a high-pitched giggle squeaking from my throat. Rearranging my face, I try to regain my totally professional, not-at-all flirty composure.

"Fine. So we've ruled out seahorses, barracuda, turtles, and crabs." I list each animal, tapping the pads of my fingers one by one.

"Does the mascot have to be marine life? Can't we be something that sounds cool, like the Storm or the Cyclones?"

"An animal is memorable, though. Easy to brand for merch."

He huffs out a breath, raking a hand through his dark hair. "Fine. We'll keep thinking then."

The cabin lights dim and the engines roar to life, the floor vibrating. I grip the armrest between us as the pilot advises everyone to buckle up for takeoff. Weston reaches over and clicks his seatbelt into place, then leans back into the leather. Relaxed and calm.

Unlike me, my insides knotting and twisting like a soft pretzel from a Central Park vendor. I've never been a huge fan of flying and somehow, the private plane feels worse than commercial. Smaller and more likely to crash.

The plane begins to taxi and we pick up speed at an alarming rate. I focus on breathing in and out. Weston cuts his eyes at me.

"You okay over there, Hurricane? You sound like you're having an asthma attack." His lips curve up slightly at the corners and I attempt a glower, although I'm very busy panicking about dying at the moment.

"I'm fine," I wheeze, in between breaths. "Maybe a touch nervous."

"Ah, she does have a weakness. So you can handle a room full of vicious reporters, but a little bit of gravity defying is too much?" His eyes twinkle, and I grimace as we lift off the runway.

"I suppose you're going to use this against me at some point in time?" I shoot back, already worrying about how he's going to spin this.

"Never. Just like you can't hold it against me that I'm terrified of moths."

"Moths? They don't do anything but fly around."

"I know. But you never know where those creepy things are going to land and they're all dusty, like they just escaped from a crypt or something. Look…" He points out the window at the fluffy white clouds rolling by. We're already airborne, and I didn't have a panic attack.

"Wow. Thanks. For distracting me." I shoot him a begrudging look of gratitude, surprised at how decent he's being.

Not making that professional distance thing any easier.

The foursome stays at the front of the plane, partially hidden behind a half privacy screen. Which leaves me and Weston here in the back, the only other people on board besides the pilots and flight attendant. And now that we're soaring high above the clouds, I'm hyperaware of him.

The casual way he stretches out in his seat, commanding space. The easy in-and-out of his breath, each exhale winding his intoxicating scent around me. The heat shimmering off his body, lighting me up inside.

Distracting me.

"Would you care for a beverage?" The flight attendant glances from me to Weston.

"I'll have a water," Weston says.

"Still or sparkling?" She bats her thick fringe of lashes at him, and a flash of irritation rips through me. I quickly shove it away. So what if she's flirting with him?

I don't even like the guy.

Besides, I'm sure he lands more than his fair share of women, like most other pro athletes.

"Still would be great, thanks." He's polite, but doesn't even look twice at her.

Interesting. And again, unexpected.

"Same." I nod curtly, and she hurries away to get the drinks.

"Serious question…" Weston narrows his eyes, peering over at me. "Is this relocation thing temporary? Or is the team moving to Florida forever?"

His question's a sucker punch straight to the gut, circling us right back to the very issue dividing us. I swipe my hands down the soft linen of my skirt, mouth dry.

"Uh...tough to say."

His full lips press into a thin line. "Not a great response, Hurricane. As someone who does press interviews for a living, I thought you'd come up with something better than that."

I bite at the inside of my cheek, wishing I had a more concrete answer.

"I know. Sorry. It kind of depends on how the season goes, I guess. Ultimately, the final decision's not up to me."

He swivels in his seat, facing me. "We're kind of damned if we do, damned if we don't then, am I right? Play great, town loves us—we stay in Florida forever. Or get down there and suck, the community angle doesn't hit, and we're back at square one. Players lose their positions, more people from the franchise get fired..."

And I'm out on my ass. Proving my father right.

You're not championship material, Harbor.

My dad's words burn in my chest. If this rebrand fails, if I don't build something lasting here, he'll have his proof I was never worthy of the Hayes name.

"Water." The flight attendant shoves a bottle in my direction, handing the other to Weston, her fingers lingering on the plastic for a beat too long.

"Thanks." Weston unscrews the lid and takes a long swig. She hovers for a few more seconds, then darts away when the GM calls her over.

I shift in my seat, take a quick sip of water to quell my scratchy throat. I didn't know I signed up for twenty questions with the grumpy captain this morning.

"That's not going to happen. We're going to get to

Driftwood Cove and nail this rebrand. At least, I'll do my part." I level my gaze with his. "Will you do yours?"

"Are you insinuating I won't?" His brow furrows, a deep V forming between his eyes.

I shrug. "I don't know. You haven't been pleased with the rebrand from the start. How do I know you're not going to tank the whole thing?"

Weston leans forward, our faces inches apart. "Don't question my integrity, Ms. Hayes. To be clear, I always do what's best for the team. No matter what, whether I like it or not. I'm the leader of this team and I don't take that responsibility lightly."

There it is again, that edge in his voice that reminds me of my father. Always questioning my decisions.

This time, I'm not backing down. I've earned my place at the table.

I swallow hard, sitting up as tall as I can in the buttery leather seat. "Remember how you said I have to earn your trust?"

His jaw ticks, a vein in his neck pulsating. "I do."

"Well, you have to prove yourself to me."

His eyes flash and a hot bolt of desire zings straight to my clit.

WTF?

But there's something about his strong, tense jaw, that spark just below the growly surface.

"Make the team believe in this plan, Weston."

"I'm a hockey player, not a magician."

I huff out a sigh. The man's aggravating as hell.

Suddenly, lights flicker and the plane bounces up and down. Gasping, I grip the armrest, hot panic flooding my chest.

"Please take your seats and keep your safety belts

fastened for the remainder of the flight. We're moving through a storm and there will be turbulence." The pilot's voice hums through the speaker, and I plant my feet firmly on the floor, digging in.

"It's just a little turbulence. We'll be fine." Weston's voice is calm as he attempts to reassure me.

The plane shakes and we drop again, a quick dip down, sharp enough to lift my ass off the seat.

"Oh my gosh!" I cry, the panic intensifying.

"Breathe, Harbor. It'll be okay." Weston's voice is low, soothing me. "Breathe in and out. Good, just like that."

He rests his fingers on my forearm, the rough pad of his thumb rubbing tiny circles on my arm. Sparks fly across my skin, all my focus on Weston's touch.

"In and out. Good girl." The words trickle through me like warm honey, my stomach swooping. "That's very good."

We drop again, steeper this time, and now I'm shaking.

"It's okay, we're okay." I don't know if he's trying to convince me or himself at this point. The sky's a dark gray as we pitch through the clouds. Sweat beads on my brow as we lurch through the air. Weston keeps his hand on my arm the entire time.

I scrunch my eyes shut and start reciting the Hail Mary, at least what I can remember of it, my lips moving fervently as I pray.

I don't want to die today.

Please don't let me die.

I can't go out like this.

Rain beats against the window, competing with the loud whoosh of blood pounding in my ears. A wave of nausea rolls through me as we bounce up and down, the water churning in my stomach.

Another spiky descent and to my horror, I scream, bracing for impact. Weston wraps his arm around my shoulders, pulling me against his strong body.

"Shh, it's okay," he murmurs, stroking my arm. His masculine scent fills my nostrils as I breathe in deeply, trying to get ahold of myself. "I've got you."

I relax into him, hot tears pricking my eyes. His T-shirt's soft on my face, his heartbeat thumping in my ear.

I cannot cry right now.

Champions don't break under pressure. Mental toughness separates the winners from the losers.

And here I am, about to break down at thirty thousand feet in front of the one person whose respect I need the most.

"If you could go anywhere in the world, do anything, what would it be?" Weston lightly squeezes my biceps, bringing me into the present.

"Besides heaven, if this plane crashes?"

"Yeah. Besides heaven."

"Uh...I don't know." *Bounce, bounce, bounce.*

I rack my brain for an answer to his question, ignoring the turbulence.

"France. I always wanted to see the Eiffel Tower in person. Sounds cliché, I guess. But I took French in school."

"Nice. Good choice."

"What about you? Where do you want to go?"

"Iceland. I want to see the Northern Lights."

"Oh, that's a good one. Me too. It seems so romantic."

The nose of the plane lifts up, gravity forcing us to lean back in our seats. But still Weston keeps a firm grip on me.

"That's a good sign, right? That we're rising up?"

"Yeah, Harbor, that's a good sign. Better than down."

My body relaxes into his, nestled under his strong arm. *We fit just right.*

"What do you think about sharks?" I ask.

"I don't love them. Especially if we crash into the ocean."

"You think we're going to crash into the ocean?" My voice tips up, chest squeezing.

"No. I'm teasing you."

"Oh, good." I swallow down the panic. "For the mascot —hammerhead sharks. Because we're the Coastal Crushers. Get it? Crush, hammer."

His body stiffens. "Not sharks."

"Why not?"

"The team can't be a Florida cliché."

The plane dips precipitously again and my fingers fly to his shirt, clutching at the solid wall of chest. His heart hammers beneath my palm.

"They're apex predators." I try to keep my voice steady, despite my frayed nerves and the turbulence. "Powerful, fast, respected."

"Fine. Hammerheads. But don't make the shark all cutesy. We're elite athletes, not cartoon characters."

"Deal."

I practically sigh with relief as the plane levels out, the sky brightening and the lights blinking back on.

"That should be all the rough skies we hit today, folks. But keep those safety belts on, just in case." The pilot's voice crackles over the speaker.

I exhale a long breath. "Crisis averted."

"Looks like."

We sit in silence for a long minute, Weston's arm still wound around me. My nervous system should be calming down now that we're not careening into the Atlantic, but that's not what's happening.

Instead, I'm acutely aware of my racing heart, the heat of my skin where Weston's making contact.

"Thanks. For talking me through that."

He unwinds his arm from my shoulders and a tiny flicker of disappointment ripples through me.

"No problem. Should have asked if you were a nervous flyer before I took this seat, I guess." He nudges my elbow, a half-smile tugging at the corner of his mouth.

"Shut up. That wasn't just nervous flying. We almost died!"

"So dramatic. We hit a rough patch. I thought PR people were calm under pressure."

"There's a difference between business challenges and facing down death, Weston."

He chuckles, the sound vibrating his broad chest, and my pulse accelerates.

I survived an almost-plane crash. But I'm not so sure I'm coming out of this job intact.

Not if I have to keep working so closely with Weston Steele.

Because my heart isn't part of the contract.

CHAPTER 7
HARBOR

D riftwood Cove doesn't disappoint. From the white sand beach to the crystal blue water, the rolling dunes buffered with tall sea oats blowing in the wind, the landscape's picturesque. And, despite my father's negativity, the town isn't a "piss-ass, backwater swamp" at all. The Main Street area's lined with charming boutiques—a wine and cheese shop, a bookstore, an old-fashioned ice cream parlor, a beachy gift shop. Every store front has a different colored awning, the prettiest pink, aqua, and sunshine yellow pastels. The entire area's walkable, with plenty of grassy spaces and sidewalks perfect for a lazy afternoon stroll. And the Southern hospitality thing? Real, y'all.

All the good things I'd read online about this super cute beach town turn out to be absolutely true. Starting with the adorable Driftwood Inn. Sitting right on the beach, the quaint two-story hotel has an amazing ocean view from the lobby. Lots of glass and white-washed wood, with plush light blue couches. There's a restaurant open for breakfast, lunch, and dinner with a small bar area. And the pool sits in the center of an old-fashioned court-yard flanked by hotel rooms. The set-up's quirky and fun, and I can envision a lot of great events in the future.

I'm staying here until I find a more permanent place to live. But I haven't had much free time to drop everything and house hunt. Mr. Prince has kept me busy, sitting in non-stop meetings from morning to night. By the time I roll into the inn, I'm too exhausted to even scour the internet for listings.

Luckily, the team's hired a relocation specialist to help the players find rentals. Smart move because while adorable, the town is on the smaller side. There's one luxury condo building, but it's only four stories high. Something about building code and beach ordinances. Even if no other residents currently lived in the condos, the entire hockey team wouldn't fit. Some players are going to have to rent houses or maybe apartments.

Kind of a logistical nightmare, and I'm glad housing isn't my problem to solve. Gia, the housing woman, set me up with a tour of the condos later this afternoon, along with a townhouse and a single-family home that looks way too big for me.

I can't focus on that right now, though. I'm running late for my morning meeting with the GM. Not ideal, consid-ering I'm pitching the new color scheme and mascot. But my alarm didn't go off—or at least I didn't hear it.

Due to the summer heat, I've traded my typical sheath dress and heels for a slightly more casual look. Throwing on a navy striped midi dress, I slide my feet into white sneakers and grab my cell and satchel. With a quick swipe of lip gloss, I'm ready to go.

Popping my sunglasses on, I cross through the empty

courtyard. It's still early, so no one's lounging in the chaises or splashing around in the pool. Being June in Florida, the temperature's already in the eighties and the curl in my hair's telling me the humidity's damn near one hundred percent. By midday, everyone's going to be boiling.

Not that New York's all that pleasant in the summer. At least here there's a constant ocean breeze.

I walk the two blocks to the arena, enjoying the warmth of the sunshine on my skin, the slight tang of salt on the air. It's refreshingly peaceful, the sound of the ocean waves crashing in the distance a lovely soundtrack for my commute.

I could get used to this.

Maybe Florida won't be so bad after all. I haven't seen a gator yet, and so far everyone's been friendly and welcoming.

The most hostile person I've encountered during the relocation is Weston, and even he's softening up a little. The turbulent plane ride showed me a side of him I hadn't expected—protective, calm and reassuring.

After that near-death experience, I understand why he's the team captain. He's great under pressure, a strong leader.

I only hope he leads the team in the right direction, getting them fully aboard the rebrand. Too much rides on the plan for him to half-ass it. He promised me he wouldn't, but I'm not sure he's sold on the whole relocation. Not yet, anyway.

The arena parking lot's fairly empty, and I notice Prince's spot is vacant. At least I made it to work before my boss. I tap my building keycard on the box and the light turns green. Access granted.

I move through the airy lobby, my sneakers squeaking on the shiny linoleum. The space is light and bright, with huge windows and a soaring atrium area. Plenty of places to hang team pennants and banners in the coming season —the sponsors will love it. The bones of the arena are good. With a little bit of work, this place will be great. A perfect home for a new hockey dynasty.

Buzz, buzz.

Fishing my cell out of my bag, I read the text from Prince.

> Prince: Meeting rescheduled to this afternoon. Have an interview this morning. See you at 4 PM

Well, guess I'm not late after all. It's fine, I can use the extra time to research different community outreach opportunities. I'd love to have at least one lined up by the end of the week so we can hit the ground running once the rest of the team shows up.

On a whim, I decide to cut through the rink to get to the offices on the other side of the building. I pull the heavy metal door open and slip into the chilly arena. A shiver rolls through me at the sudden change in temperature, chill bumps rising on my bare arms. I blink, my eyes adjusting to the darkness. The only light in the arena shines down on the ice, illuminating the rink.

I'm not alone.

Weston's out on the ice in his practice jersey, running drills. His back's to me as he skates toward the opposite goal, W. STEELE stamped across his shoulder blades. Ice flurries around the blades of his skates as he races across the rink. At the goal, he slides to a stop, then transitions into backward skating. He's quick and graceful, the thick muscles in his legs visible without the typical bulky pads. I hold my breath as I watch him skate back and forth, a blue streak against the white ice. Strong, lithe, powerful.

This is what elite-level hockey looks like. I've watched enough practices to recognize good players from great ones.

Even my father would agree that Weston Steele falls into the latter category, every inch of him confident and primed for peak performance.

He's the real deal.

Picking up speed, his skates slice across the slick surface, a rhythmic *ssshhh* bouncing off the walls. Soft and melodic, a whisper like the waves on the beach. The sound grows louder as he moves in my direction, a distinct metallic scratch with each dig into the ice. His muscles flex and ripple with the exertion and I can't take my eyes off him.

His body, the way he moves with both speed and precision. He's in the zone, oblivious to my presence as he switches to cone work. Zipping around each cone smoothly, easily.

He's gorgeous.

In a Weston-trance, I inch closer to the edge of the rink. Moving up to the glass, but careful to stay in the shadows so I don't break his flow.

From here, the ring of sweat on his jersey's visible. His breathing's labored as he slaloms around the cones. In and out, in and out, concentration etched on his face.

Seconds later, he's at the other end of the rink. He drops a puck on the ice, slapping the black disc back and forth with his stick. Skating close to the goal, he smacks the puck deep into the corner of the net. Retrieving the disc, he works his way through a seemingly familiar rotation. Hit deep left. Skate away. Hit deep right. Skate. Center. Repeat.

He cycles through this drill several times before abandoning the puck in the net. Spinning around and facing the other end of the rink, he repeats the speed drill. Knees bent, he tilts his chest forward and powers down the ice. Arms pumping back and forth, his head perfectly still as he pushes sideways off his blades.

Weston Steele's an absolute force on the ice.

A spray of ice glitters in the lights and he comes to a complete stop, his broad chest heaving. Stick in hand, he lifts his helmet.

"Like what you see, Hurricane?"

My entire body jolts.

Busted.

A hot blush floods my cheeks, creeping down my neck, and I thank the universe that the arena's dark.

I tip my chin up, though, trying to seem more confident than I feel inside. I'm not some puck bunny, sneaking in to watch the hockey star. I belong here, too.

"You look good out there, Steele." I work very hard to sound casual.

"To your trained eye?" He cocks his head, one dark brow arched high.

I shrug. "I've seen a lot of hockey. My dad dragged me to tons of practices when I was a kid and my mom wanted me out of the house."

"Fair enough." He skates to the edge of the ice and takes off his helmet. We're face to face, with only the glass between us.

His blue eyes sparkle beneath the bright white light, a sheen of sweat on his face.

Suddenly the arena's a whole lot warmer.

I shouldn't be reacting like this. I have no business getting involved with the team captain.

"Did you need something in particular, Hurricane? Or are you just here to ogle?"

The tips of my ears burn, my mouth going drier than the Gobi Desert in a drought.

"I'm not ogling."

Definitely was.

I fold my arms across my chest and square my shoulders. "I was cutting through to the offices. For a meeting." I stumble over the words, overexplaining.

"Uh-huh." He locks his eyes on mine and my stomach swoops, a tingle running straight down my spine. "Let me guess—you're pitching the new uniform design and you made them teal and hot pink."

I screw my lips up, trying to squash my annoyance. "While that color combo would likely resonate with many Floridians, no, I did not choose teal and hot pink as the new color scheme. But maybe I will now…" I let the threat hang in the air for a moment.

Weston scowls, his little dig backfiring. "Please don't. Pretty sure the *Miami Vice* vibe isn't it right now."

My cell buzzes and I leap at the distraction, checking my messages.

> Gia: Tour at noon? A few good options I
> think you should see

I tap out a quick response with shaky fingers.

> Harbor: Sure, sounds good. Where should
> I meet you?

SLAP SHOT SCANDAL 71

Gia: The Cove Towers lobby

Harbor: Great. See you soon

Dropping my phone into my purse, I rise to face Weston. He's still watching me. Stick in hand, a smirk on his too-handsome face.

"You late for your meeting now?" He tosses his stick back and forth between his palms and I'm transfixed by the white blur.

"What? No. The meeting got bumped. That was Gia. I'm taking a tour of housing options at noon."

"Noon?" He pauses, a brow lifted.

"Yes…"

"Huh. Me too."

I fiddle with the bangles on my wrist. "You're touring houses today? With Gia?"

"Yes." Weston squares his shoulders, plants his stick between his feet.

"Small world. I suppose she's trying to consolidate her appointments."

"Suppose so."

I bite at my lip, shifting from foot to foot. His eyes hold mine for a long second, then he clears his throat and glances away.

"We're both heading in the same direction. I can give you a ride if you want—my car got delivered."

I almost choke on my own saliva. "Really?"

"I mean, yeah. It would make sense. We're both here and we're going to the same place. Save gas and all that."

Trapped in a car with the grumpy hockey star who apparently makes my brain short-circuit.

Terrible freaking idea.

But, somehow, I can't refuse. Instead, I shrug and act way more nonchalant than I feel. "You offering because it's efficient? Or is this a power play to avoid hot pink and teal?"

"Strictly efficiency, Hurricane." He puts his helmet back on and pivots, going back to practice. But he steals a quick glance back at me over his shoulder.

"Besides, I look good in pink." He winks and skates away, leaving me standing there absolutely shook.

I think the grumpy hockey captain may be thawing.

At any rate, I have a ride to the condos. And I'm probably reading way too much into his carpool offer. It's a rideshare, not a date.

Yet my chest feels lighter than it has in months—and that terrifies more than the current PR crisis.

I can't get distracted.

Remember, Harbor. The moment you take your eyes off the prize, you've already lost the game.

Getting involved with Weston Steele is exactly the kind of thing my dad would predict—proof that I'm not a winner, not cut out for this game.

There's no way I'm letting that happen.

CHAPTER 8
WESTON

don't know what possessed me to offer Harbor a ride to the condos. Sure, heading over together is practical and efficient.

But spending more time with the woman responsible for uprooting my life and potentially tanking my hockey career?

Not my best idea.

Especially when she's rapidly ascending to the top of the 'highly fuckable' list.

Blonde, petite, the perfect size to tuck beneath my arm. Add that razor-sharp wit and glittering smile, and she's a force to be reckoned with.

A hurricane.

Blowing through and messing me up, screwing with every single aspect of my regimented life.

I don't date. I'm not a casual kind of guy. Unlike Bennett, I don't have the bandwidth to deal with distractions. I like to stay focused on what's most important —hockey.

I don't have time for relationships, making someone else happy.

But now, I can't stop thinking about Harbor.

Not since our first run-in at the team meeting. The way she patted at my chest, blushing and stammering. Then on the plane ride when we hit the storm and she panicked. Gripping the armrest for dear life before I calmed her down.

Holding her close to me, I felt her heart pounding, heard her breath hitch when we touched.

There was something between us in that second—and I don't think I can blame it all on the turbulence.

The woman does something to me. Much as I want to deny it, when she's in the room, I can't look away.

Which could be a very big problem.

The team's in crisis, my career's on the line. I'm the damn captain. I can't go falling for the PR consultant behind every bad idea that's rolled my way since Coach Evans was fired.

She's enemy number one.

So why am I constantly thinking about crossing the line?

Fuck. This is all kinds of messed up.

Harbor waves as she hurries out of the arena, dashing across the parking lot. Bright sunlight catches the gold streaks in her hair, and I swipe my sweaty palms on my mesh shorts.

Must be the Florida humidity.

"Punctuality not your thing, Hurricane?" I open the car door for her, wait while she slides into the leather seat of the Porsche.

"Sorry." She shoots me a sheepish look and tucks her legs into the car. "I got caught on the phone with a community sponsor."

I slam the door and hustle around, taking my spot behind the wheel and firing up the engine. The Porsche roars to life and I punch the directions to the condo into the GPS before pulling out of the lot.

Harbor fidgets with her bracelets, hands constantly in motion, like she's nervous.

"I still have to run the idea by Mr. Prince, but the youth league's interested in you guys working with the kids. That would be a great photo op. A few key players—like you and your brothers—skating with the little ones. Plus, it could help build the local fan base and stoke excitement for the upcoming season."

Her words tumble out in an excited rush. While I appreciate her enthusiasm for pumping up the team's image and fanbase, I don't particularly want to be used as a pawn in her little PR chess game.

"No." I growl out the word, the harsh sound echoing in the enclosed chamber of the car.

"What? What do you mean 'no'?" Her head swivels in my direction, her golden ponytail whipping over her shoulder.

"What part of the one syllable answer confused you?"

"All of it." Glossy lips pressing together, her nostrils flare. "You're going to have to work with me on this sort of thing, Captain."

"I don't recall 'work with me' being in my contract."

"It's implied in the fine print. Right between 'don't sabotage the PR consultant trying to save the team' and 'don't act like an arrogant asshole.'"

I tighten my grip on the wheel, something hot flaring in my gut. "I know how to read a contract, Hurricane."

"Then read the room. Your team needs help. And I'm here to do just that."

Aggravation shoots through me. "I don't want to use neighborhood kids in a cheap bid to build goodwill. That's not right."

"We're not using them. We're connecting with the children in the community and building relationships." She puts heavy emphasis on the last part, *community* and *relationships.* "You do know how to build relationships, right? Or am I overestimating you?" Her tone slips into snark and my dick twitches in my pants.

Not the time, boss. You twisted motherfucker.

"Of course I do," I snarl back at her, my gaze pinned on the road.

"Would your last three girlfriends agree with that assessment?"

"I love that you gave me three, Hurricane. Considering how little you think of me."

A tiny sigh escapes her lips and she sinks back against the seat. "I don't think poorly of you." Her voice is soft, almost gentle. "But you fight me at every turn. We're on the same team. For now. How about we act like it?"

I huff out a heavy breath, gut rolling. From nerves, anxiety.

From her.

Sliding into the Visitor parking spot in the condo lot, I cut the engine and glance over at her.

"You're a temporary member of this team. I've been here and I know what works and what doesn't. Personally, and for the rest of the guys. None of them are going to like this idea. Guaranteed."

She scrunches those full, pink lips up and stares me down.

"We'll see about that. I'm pitching the idea to Prince this afternoon. If he gives me the green light, it's likely a go. But tell you what—I'll compromise. If it's a yes from Prince, I'll float the idea with the rest of the team. If everyone hates the idea, I'll pivot."

I frown, mulling over her negotiating strategy. "Still don't like it. But fine."

"Deal?" Her voice tips up, tinged with hope.

"Deal." I force out the word through gritted teeth.

This woman's maddening. I'm not sure I'll survive an entire season with Little Miss Sunshine and all her bright ideas.

"We're late. Let's go." I hit the unlock button and climb out of the driver's seat, every inch of my body tense—and we were in the car less than ten minutes.

It's gonna be a long damn season.

"Yoo-hoo!" Gia, a busty brunette, waves us over to the double glass doors of the light blue stucco condo building.

I stomp across the pavement, Harbor jogging to keep pace with me.

"There you two are. I thought maybe you got lost!" Gia chuckles at her own joke, holding the door open for us.

A blast of cold AC hits me in the face as we step into the lobby. The décor's dated, lots of shiny gold and glass, a modern aesthetic leaning more toward retro now. A few beachy paintings hang on the wallpapered walls. A wood-paneled front desk sits empty.

"I have the keys to one of the vacant condos. The manager's at lunch, but she said to go ahead and take a quick tour. She understands our predicament and knows how busy you are, Weston." Gia shoots me an apologetic look, and Harbor's mouth opens like she's about to clap back with a comment about her own busy schedule.

She must think better of it, though, clamping her mouth shut tight. I can't help but stare at her glossy pout, caught up in an image of Harbor on her knees with my dick sliding between those pretty pink lips.

Gia smashes the gold button for the elevator and I'm back to reality.

I shouldn't have these wildly inappropriate fantasies about the PR consultant intent on trotting me and the team out like show ponies.

No matter how gorgeous she would be on her knees, begging for my cock.

"Weston, I know you and your brothers are thinking about renting a house. And that could be a great option. But at least take a quick tour here so you can report back to the guys." Gia babbles on about the building as the doors to the elevator creak closed and we begin the achingly slow ascent to the fourth floor.

Ding, ding, ding, ding.

After a few long minutes, the doors slide open and we step out onto a sea of beige carpet. The same shell wallpaper from downstairs hangs on the walls, each door marked with a gold shell bearing a number.

"Here we are, 422." Gia whips out a key and unlocks the door, letting us inside.

The condo's small but airy, with a view of the ocean from the living room.

"Million-dollar view." Gia flashes me a smile and I catch the slight tightening of Harbor's lips, one side tipping up into a strained half-smile.

Almost as if she's jealous.

I square my shoulders and puff out my chest a little before striding over to the kitchen, a small but adequate space directly next to the living room. White cabinets line the wall and the appliances are stainless steel, good enough to get the job done.

"How many available units are there?" Harbor asks, popping her head into a cabinet.

"In this building, I believe there are currently ten available units. There may be an eleventh, but it's being renovated right now," Gia says, checking the printout she's holding. "Besides these condos, I have a few single-family homes I can show you. Also, some cute townhomes only a few minutes from here."

"That's a nice thing about this location, though, right?" Harbor says. "Everything's close because we're in a small town. So convenient."

"Uh-huh," I mutter, stuffing my hand in my pocket. Always focusing on the bright side of things.

Annoying.

"Let's take a quick look at the bedrooms. This is a two-bedroom unit, so you have one bedroom for guests or an office." She leads us out of the kitchen and down a narrow hallway. "Here's bedroom one."

Gia flips on a light and reveals a small, boxy room with no window. "There's an en suite bath."

We peer into the bathroom, which has all the necessities. Shower, sink, toilet.

"Then on the other side of the hall's the second bedroom, also with an en suite."

This room's the money room, significantly larger, brighter, and better, with a sweeping view of the Atlantic.

"You could fit a king-sized bed in here, no problem." Gia's eyes linger on me, flicking over my arms, my chest.

Harbor clears her throat. "The room dimensions are adequate for standard furniture. Although I'm sure most players prioritize function over aesthetics."

"You'd be surprised what professional athletes prioritize. Right, Weston?" Gia shoots me a flirty smile, but I ignore her overture.

"Mostly just winning," I say, Harbor's knuckles whitening around the notepad she's holding.

Gia's phone trills and she holds up a finger. "Sorry, I have to get this. Take your time and I'll meet you downstairs in a few minutes."

She's already walking away, chatting into her cell. A few seconds later, the door closes behind her and Harbor and I are alone in the condo.

"Well, she's awfully friendly." Harbor's voice drips with sarcasm and my lips tip up slightly.

"Yeah, she was. Super nice." I add the last bit just to fuck with her.

It works.

"Uh-huh. Surprised she didn't ask what you're doing later tonight."

"Who said she didn't?" I fire back, tipping my head and smirking.

Harbor rolls her eyes and changes the subject, waving her hand at the view.

"Think this will meet the team's expectations?"

The ocean's dark, the bright sun hidden behind fast-moving storm clouds. A deep rumble of thunder vibrates the windows

"It'll work. Most of the guys will be fine here."

"But not you? You're renting a house with your brothers?" Harbor bites at the edge of her lip, and I try not to stare.

"Correct. I want more privacy than a condo offers."

"The captain needs his privacy," she teases, a playful glint in her hazel eyes.

"Yeah. I have my routines."

"Wouldn't want us peasants messing up your 'routines.'" She air quotes the word, and a spark flickers low in my gut.

I want to fuck the sass right out of that mouth.

No. Uh-uh. Bad fucking idea.

Still, I take a step forward, edging closer to her. "My routines keep me focused."

"On what?" Her voice drops slightly, those hazel eyes widening as she realizes how close we're standing.

"On winning." I hold her gaze for a long beat, longer than necessary, her pulse fluttering in the graceful column of her neck. "On not getting distracted."

She swallows hard, taking a deliberate step back. "Well, consider me warned about disrupting your precious focus."

"You're already disrupting it." I rake a hand through my hair, tearing my gaze from her mouth and breaking the tension. "You need to see anything else? Measure the closets or something?"

"No, I do not."

Without another word, she spins on her heel and stalks away. I follow her to the elevator.

She smashes the button and the gold circle lights up. Another rumble of thunder shakes the building.

"We may be taking the rest of the tour in the rain."

"Gia probably has an umbrella for you." Harbor glances over at me, arms folded across her chest.

"Hope so. Because I didn't bring one."

Ding.

The elevator opens and Harbor swishes inside, jamming the L. I lean back against the gold railing as the doors slide closed.

"Where are you going to stay?" I ask under the guise of small talk, although part of me is genuinely interested.

I shouldn't be, but I am.

She shrugs. "Not sure yet. Probably wherever's left after the team arrives."

"You should decide now. Get a jump. You were here first."

"The athletes are more important. I'm fine wherever. You should have seen my apartment in the city. It was tiny. About half as big as the condo we just toured."

"Wow. Did you at least have a good view?"

"If you count the building dumpster, yeah. It was great."

"Oh."

"I'm sure you can't relate," she fires back.

"I have lived in shitty places before, you know."

"Like where?"

"My college dorm wasn't amazing."

"Are dorms anywhere amazing?"

Suddenly, the lights flicker and then cut out, the elevator lurching to an abrupt stop. Harbor loses her balance, falling into me. I grab her arm, catching her at the elbow as she stumbles up against my chest.

The car drops another inch with a sickening lurch. Harbor's fingers dig into my biceps, her breath catching on a gasp.

Oh shit.

I'm stuck in a pitch-black elevator with Hurricane Harbor—and there's nowhere to hide from what's brewing between us.

CHAPTER 9
WESTON

eart pounding, Harbor's soft body presses against me in the darkness. The scent of vanilla and coconut drifts up from her hair, swirling and filling the enclosed space.

"Weston?" Her voice is quiet, barely above a whisper.

"Yeah?"

"Did the power just go out?"

"I think so."

"Oh my god." The words come out a tight, sorrowful moan.

"It'll be okay." I squeeze her arms, trying to sound reassuring. Although inside, I'm less than confident.

I hate tight spaces.

"I'm sure we'll be up and running again in no time." I'm trying to talk myself into believing the power's coming back on as much as I'm trying to calm her down.

Hot panic surges through me, chest tight. My vision goes spotty, white pricks of light dancing in the periphery, and I can't get a full breath.

"You okay?" Harbor's palm flattens on my chest. "Your heart's racing."

"I'm fine. Mildly claustrophobic." Sweat beads at my temple and I take a shuddery inhale, sucking in the sweet scent of Harbor.

"Oh shit. You want some water or something? Don't pass out on me."

"I told you, I'm fine. And I'll skip the water. A stalled elevator and an urgent need to pee's not a winning combo."

"True."

The car jerks, dropping another inch, and I instinctively grip Harbor tighter. She shrieks, her high-pitched scream reverberating in my eardrums.

"We should sit. Just in case." I slide to the floor, pulling her down with me. She's nestled in between my legs for a brief moment, her warm breath dusting my cheeks. Then she slides over and settles in next to me. Shoulder to shoulder, our thighs brushing.

I pull my cell out of my pocket and tap the screen, the light bouncing off the walls.

"Dammit. No service."

Harbor checks hers with the same result.

Tapping the flashlight button on the phone, I hold the light up to the electrical panel and pound the emergency button. Nothing happens.

"You've got to be shitting me," I mutter, panic bubbling up. "The button doesn't work."

"Probably because the power's out. Don't worry, I'm sure your girl Gia will figure it out. Hopefully she'll call the fire department or something." Harbor's tone is sarcastic.

Damn. She is jealous.

"Gia's not my girl—don't worry, Hurricane," I tease, elbowing her.

"Me? I'm not worried…" Her voice trails off and my muscles tense, acutely aware of her presence, her nearness, even in the dark.

The space is small and quiet, our breathing suddenly loud. The eerie sound of the car creaking as we sway back and forth, dangling in the air, is disconcerting. More sweat beads on my brow and my underarms are soaked.

"Tell me about you." It's a demand, from me to her. Anything to get my mind off being trapped in here.

"Uh, what do you want to know?"

"What do you want me to know?" I shoot back, mopping my face with the hem of my T-shirt.

"Well, you know I come from a hockey family. My dad's a coach."

"I remember. What level?"

Harbor hesitates, then sighs. "Professional. My dad's Doug Hayes."

"*The* Doug Hayes?" My tone's edged with awe. "The most winning coach in the league's history? Three-peat?"

"Yep. That's him."

"Wow."

Holy shit. I've been treating Coach Doug Hayes's daughter like some random PR consultant who doesn't understand hockey. No wonder she's been ready to hurt me every time I question her expertise. The woman's hockey royalty, a card-carrying member of a dynasty. And I doubted her knowledge of the sport at every turn.

Airball.

"How was it growing up with Coach Hayes as a dad?"

Harbor exhales, a long, heavy sigh. "It was…something."

Her answer surprises me. She sounds almost exhausted, with a hint of sadness coloring the edges.

"Huh. Something good or something bad?"

"Just something. To the outside world, my dad's the greatest coach who's ever lived. Unfortunately, he brought that locker room mentality back home with him. Everyone in the family was a player in need of coaching. He was tough." She takes another shuddery breath. "Still is."

Her voice drifts off and even in the darkness, worry lines stand out on her forehead.

"It's hard to compartmentalize when you're that good at something, I guess."

She shrugs. "Must be. Because he's retired and hasn't let up."

I chuckle. "So he's a hard-ass?"

"Absolutely."

"How's he feel about you working in hockey?"

"Doesn't love it. According to the greatest coach in hockey history, I'm better suited for 'behind-the-scenes' work that doesn't sully the family legacy. His words, not mine."

Biting at her lip, she plays with her bangles. "Apparently I lack the 'championship-mindset' required for front-facing hockey jobs. So here I am, trying to prove him wrong by rebuilding an entire franchise."

Now I get why Harbor's so motivated, so invested in this rebrand. She's not just proving herself professionally —she's fighting for validation from hockey's greatest legend.

Risking everything on a relocated team in a small Florida beach town, betting her family legacy on our success.

"Bold move."

She sighs again, shaking her head. "Maybe not my smartest play. Dr. Martina—that's my therapist—because yeah, I'm *that* girl. The one with daddy issues. Anyway, she thinks he suffers from a generational patriarchy complex. I chalk it up to his need to be in control all the time. Either way, it's really fucking annoying. You know he tried to talk me out of taking this job?"

"Really? So he thinks Florida's a bad idea?"

"Yep. Fought me on it until the very last second. He even got me an interview with the Lakers the day we flew down here."

"He's really committed to your success, huh?"

She rolls her eyes. "That's a lovely way of saying he's meddling above his pay grade. The man's offsides and right now he's in the penalty box."

Harbor licks her bottom lip and I can't stop staring. Maybe it's the tiny, enclosed space. Maybe it's the constant tension between us, I don't know.

Something inside me, deep-down, shifts when she's around.

I know I should keep my guard up, protect myself and the team from the shit storm swirling around us. I've worked too hard to get where I am only to throw it all away.

But there's something about her that draws me in. She's competent and professional, yet strangely vulnerable.

It's a compelling combination and I can't seem to break away.

"I take it you're not on speaking terms right now, then?"

"Not really."

"I'm sorry. That's a tough spot to be in."

She flips her hair off her neck, fanning herself. "It's fine.

We've always had a rocky relationship. What about you? Your dad was a professional hockey player too, right?"

I cut my eyes at her. "You did your research."

"Of course I did. What's he saying about the move?"

I hesitate for a second before answering. "I wouldn't worry too much about my dad's advice. Nothing I do is ever good enough for him. That is, when he bothers paying attention at all."

"Oh."

Scrubbing my hand over my jaw, irritation swirls through my gut. "When he remarried, his priorities shifted. He's mainly concerned with making his wife happy. He leaves me and my brothers alone, for the most part. Except for the occasional phone call after a game to dissect every play that went wrong."

"Sounds like our dads would get along great." She elbows me lightly and I shoot her a wry smile.

"Probably. If they could get past their own egos."

"I'm guessing your dad's not a huge fan of all three of his boys moving to Florida?"

"Not particularly. Thinks it's a big risk."

"It is. But that's what makes the opportunity so perfect. We have the chance to make the Coastal Crushers the next big thing in hockey. From the ice up. It's going to be huge, Weston."

Her eyes sparkle in the darkness, her enthusiasm bubbling over. She's fucking stunning when she's excited and all I can think about is what she's like in the bedroom — how she'd feel underneath me, what she tastes like, the sounds she makes when she's coming undone.

For fuck sake, Steele. Get it together.

"Did you leave anything behind in New York?" It's a

thinly veiled question, probably overly personal. But right now, I don't care. I want to know everything about her.

"My apartment. It wasn't that great, not a huge loss. And a book club. Other than that, not much. What about you?"

"I did have a pretty nice apartment. A color-coordinated closet, a home gym."

"Oh, you had me at color-coordinated closet," she teases, nudging my knee with hers. A spark flares low in my gut and I chuckle.

"My brothers make fun of me for that. I'll have to report back that it's actually a net-positive."

"Totally is. I'm a big fan."

"Never would have guessed…"

She blinks up at me in the dark, and my heart hammers so hard I'm certain she can hear it in the tight space. I gaze down at her, my eyes finally adjusted to the darkness, taking in her full lips, the way her teeth worry at her bottom lip. I lean in closer and her sweet perfume fills my nostrils. We're inches apart now, her breath hitching as I tip forward.

So close.

This woman—daughter of the most legendary coach in hockey—chose to bet everything on us. On me. That kind of courage…

I shouldn't be doing this, it's a mistake.

But a mistake I'm dying to make.

I brush my thumb over her bottom lip, her mouth soft against the rough calloused pad. She sighs, her breath a whisper in the dark. Leans in with a tiny hitch in her throat.

"Weston…" She reaches up and grips my wrist, her

fingers hot on my skin. Her lips part and I inch forward, aching to touch her.

A bad idea. But God, I want it.

Buzz.

The lights flicker and the elevator lurches, zooming down with the force of gravity. Harbor's fingers tighten on my wrist and I hold onto her, trying to shield her from impact.

Ding.

The doors slide open, flooding the elevator with light. Both of us mashed together against the wall, sweaty and breathless.

I blink against the sudden brightness, Harbor still pressed against me, her fingers digging into my biceps.

"Well, well, well. Don't mind me, Captain. Wouldn't want to interrupt this hot and heavy PR strategy meeting."

Bennett.

Of all the people who could be standing here in this moment, it has to be my smartass, too-observant brother, with his perpetual fucking smirk.

Harbor jerks away from me, smoothing her dress down with trembling hands. "The power went out. We were trapped in the elevator for a while."

Bennett's gaze slides from a disheveled Harbor to me, lingering on the side of my neck where I'm sure my pulse is hammering beneath the skin.

From the sudden drop, of course.

"Must have been terrifying. Good thing my brother was here to keep you company." His tone's knowing, making my jaw clench. "You two look...rattled."

I swipe my sweaty palms down my shorts and stand. "Mechanical failure," I growl, stepping out of the elevator. "Nothing more."

Bennett smirks. "If you say so, Captain."

Harbor marches out, her cheeks stained pink, gaze averted. But her face is totally neutral.

And that rattles me.

With the doors finally open, I'm breathing again.

I got my breath back—but something else stays lodged in my chest.

Her voice. Her story. The way she looked at me like I mattered.

I'm out of the confined space, but somehow, everything feels tighter.

CHAPTER 10
HARBOR

That was a close one.

I stalk away from the elevator, flushed and out of sorts. Gia has Weston and Bennett cornered at the front desk. Her dark head's bobbing, hands waving wildly through the air. Probably trying to explain the power outage and convince Weston the building's up to code and the hockey team won't get stuck in the elevator on game day.

I take the opportunity to slink away unnoticed. I'm not in the mood to defend myself to Weston's brother or stand by while Gia shamelessly flirts with Weston.

I'm entirely too flustered to do either. My heart's still racing, working hard to keep pace with my mind.

If the power hadn't come back on, I'm pretty sure Weston and I would have kissed.

And that would have been a gigantic mistake.

I could lose this job, my reputation, everything I've worked so hard for.

Champions don't let personal feelings cloud professional judgment.

Getting involved with Weston would prove my father's point—personal feelings disqualify me from this job.

Years of effort and sacrifice, gone in minutes.

And for what? A fling with the pro hockey star with an attitude problem?

Because nothing real could happen between us. I mean, I haven't had a serious boyfriend since college. Clearly, my judgment's lacking in the relationship department.

And I feel like I'm losing my grip again. Maybe it's the stress of the transition, coupled with the Florida heat and humidity.

Maybe it's Weston's stupidly oversized biceps and rock-hard abs, that sharp jawline and his sexy as fuck smirk.

Doesn't matter what's causing me to lose my edge. All I know is I need to keep my eyes on the rebrand—and off of Weston Steele.

All of him.

No matter how freaking gorgeous he is.

And also maybe—secretly, deep-down—a nice guy.

Ugh. If he starts being nice to me, I'm definitely going to lose my resolve. I'll just have to double-down on my professionalism and do my best to keep my distance.

Shoving out of the glass doors, I hurry in the direction of the arena. I can probably make it back before the storms kick up again.

"Hurricane!" Weston's deep voice stops me in my tracks.

Shit.

Digging deep, I pray for my willpower to kick in. I take a quick breath and spin to face him.

"Hey. We survived." I work to keep my tone light, although I'm high-key panicking on the inside. He can't be out here, using that nickname where anyone could hear. It's too personal, making our private connection visible, real. I fiddle with the stack of bracelets on my wrist and hope my cheeks aren't as red as they feel.

"Aren't you going to look at the townhomes with us?" His brow furrows as he squints down at me, the hulkiness of his body overwhelming. I shift from foot to foot, trying to come up with a plausible excuse. Because there's no way I'm going to be able to house hunt with Bennett hawking my every move concerning his brother.

"I'm going to pass. I have to get back." I hook my thumb over my shoulder, pointing toward the arena.

"It's kind of a long walk. You want me to give you a ride?"

"No, I could use the extra steps." I tap at my watch, pretending to check my activity tracker.

"Too bad. Who's going to talk me down in the event of an elevator emergency?" His lips tip into a wry smile and my heart skips in my chest.

This is so not good.

I can't let my guard down, not when everything's on the line—for both of us.

"You'll be fine. Your brother's here now. The two of you are probably strong enough to get the elevator moving even without power."

He shakes his head, raking his hand through his hair. "Don't think so. But thanks for the vote of confidence. You sure you're okay?"

"Yes, I'm fine. I lived in New York for years—pretty certain I can handle Driftwood Cove."

"Alright. I'll see you later then."

We stand staring at each other for a long second, the salty ocean breeze cool on my heated skin, unspoken words hanging between us.

Finally, I break away. Focus on putting one foot in front of the other at a normal pace, although my gut instinct is to run and hide.

Because I don't know exactly what happened in the elevator between us, but I do know that whatever it was definitely can't happen again.

————

Straight after the afternoon meeting, I go back to the hotel and take a long shower, washing away the sweat-and-cedar smell of Weston left clinging to my skin. I'm finally in bed, working on my laptop with a glass of wine, when a video call from my younger sister, Piper, rings through.

Saving my latest 'Hockey with Heart' document, I tap my cell and Piper's cheery face fills the screen.

"Hey, you." Piper grins and waves, her long, dark hair in a high ponytail. "How's Florida? You don't look very tan."

"Must be the lighting. Oh wait—no, it's probably because I've been working during all the daylight hours, Pipes. It's been a week and a half of non-stop meetings. One doesn't tan buried under mountains of strategic plans in a cave of an office."

"Still salty, though." She *tsks* loudly and shakes her head, ponytail swishing over her slim shoulders.

"Were you at yoga?" I motion at her tight, pale pink top and matching leggings.

"Yes. I'm doing a write-up on a spa in Arizona, with a

focus on wellness retreats. Lots of yoga, saunas, cupping, that sort of thing."

"Sounds dreamy." Not for the first time, I'm slightly jealous of my sister's career. Travel content creator sounds much less stressful than PR strategist right now.

She shrugs. "It's fine. No hot guys here, though. Unlike your position..."

"Stop." I shake my head, even as heat floods through me. An image of Weston skating this morning pops into my mind. All those muscles, barely contained in his practice jersey. His icy stare as the puck flew across the empty rink, the furrow of concentration on his serious face.

"Don't tell me you're not flirting at all? You're surrounded by hockey babes."

I heave out a sigh. "Yeah, I know. But I have to keep things professional, you know?"

Piper narrows her eyes at me. "It's more than that, Harbor. It's written all over your face. Spill."

"What?" I feign innocence, even as my heart hammers thinking of Weston.

"I know that look. That's a *there's definitely a hot guy* look. Spill the tea!"

"No tea, sis."

"Liar."

"Me?" My hand flies to my chest and I do my best to act affronted. "I would never."

"Uh-huh. Hey, I'm proud of you, showing interest in something other than your job for once."

"Gee, thanks, Pipes." I roll my eyes at my annoyingly perceptive sister.

"You're deflecting. Talk—I know there's a guy. You're blushing and your neck's blotchy. Who is he? A player on the team? What position?" Piper sits down on her yoga mat in lotus position, readying for a long chat.

"Sorry to disappoint. But there's not much to tell. I'm down here with the owner, the GM, a few office staff…" My voice trails off, throat going dry as I lie to her.

"And…" she presses, not letting the subject go. A damn yappy dog with a bone.

"And the team captain. But the rest of the team's rolling in now."

"Oh. So it's the captain. That's fine, say no more. I'll have the details here in a second."

The screen shakes as Piper does a quick internet search, tapping and then smiling at her results.

"He is cute. Kind of scowly and serious. A perfect match for you. Weston Steele." She says his name in a sultry tone, waggling her eyebrows.

"Shut up," I say, playfully slamming a pillow at the computer screen as my stomach flip-flops at Weston's name.

"Just admit it…" Piper grins like she's already won this round. "You're falling for Hockey Captain America."

"I'm not falling for anyone. I'm rebuilding careers—his included."

"Mm-hmm. And does everyone's career make your neck blotchy like that?"

I slap my hand to my throat, then glare at her. "It's the humidity."

"Sure. Blame the weather. Not the six foot-four, 225-pound hockey star, born and raised in New York. And he's a triplet? Wha-what?!?"

"Yeah, he is. His brothers are on the team too."

"Are they also single? I'm available, you know."

"Oh my gosh, Piper. I don't know if they're single. And

I'm not interested in Weston. We're working together is all. He's the captain of the team and I need him to get on board with the plan so the rebrand is successful."

"I bet he wants to get on board." She raises her perfect brows, and I crack up laughing despite how annoying she is.

"He does not. We've been fighting non-stop since we met."

Well, that's sort of true. We weren't fighting this afternoon in the elevator.

"Harbor...what aren't you telling me? Because that's your lie face." She points her index finger at me and I frown.

She's losing her mind. "I don't have a lie face."

"You do. And you're making it right now. The way your brow's scrunching and you hold your lips really tight."

I grab my wineglass and swirl the golden liquid, averting my gaze and debating how much to share here.

"Fine. We have been fighting. A lot. He hates my PR plan and has been a huge, grumpy pain in the ass."

"Until he wasn't." Piper finishes the thought for me and a mixture of annoyance and comfort swirls through me. There's nothing quite like a sister to sift through your bullshit. Cheapest therapy on the planet.

"Yeah. Until he wasn't." I sigh, leaning back against the fluffy white pillows. "Today we were trapped in the elevator together—"

She interrupts my story. "What? Did you say trapped? Like, in the movies? Oh my god, did you have *sex* in the elevator with the hockey star?" She fans herself, lips parted in shock.

"No! Of course not. It was dark and hot and we were

both kind of panicking. I was afraid he was going to pass out from a panic attack. Don't repeat that—top-secret info. Not that he told me not to tell anyone or anything, but…"

"Oh my gosh. You have it *bad* for this guy. You're protecting him. Harbs! That's so sweet. Can I be your maid of honor?"

"Piper! We're not even dating, let alone getting married. You're so ridiculous. Besides, even if we weren't clashing at every turn, the situation's tricky. I work for his team."

"Yeah, it's called an office romance. Like fifty percent of relationships begin at the office."

I huff out a breath. "But it's more complicated than that. It's not like we're peers. Not really."

"But you're not his boss, right?" She lowers her chin, staring straight through the screen at me.

"Not technically, no."

"So what's the issue?"

"Remember Kate, from Redline PR? She dated a player and once the media found out, she was fired on the spot. Besides, my job is to protect the team from scandal. I can't be *part* of the scandal, getting with the players. Especially not when I'm Doug Hayes's daughter. Any misstep gets amplified. Dad would have a field day and it would prove exactly what he thinks—I don't have what it takes to be in the hockey world."

"Right, I agree. You definitely shouldn't get with the players. Just him. Weston."

A shiver rolls through me at his name.

God, my sister's so annoying.

And also, accurate.

"I can't go there, Piper. Too much is at stake here. The team needs my entire focus to be on their success."

What I don't tell her—can't tell her, no matter how close we are—is this rebrand is every bit as much about my success, too.

This isn't just about the team. Our dad's watching, waiting for me to fail. I can't give him the tiniest scrap of ammunition to use against me.

I can practically hear his *I told you so* from here.

"And their success probably hinges on how well Weston Steele, team captain, plays. And I bet he plays better hockey when he's happy, know what I mean?" Piper gives me an exaggerated wink and I laugh.

"Knowing Weston, he probably has a strict no-sex policy during the season. To keep his focus laser-sharp."

Focus.

There's that word again. And it's starting to feel like a battle I'm losing.

"Damn, you sound like you know him pretty well already."

I bite at my lip and stare out at the dark ocean, reflecting. *Do I know Weston well already?*

Not really, but it feels like we've known one another a lot longer than a week and a half.

Because you click with him.

Shoving that thought away, I focus on my sister. "Anyway, enough about me. What's up with you? How's work?"

"It's fine. That's one of the reasons I'm calling. I have an assignment in Florida later this month and was hoping to see you."

"Sure, sounds good. Shoot me the dates and I'll get you on my calendar. I need to check the schedule, but I should be around."

"Great. I've gotta run to a nature meditation session. But I'll send you dates!"

"Perfect. Love you, Pipes." I blow her a kiss as she waves and clicks off, the screen going dark.

My sister's something else. We're nothing alike—she's a free spirit and I'm more structured, preferring a schedule and rules to the freelance lifestyle. But she is intuitive and just may be on to something.

In the elevator, things shifted between me and Weston. Maybe it was the confined space or the darkness, I don't know. But for the first time, it felt like maybe—just maybe—something could happen between us.

And I'm not sure if I should be happy about that or shaken to the core.

Because I can't afford to screw up this team rebrand. An entire team's counting on me. Jobs hang in the balance—including mine.

Even if I wanted to take a chance with Weston, it's a terrible idea.

I set aside my wineglass and open the Hockey with Heart proposal, forcing myself to focus on the community outreach calendar instead of piercing blue eyes and the scent of cedar.

My phone vibrates against the nightstand. I check the screen and nearly drop it.

> Weston: Prince wants to see updated mascot mockups by tomorrow. I've got early ice time at 5:30. Meet at Shoreline Coffee at 7 to review?

Pulse jumping, I stare at my cell. It's a professional text from a colleague.

An ordinary request.

But it doesn't feel ordinary—not with him. Not anymore.

I have a perfectly professional reason to meet with him. Alone. And it'd be suspicious if I declined.

The smart move would be suggesting a video call. Safe. Remote. Professional. Exactly what my father would expect from someone in my position.

But you know what? I'm tired of playing it safe. Tired of his voice in my head dictating every single decision.

Harbor: Sure. See you at 7

I hit send, dropping the phone on the bed.

What the hell am I doing?

CHAPTER 11
WESTON

After being stuck in the elevator with Harbor yesterday, I need to cool down. So naturally I immediately schedule solo practice time on the ice.

I have to regroup, get my head on straight.

Because being that close to Harbor—trapped in the dark, her body smashed up against mine—unlocked something inside me. Something I thought was broken forever.

Desire.

And it couldn't be happening at a worse fucking time.

I've had my eyes on the puck since I got drafted into the pros. I'm singularly focused, every fiber of my being locked in on hockey.

Hockey, hockey, and more hockey.

This game is everything to me.

Well, at least it was until yesterday.

Now all I'm thinking about is the tiny blonde making my heart race faster than a breakaway. Those wide, hazel eyes with the thick fringe of lashes, staring straight into my soul. The way she gnaws at her full bottom lip when she's deep in thought, the slightly sweet scent of her perfume mixed with sunscreen drifting from her skin.

Dammit.

Just thinking about her has my dick hard and it's not even light outside yet. Hopefully, an early morning practice will help me sort things out before I see her again. I need to have my game face on for our meeting at Shoreline Coffee later today. Not acting like some simp looking to get laid.

I skate onto the ice, rolling my shoulders back. Trying to get into the proper mindset and forget about Harbor.

Easier said than done.

I drop down into my hip stretch, the coldness of the ice leaching through the gloves.

Thrust, stretch, thrust, stretch.

Everything that's happened in the last couple of weeks swirls through my mind. Coach Evans's betrayal. Saying goodbye to Manhattan. Flying down here on the team jet. Harbor hanging onto me for dear life when we hit turbulence, her chest flushing. The way she gazed up at me, pupils dilated.

Aroused.

Purely a sympathetic nervous system response to almost crashing, but I bet that's what she looks like after she comes.

Damn, Steele. Way to take it there.

But I can't help it. There's something about her—the fire in her eyes, those snappy retorts, the push-pull thing we have going. All of it combined has me unbalanced, off my game.

I move from stretches to easy skating, warming up my

muscles. Gliding side to side, the sluicing of the blade loud and rhythmic in the empty space.

In a trance, I skate up and down the ice, my breathing even and controlled.

Not like it would be if Harbor was under me right now.

Her round breasts bared to me, nipples rosy and diamond-sharp. I'd suck each one hard until she moaned my name, begging me to fuck her.

I lower my head and pick up speed. Getting into a quicker pace, ice flying around the blades of my skates.

Please, Weston. Please fuck me.

I'd tease her, sliding my fingers into her hot, wet pussy. Working her until her body bowed to me. Arching up and wanting more.

So much more.

Keeping my center of gravity low, I apply pressure to the edges of my blades and stop on the line.

Spin and repeat. This time harder, faster, more explosive.

Please.

I'd ease into her, slowly, so slowly. Finally giving into the tension we've been fighting since the moment we met. She'd wind her arms around me, her fingers dancing across my lats. Then I'd press all the way inside her, filling her up with my rock-hard cock.

Hips thrusting, pounding into her. Her entire body flushed, eyes fluttering closed as I hammer into her.

Please, Weston. Please.

Begging for me. Wanting me. Needing me.

The overhead lights flip on and I blink against the brightness.

What the fuck? I reserved the rink this morning. No one else should be here.

"Hey, bro." Bennett skates onto the ice and my gut tightens, aggravation flaring.

"Hey."

He does a few quick stretches, then skates over to me.

"Surprised to see you here so early. Thought you'd still be sleeping, adjusting to the heat." I lean on my stick, assessing my brother. He's suited up in his practice gear, ready to go.

"Nah. I spent the last few days packing. I need to get back on the ice, stay sharp. Wanna run some drills together?"

I consciously shrug away my agitation. I should be happy to have someone to run drills with.

"Sure."

Bennett slaps the puck toward me and wordlessly we break into the same warm-up drill we've been doing since we were kids at rec league. Moving down the ice, Bennett drives wide. I drop the pass back to him as we skate toward the goal. He takes aim at the water bottle set at the corner of the net, the puck flying across the ice.

"Score!" Bennett pumps his fists into the air as the water bottle falls. He cups his hands around his mouth, cheering. "Go Steele!"

"You're such a ham, bro." I retrieve the puck and we repeat the drill, switching positions this time.

Skate, drop back, slice, aim, shoot.

The puck ricochets off the bottle, the plastic toppling and the black disc bouncing back.

"Denied!" Bennett cries, his voice echoing off the empty bleachers. "Boo! Hiss!"

"Shut the fuck up, Puck Bunny." I scowl at him, slapping the puck against my stick.

"Captain losing his edge?" His brow arches as we skate the other direction.

"No. Just an unlucky shot."

"Uh-huh." Bennett lines up and shoots, the puck pounding into the bottle. "Another point for Bennett Steele. He's gonna be tonight's MVP for sure!"

"Oh brother," I mutter, skating away from my egomaniacal triplet.

"What? It's called manifesting, bro. You should try it sometime. Maybe with PR Barbie?"

Jaw clenching, I dig my blades into the ice and pick up speed.

My words whip out, landing in the space between us. "Her name is Harbor. Not PR-fucking-Barbie. Or Malibu Barbie."

"Right. Har-bor." He draws her name out, two long syllables. "You two looked pretty cozy in the elevator yesterday. Sorry I interrupted."

Redemption time.

Eyes pinned on the goal, I fire off my shot. The water bottle flies up into the air as the puck slices into the corner of the net.

"There. Happy now?" I come to a hard stop, ice flying. "Goal. And we weren't anything. Aren't anything," I correct myself, driving the point home.

"So you'd be cool with me making a move then?"

I grit my teeth, trying hard to tamp down the emotions flooding through me. Irritation, anger, jealousy, all swirling together.

Jealousy. What the fuck?

I have no right to be jealous of anything when it comes to Harbor. Yet the thought—the very idea—of my brother flirting with her, asking her out—grinds my gears.

Hard.

"No, I would not." I spit out the words, knuckles flexing in my gloves.

"Because there's nothing going on between you two, right?" Bennett tips his head, his blue eyes narrow as he goads me.

"For fuck's sake, Bennett. Do you have to try to get with every female you come into contact with?"

Bennett shrugs. "I mean, I don't *have* to. But I do love a good challenge. And PR Barbie—sorry, Harbor—is pretty hot, in that uptight, corporate kinda way."

Anger simmers low in my gut. "She's not all that uptight."

"Whoa—" Bennett holds his hands up. "Heard, loud and clear. You're into her. I'll consider her off-limits."

He skates around me in a tight circle, stopping at my elbow. "I haven't seen you this worked up over someone since Bee."

I flinch at her name.

It's been a long time since anyone's brought Bee up around me. My one and only long-term girlfriend, the girl I cut loose after I got drafted. Instinctively, I knew I needed to focus on my hockey career.

So I unceremoniously broke up with her after three years of dating. Not because I didn't care about her or love her. I did.

But not more than hockey.

I haven't spoken to her since, and guilt still gnaws at me about that. I should have handled the entire situation better, more gracefully.

But I figure she's better off without me. It's not like she tried to connect. I haven't either.

Best to leave the past in the past.

I've been single ever since, never wanting to choose between love or hockey again. Instinctively knowing there's only room in my life for one of them.

Glancing over my shoulder at my brother, I lock a steely gaze with him. "I'm not worked up over Harbor. I just don't think you—or anyone else—should be flirting with, dating, or otherwise engaging—with the PR consultant hired to rescue the team. It's not a good look."

Bennett snickers, and now I'm even more pissed off.

"What?"

"I'm gonna remind you of this conversation in a few weeks, Saint Weston."

"Fuck off, Bennett."

He lifts his helmet, shaking his shaggy hair loose. "Gladly. Thanks for the practice."

Then he skates away, leaving me stewing over the Harbor situation and the ominous prediction he left in his wake.

———

I pull up to Shoreline Coffee a few minutes before seven. There's plenty of parking outside the town's one and only coffee shop.

Maybe Driftwood Cove won't be so bad after all.

I banish the thought immediately. Clearly, Harbor and all her bright and sunny optimism's getting to me.

Locking the Porsche, I stride into the empty shop. The place is light and bright, very beachy, with whitewashed chairs and tables and a few booths along the side wall. Instead of the typical dark tile flooring I'm used to back in New York, here the floors are some type of light wood. A lone barista stands at the white marble counter, scrolling through her phone and looking bored. No sign of Harbor.

I take a few seconds to browse the chalkboard menu, then go with my usual order.

"Morning. I'll take a cold brew with a splash of half and half, light ice."

"What size? We have mini, regular, and tidal."

"Um...regular?"

"Cool." She rings me up, then sets about making my coffee, avoiding both eye contact and conversation which I don't mind a bit.

I take a seat at a table in the back. Eyes pinned on the door, my knee's bouncing up and down like a jackhammer and I haven't had any caffeine yet.

Not a great sign.

The early morning sweat sesh was supposed to calm my nerves. But Bennett derailed that plan with all his little digs and innuendo.

Asshole.

Now I'm more amped up than before I went to the rink.

The door swings open and Harbor sashays in, the sunrise a golden glow behind her.

Fucking stunning.

I swallow hard, adjusting my rapidly stiffening dick in my joggers. She waves and walks over to me.

"Hey. Did you already order?" She tips her head at the counter, and I nod.

"Yeah. I didn't know what you wanted or I would have ordered for you too."

Oh geez. Tell her you're into her without telling her you're into her.

She waves her hand through the air, her gold bangles tinkling on her delicate wrist.

"It's fine. One sec." She spins and glides up to the counter and I can't help but stare at her ass, perfectly showcased in a tight black pencil skirt.

I drum my fingers on my knee, trying to focus on the purpose of this meeting. The team needs a new mascot, and I have to make certain it's a good one or I'll never hear the end of it from the guys.

A few seconds later, Harbor's back at the table with both coffees in hand.

"Here you go." She slides my drink to me, then takes a seat and opens her laptop. All business, a great start. That's gonna make this easier on me.

Although a tiny part of me can't help but be disappointed. Maybe I'm reading the room wrong…

"So…here are the options." Harbor scoots around, moving her chair up next to mine and spinning the laptop so we can both see the screen. We're side by side now at the small table. Her body so close to mine I feel her energy, buzzy and shimmering, rolling off her in warm waves. The gold bangles on her wrist tinkle as she moves her finger on the mousepad, her sweet vanilla scent drifting off her skin, her hair.

After a few quick clicks, three mascot options pop up.

It's damn hard concentrating on mascots right now.

"Option 1—Hank the Hammerhead." She points to the shark on the far left. He's wearing a T-shirt with the new Coastal Crushers logo and sunglasses.

I press my lips together, withholding judgment.

"Option 2—Smash the Shark." Smash is less cartoonish, wearing a white hockey jersey and holding a stick.

"Smash is moving in the right direction." I wipe a drop of condensation from the iced coffee cup and keep my eyes glued to the screen, avoiding dropping my gaze to her sheer blouse.

"And option 3—Riptide." The last shark is fierce, wearing a helmet and dark blue jersey. "I was thinking we could have a kids' version and call him Lil Rip. Kind of a father-son combo. Really lean into the family aspect we're trying to promote with the whole 'Hockey with Heart' vibe."

"Hmmm..." I take a sip of my drink, slightly annoyed that I don't hate any of them.

Harbor sits back, her hazel eyes flicking from the screen to my face, then back to the screen again. She taps her index finger on her coffee cup—three quick taps, followed by two longer ones—a type of private morse code she uses when she's thinking.

I take another long drink, dragging the moment out longer than strictly necessary. Before yesterday, I would have done this just to be a dick. Now I'm doing it because I want to sit this close to her, watch as her skin flushes pink and her pulse flutters in her neck.

Dammit.

This isn't supposed to happen.

Things between me and Harbor need to stay strictly professional, no feelings involved.

Not lust, not longing—even like feels too risky.

"You hate them all." Harbor swirls her coffee, the ice sloshing against the plastic cup.

"No, I don't. Hank the Hammerhead's a little too cutesy. But the other two both work."

"Really?" A slow smile spreads across her face, and an ache burns in my chest.

The way she lit up just then—it's like watching the sun

rise over the ocean after a storm, the golden rays bursting through the clouds.

I catch a glimpse of the tiny freckle sitting right below her earlobe, normally hidden by her hair but visible now as she tucks a strand behind her ear. That freckle taunts me —I want to kiss her in that exact spot. Lick the pale skin and hear the hitch of her breath at my touch. My throat tightens as I stare at the solitary mark, somehow more intimate than anything else about her.

It's fucking painful sitting here—so close I catch the hint of mocha from her coffee mixing with her shampoo—and not being able to touch her.

Especially after yesterday, when we were so close in the elevator.

My fingers itch to reach over and touch the soft skin of her cheek, to brush her hair away from her eyes.

Steele. Fucking focus.

"You pick. Either one works."

I grab for my coffee and Harbor reaches for her laptop at the exact same moment, our fingers colliding mid-air as she slides the computer back toward her. The brief contact sends an electric jolt straight up my arm, her skin impossibly soft against my calloused fingertips. She jerks back, knocking over her coffee with her elbow. The lid pops off, sending a waterfall of ice and the remaining drink spilling over the table. Harbor swoops in to rescue her laptop as coffee drips onto my lap, the cold liquid soaking through to my skin.

"Oh my gosh, I'm so sorry." She flings her laptop aside and grabs for a napkin, dabbing at the wet spot on my joggers, dangerously close to my dick.

"It's fine." My voice is gruff as I fervently try to think the least sexy thoughts possible.

I cannot get a hard-on right now.

But she's making it damn near impossible, leaning in and patting at my crotch with her delicate fingers.

"Use your focus group thingy or whatever. You're the expert." I shove away from the table and stand abruptly, needing distance before she notices the effect her touch has on my breathing—and everything fucking else.

Her lips turn down, but I don't stick around to hear any of her protests or clapbacks.

Instead, I hustle out of the coffee shop before I do something stupid I'll regret.

As I push through the door, my cell vibrates in my pocket.

> Puck Bunny: Team dinner tomorrow night at the Rusty Anchor. Prince says bring Harbor. Guys want to meet the woman behind the move

The thought of Harbor surrounded by my teammates—especially fucking Bennett and his knowing smirks—has me all the way on edge.

Heat roars through my chest—and the warmth's not from the beating of the Florida summer sun.

CHAPTER 12
HARBOR

ammit.

I blink at the dark blue streak of Weston's T-shirt as he darts out of the coffee shop, practically running to get away.

What possessed me to pat him down like a freaking TSA agent, my fingers all over his coffee-stained junk? Very sizable junk, too, impossible not to notice through the thin fabric of his pants.

I just made things a million times more awkward.

And right when I thought we were making real progress—starting to see eye to eye on the rebrand—things between us are all weird again. Something between us shifted, then shifted back again the instant I spilled my drink all over his lap.

Le sigh.

I hoped we'd turned a corner after our time in the elevator together, but I guess not. He couldn't get away from me fast enough.

Which is probably for the best but still stings a little.

Maybe I'm reading too much into his body language, those smoldering stares. It has been a minute since I waded into the dating pool. I'm out of my element, most likely overanalyzing all the things.

Still, the way he acts when he's with me—so focused and attentive. Like I'm the only person in the room.

Shit.

I need to stop thinking about Weston.

His ice-blue gaze, the shadow of stubble on his sharp jawline. The way the cotton of his shirt stretches to try and contain his muscles. Those abs.

All of him.

I shouldn't be thinking about him, full stop.

We're colleagues, nothing more.

Keep it professional, Harbor.

It's safer that way.

Being Coach Doug Hayes's daughter means every single move I make is analyzed, scrutinized.

Broadcasted.

I can't date a player. That would be catastrophic, career suicide. *Hello, puck bunny!*

And I certainly can't date Weston Steele. Falling for a man like him is dangerous.

Because he's the type of guy you fall in love with—and never get over.

I can't afford a heartbreak like that. Not now. Not ever.

Buzz, buzz.

I glance down at my phone.

Prince: Head coach interviews done.
Need press conference set up to
announce team move, name change,
etc ASAP

Okay, then. Guess we're full speed ahead with the rebrand.

Harbor: On it. I'll see what I can do and
get back to you with day and time

Prince: Later today or tomorrow would be
ideal

Shit, no pressure.

Harbor: I'll reach out to my contacts at
the networks

Prince: Great

I tuck my cell back into my bag along with my laptop, chuck my empty coffee cup, and head to the office. It's going to be another long day. But at least I'll be busy. Gives me less time to think about a certain grumpy hockey captain and the stupefying effect his burning gaze has on me.

————

At four PM, I'm still working at my desk in the office when a good news email hits my inbox. By some miracle of God, the press conference is all set for tomorrow morning.

I immediately text Prince, letting him know all systems

are a go for the rollout. Now I have roughly a million things to do to prepare for the big announcement.

So much for sleep.

I've pretty much resigned myself to pulling an all-nighter here in my office. Maybe I should request a couch be brought in for the late night work sessions.

> Weston: Have you heard about the team dinner tonight?

What? No, I have not. And I don't have time to sit around and eat, either.

> Harbor: No. Why?

> Weston: Prince wants you there

Not sure why Weston's telling me this and not Prince himself. I sat across the table from him half the day and he never once mentioned it.

He is pretty caught up in all the planning. Not to mention meetings with his divorce lawyer. Maybe it slipped his mind.

> Harbor: When and where? I'm pretty busy with the press conference on the schedule for tomorrow AM

Blue dots swirl, then disappear, then swirl again as buzzy anxiety zips through me.

> Weston: The Rusty Anchor, 8 PM

> Weston: The team wants to get to know the brains behind the rebrand

I stare at my screen, blushing like a teen girl with a crush on a sports star.

Weston thinks I'm smart.

I mean, I guess "the team" does. But I'll take what I can get.

> Harbor: Well, when you put it that way...
>
> Harbor: Fine. I'll stop by for a minute. Just to say hi and show my face

> Weston: Your presence will be most appreciated

By him?

I have my doubts after this morning. He's probably worrying about me spilling another beverage all over him, maybe groping his ass the next time.

Dammit.

Anyway, I promised myself I'd stop thinking like this. Nothing good is going to come from lusting after Weston Steele. Right now, I need to focus on this press conference and nailing every last detail.

Not the captain.

Argh. I have a freaking one-track mind right now and it's not on PR strategy.

Dad's voice echoes in my head: *The moment personal feelings interfere with execution, you've lost the game.*

Here I am, sitting at my desk and fantasizing about the team captain instead of focusing on tomorrow's press conference.

Way to prove his point, Harbor.

Smoothing my hair over my shoulder, I toss my cell

down and click into email. I still have so much to do and tons of unfinished tasks on my list.

Yet all I can think about is Weston's sudden retreat this morning. I dried him off instinctively, not thinking about the logistics of my hand placement. Hopefully he won't read anything into that.

Shit, this is awkward.

And I hate that I can't stop thinking about him. That I'm letting him get to me like this.

With a heavy sigh, I refocus on my inbox.

Crap. ESPN wants an exclusive interview—with Weston.

Of course they fucking do.

I pick up my cell and text him again.

> **Harbor:** ESPN wants an exclusive with you tomorrow after the press conference

> **Weston:** Me or the team? And do you know the specifics?

> **Harbor:** You. And I'm assuming it's about the move and the new coach. But I'll get more details for you. You in?

Subtext 'pretty please.' Because I called in about ten favors to get this press conference together on such short notice and the last thing I want to do is piss off a major network.

> **Weston:** I guess

> **Harbor:** Thank you! I'll get the specifics for you ASAP

He hits a thumbs up on the message and I breathe a sigh of relief. At least I didn't have to beg.

Not that you wouldn't.

An image of me on my knees in front of a naked and gorgeous Weston pops into my mind.

For fuck's sake, Harbor. Get your mind out of the gutter.

I banish the vision and type out a response to the email requesting a time and detailed questions so I can brief Weston.

Hitting 'send' on my reply, I check my to-do list.

Find locations for official player photos

A dull headache's coming on, tension creeping up my neck into my jaw. I massage my temple with my fingertips, trying to fight off the throbbing.

I don't have time to sit around and nurse a headache. It's already late and I need to check the majority of tasks off this massive list before I leave today. And now I also have interview questions to get over to Weston and a team dinner to attend.

This day keeps getting better.

Clipboard in hand, I push away from my desk. Ignoring the pounding in my head, I hustle out of the office in search of good spots for photo ops. The obvious choice is on the ice. The goalie and a few players can use that location. But I still have at least fifteen to twenty more player photos to arrange and I don't want them all using the same background. If I use each spot five times, I need four more locations.

Hmmm.

What about the locker room? I peeked in there the other day, but I don't remember too much about the space. I recall it being kind of dark—the photographer's probably going to need more light.

I hurry down the hallway toward the locker room. I'll just pop my head in and snap a few quick pics, then send them to the photographer and see what he thinks.

The hallway's empty, my heels clicking loudly on the concrete floor. Most of the team's out searching for housing and unpacking. The players had some ice time this morning if they wanted it, but nothing's formally on the schedule yet. The locker room should be vacant.

Just in case, I rap on the door twice. No response. The coast is clear.

I push into the locker room, glancing around and sizing up the space. It's a nice locker room, with light oak benches and freshly painted lockers in the dark blue of the new team logo. We could take photos in front of the lockers. With the proper lighting, this could be a great spot for individual portraits.

Snapping pics with my cell to send to the photographer, I jot rough dimensions down on the clipboard. While I'm all the way down here, I may as well check out the rest of the space, make sure there's no better spot. Mindful of the time crunch, I hurry around the corner lost in thought.

"Oof."

My clipboard clatters to the ground as I run straight into a wall of solid muscle.

Shirtless, solid muscle, broad pecs on display for anyone to see.

My palms land on rock-hard biceps and I teeter on my heels. A large hand reaches out to steady me, grabbing me by the waist before I topple over. My breath hitches as I'm thrust closer to him. Heart pounding, I tear my gaze from the rippling abs and dare to lift my eyes to his face.

The pulse point at his throat quickens, a rapid flutter beneath the still-damp skin. His pupils dilate as he locks eyes with me, the thin ring of blue almost swallowed by the black.

Weston.

"I'm sorry," I stammer, high-pitched and breathy. "I didn't mean to run into you like this. I'm scouting locations for the player photos. I knocked but no one answered."

The words tumble out, spilling from me like a babbling waterfall as my face burns.

Damn, Weston is fucking hot.

Hotter than I even imagined. I can't keep my eyes off his golden skin, that deep V at his hips where his pants sit low on his waist.

He stares down at me, his eyes dark and stormy. A tiny furrow creases his brow, like he's struggling to hold something back. Blood roars in my ears, drowning out everything besides me and Weston, the space between us shrinking. Every nerve in my body hums in anticipation, and I'm torn between fear and desire.

Should I run? Or should I stay?

Heat radiates off his body, clear droplets of water still beading on his corded shoulders. Dark hair damp and messy, he smells so damn good. Fresh and clean, manly. The air around us vibrates, charged with something I don't dare name, and I wonder if he feels it too.

"Harbor—" His voice is low and husky, my name a whisper on his lips.

I'm paralyzed, locked in the forcefield of his gaze, my heart slamming against my ribcage. The seconds stretch between us. I should step back, walk away. Anything.

But I can't.

Can't think, can't move. I can barely breathe.

I open my mouth to say something—anything—but the

words die on my lips as he inches closer to me. His hand finds my hip, pulling me closer to him, fingers searing me through the fabric of my skirt.

"I'm..."

But he cuts me off, dropping his mouth to mine.

Swear to God, trumpets and harps swell in a romantic interlude in my head, all my focus on the sensation of his lips on mine.

Weston Steele is kissing me.

And it's fucking amazing.

I'm lost in him, the taste of him—the most delicious temptation on this earth. His lips soft and full, moving over mine with a heated fervor. Like he wants to leave his mark on me forever.

My whole body trembles, a shiver of pleasure rolling through me as I melt into the kiss.

The Kiss, with a capital 'K' because that's how damn good this kiss is.

Weston Steele's a phenomenal kisser.

Of course he is.

One hand splayed at my hip, he lifts the other and cups my cheek. The gesture's so tender, so intimate, his skin rough against mine. My skin burns under his touch, and I struggle to swallow.

I don't know what we're doing right now, the line we're crossing. All I know is I want to keep going.

He pauses and staggers back, dropping his hands to his side.

"Sorry. I'm sorry."

His skin flushed, bare chest heaving, he holds up his palms. "I shouldn't have done that. I'm sorry."

Heart still pounding, I feel like I'm drowning. *What just happened?*

This is it—the moment I've been warned about my entire life. The exact second when feelings override judgment. When I prove I don't have what it takes at this elite level.

Focus blurry, priorities shifting.

I should run away, like he did this morning. Save myself, my job, my career.

"Weston—" I lick at my bottom lip, tasting him.

Instead of running, I do something so out of character, so un-Harbor-like. I channel my inner Piper and step forward. Breathless.

"Please don't be sorry."

He stares down at me, pupils dark and wide, and I'm afraid I might actually pass out. From nerves, embarrassment, longing…a combo of all of the above. There's an almost imperceptible tremor in his hands, like he's holding back.

The fact that someone like him—a professional athlete, always so controlled, so disciplined—is thrown right now sends a rush racing through me.

I'm tired of being afraid. Of my father, what other people might think, their perceptions of me.

Tired of proving my worth by denying every single thing that feels good to me.

His fingers grip my waist with careful restraint, but tension vibrates through him—the same controlled power I witnessed on the ice held in check by sheer willpower. A muscle ticks in his jaw as he fights some sort of internal battle.

"I've been trying not to—" His voice catches, rougher than I've ever heard it before. He swallows hard, those deep blue eyes never leaving mine. "I shouldn't…"

But he inches closer, grasping my hips and pulling me

into him. His initial touch is tentative, almost questioning. His palm splays across the small of my back, sending a delicious shiver up my spine. My heart's pounding so hard I'm positive he can feel it through my blouse.

"Fuck it," he growls, seizing my lips in the most possessive kiss of my life.

All good sense flies away as his hand cups my ass, wetness flooding my panties. His tongue slips into my mouth and he swallows my tiny moan.

In this moment, I give into Weston Steele. Wave the white flag and surrender.

Bye-bye, perfect Coach Hayes's daughter.

I'm so fucked.

CHAPTER 13
WESTON

Harbor tastes like vanilla and sunshine. I know I shouldn't be kissing her—it's a terrible fucking idea. But now that I've broken through that barrier, I can't stop.

Don't want to stop.

She's a magnetic forcefield drawing me in, invisible beams of desire pulling me toward her.

I need to touch her, taste her.

Make her fucking mine.

Sliding into her mouth, I swirl my tongue around and get lost in the moment. I'm done fighting my instincts. My self-control's shattered and there's no going back.

Her body melts into mine, our breathing ragged as we finally give into temptation. I palm her firm ass and she sways a little, off-balance.

She's not the only one.

I've been off-balance from the moment we met.

I've tried to fight this—fight her—but it's useless. I'm losing this battle. And I don't even care.

Her arms wrap around my neck and I breathe her in. Her shampoo mixes with the floral scent of her perfume and I'm a fucking goner. I'm gonna have an instant boner the next time I catch a whiff of rose petals.

Every muscle in my body's tense and needy, my dick throbbing in my pants.

I want this woman.

More than I've ever wanted anyone, and that thought freaks me the fuck out. But now's not the time to reflect on anything other than what's happening right now.

A tiny moan slips from low in Harbor's throat, and I know this thing's not one-sided. She feels it too.

"Whoa. Sorry to interrupt the strategy meeting." Bennett's voice barrels through the empty locker room.

Harbor stiffens in my arms and shoves away with a force that knocks me backward.

"I...I'm...I have to go." Red-faced, she spins on her heels and jets out of the locker room before I can say a word.

I glower at a smug-as-fuck Bennett leaning against a locker.

"Nice one, bro. Didn't think we'd be circling back here so soon." Bennett raises a brow, smirking. "Can't blame you, though. She's hot."

I blow out a long, steady breath, aggravation brewing in my gut. "Fuck off, Bennett. Anyone ever tell you your timing's fucking terrible?"

"Nah. Haven't heard any complaints." He folds his brawny arms over his stomach.

"Well, now you fucking have." I rake a hand through my hair, my mind spinning.

The last thing I need is anyone else finding out about this. I don't even know what *this* is. And I don't want

Harbor to lose her credibility—or even worse, her job. Not when she's already fighting to prove herself as the daughter of the great Coach Hayes. The hockey world will be watching and waiting for any slip-up, any chance to scream about nepotism hires. Plus, the team needs a strong start here, and she's already proven herself to be the best person for the job.

"Listen—please keep what you just saw to yourself." I raise my eyes to his in a level gaze, stopping just short of pleading. "I don't want the guys questioning Harbor and the rebrand. This move is tough enough. We don't need more complications."

Bennett shrugs, one broad shoulder lifting. "Whatever, bro. I won't go spreading news about your little affair around."

I grimace. "It's not an *affair*, Bennett."

"Hook up, fling, whatever you're calling it. Your secret's safe with me." He shoots me an exaggerated wink and I wonder what I'm going to owe him for keeping the juicy gossip to himself.

"You know people are gonna figure it out, right? It's pretty obvious the two of you have a thing for each other."

"What? No, it's not." I scrunch my brow and frown at him.

"Bro. I figured it out in less than an hour."

"You're different, though. You're my brother."

"So you know Callum's gonna see through your little charade."

He does have a point there.

"If Callum asks, I'll tell him the truth. But other than him, I'd rather not have anyone else know about what you just walked in on."

"Fine." Bennett holds up his palms. "But you're not as slick as you think you are. And PR Barbie isn't either."

"Her name's Harbor…" I grit through my teeth, scrubbing my hand over my jaw. I'd love to punch him in his smug face for calling her that again, but figure now's not a great time to fight with my brother. Not when I need him to keep what he just saw to himself.

"My advice?"

"Not that I asked…"

But Bennett forges ahead with his words of wisdom. "The two of you need to stay away from each other as much as possible or figure out how to break it to Prince and the team that you're an item."

"We're not 'an item.' We kissed one time."

"It was a helluva kiss, though. Like, you're not going back for seconds? Or thirds? I'm betting you're not going to walk away from that."

I hate to admit it, but my brother's right. It *was* a helluva kiss and the touch of Harbor's lips on mine didn't scratch the itch that's been tickling at me since we met.

No, that kiss did nothing but make me want her more.

Dammit.

Bennett slaps me on the shoulder. "It's fine, Wes. She's single, right? You're single. The two of you did nothing wrong, really, except maybe violate some HR office fraternization policy. Shouldn't be a big deal."

Except I have a sinking feeling it is a big deal.

I'm certain it is to Harbor, given the fifty-yard dash I saw her sprint in stilettos a few seconds ago. And now that I know who her father is, I understand why. She's not just worried about the professional fallout—she's terrified of proving her dad right about her career choices. I saw the flicker of panic in her eyes, felt the tension in her body when she mentioned her father.

Fuck. No wonder she bolted.

We definitely have to talk about what just happened and go from there. For all I know, she's going to call it quits before anything gets started.

"She's cute, dude. You should go for it." Bennett chucks my biceps.

"Glad I have your blessing," I grumble, opening my locker and grabbing my T-shirt.

Bennett has the worst track record out of all of us. He's the last person I'm taking relationship advice from. Pretty sure his longest relationship was a few months, tops.

"You going to have a chat with your gal pal right now or do you want a quick tour of the short list of houses Gia found? That's what I was coming in here to talk to you about anyway."

"Oh." I glance at my watch. We have a few hours before the team dinner, and I'd love to get settled in a house sooner rather than later. "Let's take the tour."

Shrugging into my T-shirt, I slam my locker shut and follow Bennett out of the locker room. I'll tackle the Harbor issue later.

———

Spoiler alert: I run out of time to tackle the Harbor issue before the team dinner. The housing tour takes longer than expected, leaving us only about twenty minutes to change before heading over to the restaurant.

I shoot Harbor a quick text while I wait for my brothers in the lobby of the Driftwood Inn.

Weston: We need to talk about what happened this afternoon

But she never responds.

That silence feels louder than anything she could've said.

Now I'm pulling up to The Rusty Anchor with Callum, Bennett, and a truckload of anxiety.

At least I'll be able to pin it on the move and the coaching changes. In reality, though, most of the gut-churning is due to a certain blonde PR consultant.

"Wow, this place is...special." Bennett lets out a low whistle as we take in the weathered façade of the local bar. The siding's a chipped and faded brown, with salt-crusted windows flanked by shutters still mostly attached. A wrap-around porch holds a few old wooden rocking chairs— you'd be risking a splinter in your ass if you sat in one. The place is aptly named, the sign sporting an actual rusty anchor.

"Gia said this restaurant's a Driftwood Cove landmark. Best burger in town." Callum grips the hook of the anchor serving as a handle, holding the wooden door open for us.

"They must have something going for them. Otherwise, I imagine this place would've closed down a long time ago." I blink, eyes adjusting to the darkness of the bar as I step inside.

The air's only semi-cool and musty, with lingering hints of stale beer and fried food. The wood-paneled walls are covered with black-and-white photographs, a tribute to Driftwood Cove's past.

"You boys here for the hockey dinner?" A hostess in a tight, white Rusty Anchor T-shirt tips her head at us.

"Yes, ma'am," I say.

"Of course they are. Look at them." A man in a white Rusty Anchor T-shirt and khaki shorts sporting a reddish beard strolls over and extends his hand. "Beau Lawson. Owner of the Rusty Anchor. Welcome to Driftwood Cove."

I shake his hand, and so do Bennett and Callum.

"Happy to have you boys here. Rachel, take them to the private room?" Beau cuts his eyes at her and she blushes.

"Absolutely. Follow me." She spins and guides us through the main dining room. A few families sit in booths around the edges of the space, with larger tables filling the center. A long wooden bar takes up the back wall, a large fishing net hanging behind.

"Here ya go." She waves her hand at a smaller second room, already filled with several players and Prince.

"Thanks." Bennett smiles, giving her a quick once over, and she blushes.

"Anytime." She spins and struts away, and I elbow Bennett.

"Remember—we're not just visitors. We're living here, at minimum for one season. Don't hook up with every local. It'll make things real awkward around town. This isn't Manhattan."

Bennett shoves a hand in his pocket, glancing around the dingy room. "Don't I know it."

"Boys, glad you could join us. Where's Harbor?" Prince smacks Callum on the back but directs the question at me.

"Uh…she's coming. She was finishing things up at the office." I purposely keep things vague. Now's not the time to tell Prince anything about the two of us and what happened in the locker room.

"Good, good. I want the team to get to know the mastermind behind this rebrand. We're already getting great feedback from sponsors on the 'Hockey with Heart' slogan. Everyone's loving the new direction the team's taking and the charity tie-ins. Great for our image." Prince bobs his head, self-satisfied. "Weston—the two of you have been working together closely on the campaign. How are things going?"

Bennett scoffs under his breath next to me as my face burns. Hopefully I'm not as red as I feel.

"Fine. Things are going fine."

"Yeah, Weston told me he's loving the direction things are heading." Bennett's lips tip up in a smirk and I want to punch him. Knock that stupid grin right off his smug face.

Callum stays silent, his watchful eyes flicking from me to Bennett. I swear the proverbial lightbulb flashes on over his head.

"Super. I was hoping the two of you would hit it off. She's going to need your full support."

"You've got the right man for the job, Mr. Prince. Weston understands the assignment." Bennett slings his arm around my shoulder in a showy act of brotherly love, and I desperately want to tell him to fuck off.

Instead, I nod and try not to grimace at Bennett's nuanced statement. I'm not sure Prince would be thrilled at how well Harbor and I hit it off this afternoon.

Clearing my dry throat, I force myself to respond. "Understood, sir. Happy to help any way I can."

Bennett punches me in the back, right in the lat, but I ignore him.

Asshole.

After this, I'm definitely taking the bigger bedroom.

"I know I can count on you. All of you." Prince glances at each of us. "Best decision I ever made for this team was drafting the three of you. A few owners thought it was a rookie move. They're all regretting their life choices now."

Pride surges through me. At least he's happy with our performance on the ice, even if we didn't bring home the Cup.

"Grab some food." Prince gestures at a buffet in the far corner of the room. "We'll talk business later, once Harbor gets here."

Prince waves at some of the other players walking in and moves off to greet them. I stalk toward the buffet, Bennett and Callum following in my wake.

"What was that about?" Callum keeps his voice low so only the three of us can hear. "What am I missing?"

"Nothing. Bennett's being his usual dickhead self," I grumble, not wanting to get into the details here.

"I'm offended." Bennett grabs a plate and loads it up with chicken wings. "It's not *nothing* exactly, bro."

I scowl over at him. "Drop it, Bennett. We'll talk about it later."

"Did something happen between you and Harbor?" Callum takes the silver tongs from my hand, one brow arched.

Dammit. I can't lie straight to my brother's face.

I drop my voice to a whisper. "We kissed. Once. Doesn't mean anything's happening."

Even as I utter the words, I know they're bullshit. That kiss meant something. At least to me.

And I'm pretty sure to Harbor too, judging by how fast she bolted from the locker room.

Lines were crossed. Now everything's blurry, messy.

Not how I operate.

Callum doesn't comment, his lips pressed in a thin line and his brow furrowed. He's the opposite of smartass Bennett, always firing shots. Callum's capable of being discreet—a word not in Bennett's vocabulary.

We move down the line and fill our plates with salad, calamari, fried shrimp, and mini burgers, then head to an empty high top. A waitress comes by and we each order a beer. Still no sign of Harbor, and the room's packed. Most of the team's here, along with the GM and a few front office people I vaguely recognize.

"So what's your plan? You gonna tell Prince?" Callum finally asks, stabbing a leaf of lettuce.

I shrug. "No plan. We haven't talked since. For all I know, it was a one-time thing."

"Uh-huh, sure." Bennett snickers and I glower at him.

"I don't know. This rebrand means a lot to her." I steeple my fingers, trying to transfer the tension in my chest to somewhere else—anywhere else.

"You don't think she'd risk it on you?" Bennett knocks my elbow, sloshing beer across the table and ignoring the fact he just launched a grenade into my gut.

"I'm not sure." My voice is tight. "Can we drop it?"

"Don't think so, lover boy." Bennett kicks at my foot and jerks his chin toward the door. "Your girl just walked in."

I swivel around and the air's punched from my lungs. Harbor's standing next to Prince, every inch the smiling and polished PR professional. Blazer. Jeans. Blond hair smoothed over one shoulder.

She's poised. Confident.

Stunning.

She glows in the pendant lights of the bar, and my heart stutters in my chest. I can't breathe. I'm acting like a fucking middle school boy with a crush right now. Too scared to talk to the girl.

I swallow over the lump in my throat and straighten my shoulders. "She's not my girl."

"Okay. Whatever, Captain." Bennett's tone is dry as he lifts his beer to his lips.

Then she glances over at me.

Pink cheeks, her bottom lip slipping between her teeth.

My entire body tenses and I'm immediately back in the locker room, tasting her.

Harbor smiles at Prince, reacting to whatever he's saying. But there's a tremble in her jaw, a flicker of nerves behind her calm exterior.

Does she regret what we've done?

Or is she afraid of what it means?

Then it hits me like a slap shot to the chest, sucking all the oxygen from my lungs.

This isn't just attraction or desire.

For the first time in a decade, I'm falling for someone. Someone who's risking everything—her career, her family's approval, her father's legendary reputation—just by being here.

She chose to risk her legacy on this team, on rebuilding us from the ground up.

And now I've complicated things by crossing the professional line she tried so hard to maintain.

And that could cost us everything.

CHAPTER 14
HARBOR

I knew I'd see Weston here. Still, I'm unprepared for the firestorm raging inside me when I spot him. All hard muscle and determination, in a dark blue T-shirt that highlights every beautiful inch of his broad chest.

Red-hot desire sparks in my gut the second he locks his icy gaze on mine. A shiver rolls down my spine, his eyes tracking my every move. I twirl my bracelets on my wrist and try to remain calm, not give myself away in front of my boss.

"Harbor? Is everything lined up then?" Prince strokes his jaw and waits for a response.

"Pardon?" *What's he asking me?* I can't concentrate when I'm in the same room as Weston.

I need to get my shit together.

"For the presser. We're good to go, right?" Prince's brow squishes together and I nod, relieved I at least have the correct answer here.

"Yes, sir. We're good to go. The presser's scheduled for

the afternoon and then ESPN will interview Weston right afterward."

"Excellent. Nice work. National press coverage will go a long way in establishing the franchise."

"My thoughts exactly." I smile and try to ignore the hammering of my heart.

It's just anxiety over tomorrow. Has nothing to do with the hockey star watching me from across the room. Or that kiss in the locker room.

A mistake.

A delicious, tempting mistake.

But not one I can risk making again.

Not if I want to keep my job. Not to mention doing my best work and proving myself to my father.

I can't afford to take my eye off the prize.

Even if the distraction is downright drool-worthy. That sharp jawline, the way his muscles ripple when he flexes. And his scent, like a dark, manly forest I want to get lost in.

Harbor, focus.

This is exactly the sort of thing my dad would reprimand me for. Getting so caught up in a player that I can't keep my mind on the job. Elite hockey professionals don't get distracted by players. Success at this level requires unwavering focus, and here I am getting caught up in personal complications.

Not ideal.

"Tomorrow morning before the presser I'll be introducing the new head coach to the team. I'd like you to be there, snap some photos for social media." Prince pulls his cell out of his pocket and checks his schedule. "Locker room, ten AM."

Shit.

Of course the meet-and-greet's in the freaking locker room. Hopefully I'll be able to keep my mind on the job—and off of what happened there with Weston.

"Got it." I update my calendar, nerves coursing through me.

Clink, clink, clink.

Prince taps the side of his glass with a knife, commanding the room's attention. Since I'm beside him, all eyes are on me. My face flames and I stare straight ahead.

"I'll keep this short." Prince's smooth voice is authoritative. "Many of you have already met Harbor Hayes. For those who haven't had the pleasure—or have been hiding in the weight room—Harbor's the reason we haven't completely imploded."

A ripple of laughter goes up, but Weston's not smiling. His expression's painfully neutral and my stomach clenches.

"She's our PR secret weapon. Smart, strategic, and tougher than most of you."

More laughter and I low-key want to duck into the restroom right now. I clasp my hands in front of me and plaster a smile on my face.

"She's been working around the clock to clean up the last few months, and frankly, we're lucky to have her."

Prince heaps on the praise and heat prickles at the back of my neck. I can't bring myself to make eye contact with Weston. I'm unsure of his reaction to all of this—and I'm not sure I want to know.

"She'll be with us through the upcoming season." Prince raises his glass. "So if she asks you for something, give it to her. She's here to help us turn the page. That means full access, full trust, full respect."

These words hit me hard, the air knocked from my lungs.

The validation I've been craving—not specifically from Prince. But the hockey world in general. For one brief moment, I feel like I've made it, I'm finally in the club. Proof I'm here on merit, not just bloodline.

The team claps and nods, raising their drinks. I smile politely, even though I'm slightly embarrassed by the praise.

Finally, I bring myself to take a quick glance over at Weston. His jaw's tight as he lifts his glass, tipping it at me.

I need a minute to regroup.

"Thank you, Mr. Prince. I appreciate the warm intro." I touch his arm, his suit jacket silky smooth and clearly expensive.

"Absolutely. You've more than earned it."

"Thanks. Would you please excuse me for a second?"

"Sure, no problem."

Without hesitation, I spin on my heel and search for the closest exit. I need fresh air, space from the pressure.

Pushing through a side door, I stumble into a dark alleyway. I lean back against the building and close my eyes, inhaling a deep breath of warm, salty air. The door clicks shut behind me and probably locks, but I don't even care. The last thing I want to do is go back inside. I can't think, can't breathe this close to Weston. Let alone stand around and make small talk with his teammates and boss.

Fuck. What am I doing?

My entire job is anticipating PR crises and here I am, getting involved with a player on the very team I'm trying to save from scandal.

This is exactly what my dad predicted—the moment when personal feelings would override professional judgment. When discipline collapses and everything falls apart. Every criticism he's ever made about me—about my focus, priorities, my choices in general—runs through my head and I'm spinning.

"Hey."

I jump a foot in the air, eyes flying open as I whirl to face the deep voice I already recognize and respond to.

"We need to talk." Weston steps closer, his heady masculine scent swirling around me and making me dizzy.

I shake my head, ignoring the quickening of my pulse and the flutter in my belly. "No, we don't. What happened earlier…" I lick the corner of my lip, face flaming. "It can't happen again. There's too much on the line. For both of us."

"Right." Weston pins his steely gaze on me, the blue dark in the dim light. Desire rolls through me and my already shaky resolve wavers more.

"It's too risky." My voice is quiet and frankly, unconvincing, even to me.

"You're right. It is." He takes another step closer, and my breath hitches as heat shimmers between us.

As much as I want to lean in and have a repeat performance of this afternoon, I know what I have to do. For me, my job, for Weston and the team.

"Here." I fish the folded printout from my pocket. "These are the interview questions for tomorrow. You don't have to memorize anything. Just skim them tonight, so you're not caught off-guard."

Weston takes the paper, our fingers touching for the briefest of seconds. Sparks fly up my arm and I do my best to ignore them and the accompanying jitters rocketing through me.

"The questions are mostly about the rebrand, the relocation, community outreach and your role as captain. Happy to help with anything you may need. Wording or whatever."

He scans the folded sheet of paper, silence stretching between us. I force myself to stand still and not fill up the empty space with babbling, but it's difficult. Being this close to him—his body inches from mine—and not touching him hurts.

I fold my arms across my chest, building a wall I know I can't cross.

Won't cross.

"This is a big deal. If the segment goes well, it could anchor the entire media rollout. Give us good press right from the get-go."

"I get it, Harbor." Weston shoves the paper into his pocket, his voice neutral.

I totally blew this, every part of it.

I swallow hard, my stomach sinking. I don't want to push him away. Not really. I just don't know how to hold him without dropping everything else.

"Don't worry, Hurricane. I'll play my part." His tone is calm, controlled. All I can ask for.

"Just like you're playing yours." He shoots me one last hard stare, then walks away without a second glance.

The alley falls quiet, waves crashing in the distance.

But nothing drowns out the sound of him leaving.

Or the whisper in my head that sounds suspiciously like my sister: *What if you're protecting yourself right out of the best thing that's ever happened to you?*

Tomorrow's press conference will make or break this rebrand.

But tonight, I can't shake the feeling that I've made the biggest mistake of my career.

And it has nothing to do with the hockey scandal.

Is pushing Weston away actually proving my dad right?

When pressure mounts, I choose fear, holding back. Staying in the safe position.

Maybe I'm not championship material after all…

CHAPTER 15
WESTON

t can't happen again.

Harbor's voice echoes in my head, drowning out my brother's banter.

I know she's right. Everything's fucked if we screw this up—for both of us.

But that doesn't make walking away feel any less like giving up the game before the buzzer.

I've never wanted anything more than hockey.

Until now.

And that terrifies me more than any hit I've ever taken.

"You going to bed already?" Bennett elbows me as we walk through the lobby of the Driftwood Inn. A few of the guys from the team are hanging at the bar, but I have zero interest in drinking or small talk.

"Yeah. I have an early ice time, followed by the presser and the ESPN interview."

"Oh, fancy. The ESPN interview." His voice raises an octave as he razzes me. "Better get your beauty sleep then."

"Exactly. Callum, you gonna babysit this guy tonight? I'm afraid to leave him alone. We're collectively trying to stay out of trouble, at least for a little while."

"Hey." Bennett throws his palms up in protest. "I'm right here, guys."

"We know." I level my gaze on Bennett. "I can't emphasize this enough. We have to kick things off right. Please don't do anything stupid. I'd feel better if you went up to bed right now."

"Geesh." Bennett huffs out a breath, then tosses an arm over Callum's shoulders. "Don't worry, Dad. I have Callum to babysit me."

"I'll make sure he doesn't stay out too late, Cap." Callum pats my back. "You can head up."

Bennett leans in. "You sure you're not having a late-night strategy session with Harbor? Because hooking up with the woman whose been hired to save our asses from scandal is peak irony, bro."

My chest tightens, a mix of anger and disappointment surging through me.

"No. Believe it or not, just going to bed. Alone."

"Too bad. You'd probably be less of a hard-ass if you got laid."

My jaw clenches, but I ignore the jab. Fighting with my brother's going to accomplish nothing.

"Night." I stalk to the elevator and mash the button. I just want this day to end.

Mercifully, I'm alone in the elevator and there's no power outages, so I get up to the second floor without incident. The doors slide open and I step into the quiet hallway, making my way to my room.

I'm swiping my key when I catch a glimpse of a dark

blue blur two doors down from me. Out of the corner of my eye, I spot her.

Harbor.

Of fucking course I run into her.

I can't seem to avoid her, no matter how hard I try.

I should duck into my room and pretend I don't notice her standing there. Ignore her and the thudding of my heart.

I hesitate for a split second, then click my door shut and take three long strides until I'm standing in front of her.

"Weston." Her voice is surprised and breathy. But it's her pulse fluttering in her neck that gives her away. She's as affected by what happened today as I am, I'm sure of it. "Do you have questions for me about the interview?"

"Questions, yes. But not about the interview." I all but growl the words, fists clenched at my side to keep from reaching out and touching her. She smells sweet, her intoxicating scent winding around me in the close space.

Her wide eyes flick to my face, two bright pink stains coloring her cheeks.

"We can't," she whispers, the briefest flash of regret filling her pretty face. "You know we can't. It's too risky."

"Because of the job? Or because you're scared?"

"Both. Everything I've worked for, Weston. I can't—I won't be the cautionary tale."

A rock settles low in my gut. I know she's right. But I don't have to like it.

I scrape a hand over my jaw, heavy disappointment settling over me.

"I know. You're right."

Not waiting for a chance to second guess myself, I step in and scoop her close to my chest, pressing my lips lightly to the top of her head. Her sigh tickles my throat as she closes her eyes, seemingly savoring the connection. But before she can blink those beautiful hazel eyes open again, I step back and turn away.

"Night, Hurricane."

Before I do something I'll regret, I hustle back to my room and shove inside. I have to forget about the locker room. Pretend nothing ever happened and move the fuck on with my life.

It's the safe play. And now's not the time to take a risk, no matter how badly I want to.

———

Practice is a disaster. No sleep. No rhythm. Every break is off, every pass mistimed.

Finally, I give up and hit the showers to get ready for the team meeting. Prince hasn't looped me in on the coaching situation and I'm kind of pissed about it. Not that I have any say, really, but an intro before the meeting would have been nice.

I'm buttoning my dress shirt when the team starts to file in a few minutes before ten. Callum lopes over to me, looking uncomfortable in his dark gray suit. He's not one for dressing up, always more at ease in his athletic gear than anything else.

"Morning." He tips his head, shoving a hand deep in his suit pocket. "How was practice?"

"Shitty."

"Sorry to hear. You nervous about the interview?"

I shrug. "Not really. Just a little off out there."

"Happens to the best of us."

"I'm almost afraid to ask, but how late did Bennett stay out last night? Did he get into any trouble?"

Callum shakes his head. "No. He was on his best behavior. All good."

I tuck in my shirt and try to ignore the tightness between my shoulder blades creeping up into my neck. I can't seem to shake the anxiety that's been my constant companion for the last few weeks.

Then Bennett strolls in—and he's not alone.

My blood boils as he grins at Harbor like she's a fucking game he wants to win. Flashing his damn dimple, he knows exactly what he's doing.

Oh, hell no.

He's not allowed to flirt with her. Now or ever.

Jaw clenching, I snatch my tie from my locker and wind it around my neck, doing my best to ignore the two of them laughing and chatting across the room. Now's not the time for a confrontation with my brother. But I'm definitely addressing this situation with him again later.

I loop the silky fabric of my tie into a knot, sneaking a quick glance over at Harbor. In a navy pencil skirt and a light blue silky blouse, her hair falling across her shoulders in loose waves, she's professional and polished and very, very fuckable.

Holy hell.

It's gonna be a long fucking day.

Prince breaks my focus on Harbor, strolling in with a man I don't recognize. He's clean-cut, with sandy brown hair and a suit he probably had custom-made because he's easily twice as broad as Prince. Doesn't look to be much older than me.

Has to be the new coach, and I'm guessing he's a retired player himself based on size alone.

Prince claps his hands once and the locker room falls silent.

"Boys, I'd like to introduce you to the new head coach for the Coastal Crushers. New season, new town, new branding—and most importantly, new leadership."

My chest squeezes with each *new*. All this change might just kill me.

"After an exhaustive search, I believe he's the absolute best man for the job. He can take this team where it needs to go. He's got the mind, the experience, and the edge to lead the Crushers to victory. Meet Coach Mike Keller."

The man steps forward and scans the room like he's already clocking everyone's weaknesses.

Prince continues. "He comes to us from the AHL. Last season, he was assistant coach for the Milwaukee Icehounds. Ran defense and special teams. Top five in the league in both categories. Three of his guys got NHL call-ups this year."

A flicker of surprise goes up around the room. Clearly, this guy is good.

"He also coached in the OHL and turned a bottom-ranked junior team into playoff contenders. Player development is his thing—but don't mistake that for soft. Under his guidance, next season's going to be great. Coach—" Prince gestures to the coach and he steps forward, shrugs his shoulders.

"Appreciate the intro, Mr. Prince." His voice is clear and calm. "I'm excited to be here with you all and I'm looking forward to the months ahead. As Mr. Prince mentioned, I was with Milwaukee. I'm a former player myself—D1 before I pivoted to coaching. My style's fair, but firm. I'm not here to be friends, I'm here to win. So long as we're all working toward the same goal, everything's good." He locks eyes with me and my gut tightens.

This is what real leadership looks like. Calm authority, the kind that doesn't need to prove itself. Presence that commands respect without demanding it.

Everything I'm supposed to be for this team.

Except I'm failing because I can't keep my focus off the blonde PR consultant who's supposed to be saving us from scandal.

I've never had problems with a coach before and I sure as hell don't want to start now.

I stand straighter, shoulders squared.

"I'll be holding individual team meetings with each of you. Mini strategy sessions to go over strengths and weaknesses and what we'll be focusing on during the preseason. Sign-up sheet's on my office door. This is mandatory."

He shoves a hand in his pocket and steps back in line with Prince. Harbor snaps a few quick photos and I do my best to ignore her.

"Okay, meeting adjourned. We'll be holding the presser in the lobby. Meet in the hallway in the next fifteen minutes." Prince waves his hand and chatter immediately resumes.

"What do you think?" Callum leans over, a brow raised.

I shrug. "Seems fine. I like the winning part."

"Same. Not sure how it's going to go down with Bennett, though. He's gonna have to tone it down and focus this season."

"Bennett should be fine here. Not much to do in this town, from what I've seen." My gaze flicks over to him, one hand propped against a locker while he continues to flirt with Harbor. Jealousy roars through me, along with the realization that Bennett can laugh with her, joke around and be normal. While I'm trapped between wanting her and protecting the team that depends on my leadership.

He gets to sail along, carefree, while I watch from a distance and pretend my chest doesn't tighten every time she smiles at someone else.

Nope.

I stalk across the room, Callum on my heels, hot aggravation buzzing through me.

"Hey." I step in—closer than necessary—and wedge myself between them. Chit chat's over. My arm's nearly touching hers, and a pink flush climbs from her chest up her neck. Her eyes flit to mine, then away again just as quickly.

Bennett gestures toward the door the coach walked out, but doesn't back away from Harbor. Still standing too close to her for my liking.

"Morning, boys. What did you think about the new guy?"

"Seems like he'll be good. You?" Cal asks.

"Seems like a hard-ass to me. But I'll give him a shot. Not like we've got options." Bennett shrugs, a furrow between his brows.

"After last season, we need someone like him. He's hungry and wants to win." I only partially believe these words, but it feels good to contradict my brother.

Harbor's phone buzzes in her hand and she taps out a reply.

"I'll see you all out there." She flashes us all a quick smile, but her gaze lingers on mine for a second longer than the others and a bolt of electricity shoots through me.

As she darts from the locker room, Bennett elbows me in the ribs. "So, did you two get cozy last night?"

"Not that it's any of your business…" I drop my voice low so no one else can hear. "But no. I went to bed. Alone."

"Damn, Cap. You gonna shoot your shot or what?"

"Coach made it clear—we're here to play hockey. Focus. Keep our heads down."

"Bor-ing…" Bennett sing-songs. "Besides, you could 100% use the stress release."

"Shut up, I'm fine." I straighten my jacket and stalk out of the locker room, officially dropping the subject.

Most of the team's already lined up in the hallway, clustered in small groups. We walk toward the doors that lead out to the lobby, taking our place at the front of the line. I catch snippets of conversation, the word *coach* dropped more than once. The tight space grows louder by the minute and I'm sweating beneath my jacket. I don't know if it's from the heat or the stress, but at this rate, I may have to change shirts before the ESPN interview.

At exactly eleven AM, Prince, Coach Keller, and Harbor file into the hallway. Players move out of their way as they march toward the doors, shoving into the lobby swarming with media. Cameras flash as we take our place behind the team owner, new coach, and Harbor.

I'm damn glad I'm not the one in charge of this press conference.

Prince steps forward, adjusting the mic. "Good morning and thanks for being here. I'm excited to unveil my new team, the Coastal Crushers. Here to lead the team to victory is Coach Mike Keller."

Prince pats Coach Keller's shoulder and he steps forward as eager hands shoot into the air. One reporter doesn't wait to be called on.

"Why'd you hire a rookie?"

Prince's brow furrows, and Coach Keller stands up straighter.

"Coach Keller has years of experience in the AHL and OHL. He has a proven track record. More importantly, we share the same aspiration—winning the Cup."

The reporter fires off a second question.

"So Samson from Vancouver said no?"

Prince clears his throat loudly into the mic. "Samson was never on my radar. Next question."

"Do you have any further information about Coach Evans and your wife?" The reporter smirks at Prince and Harbor steps forward, her expression stern.

"This presser is about the Crushers and the team's new direction. Further questions should focus on the matter at hand." She glares at the reporter and he shrinks at her reprimand, sitting down.

Another reporter asks about the team's relocation and Prince gives vague, PR-worthy responses. He fields questions about the logo, the mascot, the coach.

But all my attention's on Harbor. The way she engages with the media, handling the toughest inquiries with ease. Her poise, her quiet confidence. The don't-fuck-with-me vibe she's got going.

She's everything I want in a teammate—smart, tough, unshakeable under pressure. The kind of person who makes everyone around them better.

Which makes me wanting her the most selfish thing I could do. She's here to save this team. Save our careers—not risk hers on a captain who can't keep his priorities straight.

Sure, she's hot as hell.

But she's completely off-limits for all the right reasons.

"Last question—Robertson?" Harbor points at a tall, skinny dude sitting in front.

"The team's making a big charity push in the community with the Hockey with Heart campaign. I'd love to hear from a player how they feel about this."

"Absolutely. The team captain can speak to this." She glances over at me and I clear my throat, my chest tight.

Nothing like putting me on the spot.

I step forward to the podium, my fingers tightening around the edges. "I believe I can speak for the team on this. We look forward to being an integral, positive force in the community of Driftwood Cove and giving back."

Harbor's shoulders drop. A subtle breath of relief. I don't know if she's grateful, or just glad I didn't screw up. Hopefully I can get the team on board with this plan.

It's not like we have much choice.

"Any idea which charities you'll be focusing on?" The reporter drills me.

"Um…" My palms slick and I search for any detail that's been discussed. "We'll be focusing on youth hockey and um, other important charities this season."

"Do you believe you and your teammates will be good role models for youth players?"

"Absolutely." I swallow hard, pushing down my doubts. Surely we can all keep it together for a few hours in front of a group of kids. Even Bennett.

"We look forward to the full report on that, Captain." The reporter shoots me a cocky smile, then takes his seat.

I step back from the mic, palms still damp. The captain title feels a little too heavy today. Harbor gives a small nod. Barely perceptible, but I catch it. Approval. Or relief. Hell, maybe both.

"Thanks for coming, everyone." She clicks off the mic and cameras flash as the media disperses.

The team filters toward the hallway and I follow, but not before taking one last look at her.

Calm, cool, in control.

I hate how much I want to unravel her. How much I want to press pause on this whole damn season and *feel* something again.

Something I never thought I'd miss.

Bennett sidles up beside me, elbowing me in the ribs. "Nice speech, Captain America."

I don't answer, ignoring him. My gaze is still on her.

Harbor's eyes flick to mine and for a quick second, it's just me and her. The room fades away—the reporters, my teammates, all of it.

It's just us and the fire between us.

The fire we're both pretending isn't there.

In that second, I see it all.

Longing. Regret. And something that looks a hell of a lot like hope.

Then she turns away and disappears behind Prince and the new coach.

And I let her go.

Again.

Because that's what captains do. Put the team first— even when watching her walk away feels like losing the playoffs and the girl in the same damn breath.

I've spent my entire life learning how to win.

But Harbor Hayes might be the first battle I need to lose on purpose.

CHAPTER 16
HARBOR

"Anything you want to go over before the interview?" My eyes flick to Weston's and for a split second, he meets my gaze with a stare so intense I'm pretty sure I stop breathing.

Heart pounding, I wait for his response.

"I'm good."

I twist the stack of bracelets on my wrist, burying the sharp twinge of disappointment.

Of course he doesn't want any help from me. He still doesn't trust me, doesn't believe in the plan.

I drop my voice, taking a risk and stepping in closer to him, the fresh scent of his cologne winding around me.

"We're on the same team, you know. I want this to go well, just like you."

He swallows hard, the muscles in his neck moving with the effort. "I know. I appreciate that."

Warmth floods through me at his comment.

Finally, we're getting somewhere.

One thing I am good at is reading people, understanding what they need to succeed. The kind of strategic insight my dad thinks I lack, at least when it comes to hockey.

For the first time since taking this job, I actually believe he's wrong.

I do have what it takes. I belong here. I just need to make Weston see it, too.

"If you change your mind, let me know." I tuck my hair behind my ear and pivot to walk away. His hand grips my elbow.

"Harbor, wait..."

Spinning to face him, I try to focus on the task at hand. Not the man in front of me, with the sharp jawline and the perfect amount of stubble, looking beyond sexy in his dark blue suit.

The man whose lips were on mine less than twenty-four hours ago.

Keep it professional, Harbor. Forget about what happened in the locker room.

"Yes?"

"Can we do a trial run together?"

"Sure. We have enough time to run through the questions. Let's do it. Take a seat here—" I pull out a chair, patting the fabric. "And I'll be here. That's the most likely scenario for an interview like this. It'll be you, the interviewer, me, and the camera crew. That's it."

Weston sinks down into the chair, crossing his feet at the ankles. His posture's hunched and defensive.

I hop up from my chair, placing my hand on his shoulder. "Chest out, shoulders back, head up. You want to exude confidence."

He lifts his chin, blue eyes flashing and his jaw set. "Better?"

"Much." I take my seat again and get into my interviewing position, leaning slightly forward and staring at Weston intensely. The reporter stare, we call it.

He stares right back and my mouth goes dry, butterflies zooming around my belly—and it's not only from nerves.

This man does something to me.

"So, Weston—how do you feel about the change in leadership? The relocation and new team name?"

"Cutting right to the chase, huh?" Weston's full lips tip up at the corner as he scrubs a hand over his jaw.

I shrug. "Sorry, but we don't have much time. Figure I'll start with the harder questions."

He nods. "It's fine. How do I feel about the new leadership? I think Coach Keller could be a great asset to the team."

"Could be or will be?" I frown at him. "Word choice matters here."

"Right." He rubs his face, wiping away the look of doubt. "Coach Keller will be a great asset to the team."

"Perfect." I smile at him and he relaxes a touch, sitting back in his chair. "This is your first time playing for a team outside of your hometown of New York City. How are you feeling about the move? Homesick yet?"

Weston hesitates for a second and I pounce, pointing at him. "That. No pausing. Roll right into an answer. Pause in the middle, but never at the beginning of a question. That gives the reporter time to extrapolate and interpret. You don't want that."

He huffs out a sigh. "Got it. Ask again."

I clasp my hands together and lean forward. "This is your first time playing for a team outside of New York. How do you feel about that?"

"It's new and different." His eyes lock on mine and my

heart hammers hard against my ribcage. "I'm looking forward to the season, seeing what we can accomplish together as a team."

Not breaking eye contact, I ignore the ripple of electricity coursing through me and forge ahead with the mock interview.

"The Hockey with Heart campaign is something new this season. How do you feel about the team's commitment to charity? Do you think the campaign's a publicity ploy to help bolster the team's image?"

Weston licks his lips, a surefire tell.

"Pause right there." I hover my finger just over his lips, his breath warm against my skin. For one terrifying second, I forget what I'm about to say. "Don't do that."

"What?" His brows knit in confusion.

"Anything with your mouth." I wave my hand around his face. "It's a tell. You seem nervous."

He huffs out a sigh. "Damn, you must be great at poker."

I have to laugh at that. "I am pretty good. Sit back and try again. Weston, do you think the campaign's a ploy to help with the team's tarnished image?"

This time he meets my gaze head-on. "The team's excited to build strong community ties and we're looking forward to giving back."

"Yes!" I beam at him and he finally cracks a smile, his teeth gleaming in the fluorescent lights of the conference room. "Great answer."

The door creaks open. "Harbor, we're on in five. Time to mic up." One of the sound technicians pops her head in, glancing from me to Weston. I scoot back a little, my cheeks heating. The last thing I want is to give the wrong impression to the crew.

"Got it. We were just rehearsing." My words come out in a hurried jumble as she hustles over with Weston's mic. She hands him the earpiece and he shoves it in, then she winds cords around and tucks the receiver box into his back pocket.

"All set. We go live in a few." The technician scurries away, and Weston swipes his palms down his thighs.

"You ready?"

He nods, his expression serious, tiny lines crinkling his eyes.

"One last thing."

"Oh?"

"Your tie."

Instinctively, I reach out and adjust the knot, straightening the silky fabric until it lays just right against his thick neck. "There."

I gaze up at him and my stomach swoops as he locks those deep pools of blue on me. Hot desire rolls through me and I can't move, can't think rationally.

The only thing on my mind is Weston Steele and the magnetic forcefield of want between us.

This is what my father warned me about.

Personal feelings overriding professional judgment. The ultimate sin.

Don't ruin my reputation, Harbor.

"We're on!" the technician shouts into the room, and I jump away from Weston so fast I create a gust of wind.

"Coming!" I call out, putting maximum space between us as I race toward the interview room.

Weston follows behind and we file into the press area. Several people from ESPN line the wall and the reporter's already sitting, glasses of water on a round table between two leather chairs.

He stands as we approach, jutting out his hand. "Weston, great to meet you. I'm Pete Faulkner from ESPN. Thanks for chatting today."

Weston pumps his hand once, twice, then slides into his seat gracefully. "Happy to chat."

"Sound check, one, two, three…" The technician fiddles with the sound equipment and the camera crew adjusts the lighting slightly, tilting the lights up to account for Weston's height.

"And we're recording…"

Pete the reporter launches into a series of softball questions, easy things about hockey and Weston's early career. Then the interview takes a quick turn to the scandal.

"You were close with Coach Evans, right?" Pete doesn't wait for Weston to respond before he forges ahead. "Were you surprised to hear about the gambling accusations?"

Weston clears his throat. "I was. And that's all I can comment on the matter, Pete."

"So you had no idea about the gambling ring? How do you feel about the team moving? This is your first time playing out of New York, right?"

Weston nods, straightening his shoulders. "It is. I've spent my entire career in New York. But it's an exciting change for the team and the community. We're looking forward to building the franchise, getting involved with the people here. The Hockey with Heart campaign's going to do great things for some great people and I'm happy to be a part of something that makes a difference."

Pride blooms in my chest at his absolutely perfect response. Even better than what we rehearsed.

This is what comes from championship-level preparation. The kind of strategic excellence that would make Dad proud. Reading the situation, anticipating challenges, and preparing responses that exceed expectations.

"Sounds like a great PR campaign."

"It's more than that, Pete. We're here to do more than play hockey. We're here to grow the game and change lives."

"Wow, those are big plans, considering this is kind of a rebuilding year for the team. Coach Keller's a rookie in the league—how do you feel about that?"

"I trust Mr. Prince and the GM to have the team's back. They conducted a thorough search, and I'm confident they have the best coach for the team."

"That's an awful lot of trust, Steele." Pete raises a brow at Weston. "Especially after the season you all just went through."

Weston's eyes find mine. "In hockey, you have to work together and trust your teammates. That's the only way to win out there."

Warmth floods my veins as my dad's words echo in my head.

Trust your team. It's the only way to win.

"Sounds like you're ready for a new season, Steele. I look forward to seeing you out on the ice."

The cameras click off and the lights go up, cool relief rushing through me.

We did it.

Weston stands and the sound technician scurries over, unclipping the mic from him. He shakes Pete's hand and then steps away from the stage, moving in my direction.

"Great job." I beam at him, resisting the urge to reach out and hug him I'm so happy.

"Thanks." He scrubs his palm over the back of his neck. "We good?"

The question stings, disappointment creeping around the edges of my happiness. The professional distance is back, his easygoing demeanor gone the second the cameras stop rolling.

"Yeah. We're good."

"Cool. Thanks for your help." Loosening his tie, Weston strides out of the room and I'm left staring at his broad back.

I should be celebrating. Together, we just delivered a flawless media performance, the kind of interview that gets played and replayed.

Instead, I'm standing her crushed and alone.

A professional victory's never felt more like a personal defeat.

CHAPTER 17
WESTON

can't get out of the media room fast enough. My tie's choking me out, and I'm way too fucking hot.

I'd love to blame it on the pressure from the interview, but I know it's not that.

It's her.

Harbor.

The way the golden flecks in her eyes sparkle when she laughs, the tinkly lilt of her voice, that damn freckle behind her earlobe taunting me.

I have to get away from her before I do something I can't undo.

I'm so amped up, I head straight to the locker room and change into gym clothes, then hit the treadmill. I'll run her out of my system, get back to where I was two weeks ago.

Focused.

On hockey, the game I'm getting paid to play. The game I love.

Not on the beautiful blonde PR consultant who's

making me question everything I thought I knew about priorities.

My entire identity's built around being the guy who puts the team first. The captain who never lets personal wants compromise professional responsibilities.

But Harbor Hayes is unraveling that discipline one dazzling smile at a time.

My head's all fucked up.

I crank the speed on the treadmill and sprint until my chest heaves and my shirt's ringed with sweat.

Still, her words echo in my head.

That was perfect.

Not just the interview. Me.

She saw something in me I don't let most people see.

I can't erase her smile, the way she lit up and fucking glowed after the interview.

And I ran away.

Again.

Bennett's annoying voice rolls through my mind: *You gonna shoot your shot, Cap?*

But I can't. We can't. We both have too much to lose.

It's a terrible idea.

I hit the locker room showers and try to wash away the jumpy agitation. Hot water streams around me, but it's not enough to rinse away the ghost of her touch when she adjusted my tie. The way her fingers trembled at my throat, the hitch of her breath.

I can't escape her, no matter what I do, where I go.

Finally, I give up and cut the water, towel off. Throwing on my last clean set of gym clothes, I head out for the day.

The building's empty now, my teammates, the coaches and staff, all the reporters and media crew long gone. My footsteps echo down the long hallway as I trudge toward the lobby. I'm almost at the main entrance when I spot an open door, black-and-white shadows dancing on the linoleum floor.

Intrigued, I move toward the flashing light. Hovering outside the dark room, I watch as Harbor studies video footage from the interview. Headphones over her ears, her fingers fly across the remote, pausing and restarting the film as she takes notes. Light reflects from the monitor, highlighting the apples of her cheeks, the slight curve of her full lips.

She's beautiful and I can't stop staring, every muscle in my body tight.

So much for working off the tension.

Every bit of it comes back full force, my heart pounding hard. She must feel my eyes on her because she swivels toward the door, her hand flying to her chest.

"Weston! You scared me."

"Sorry. I didn't mean to creep up on you."

She laughs, the sound drifting around me and lighting me up inside.

"It's fine. I was reviewing the film from this afternoon. You looked great out there."

"Thanks."

"You want to watch with me?" She tips her head, a golden wave of hair cascading over her shoulder.

I should walk away. Maybe run.

"Sure."

Instead, I step into the dark room, drawn to the glow of the monitor.

To her.

Moving in the exact opposite direction of common sense.

She scrolls through the footage, freezing the screen and

pointing. "Here. The way you handled the gambling question? Fantastic. Authoritative, but not defensive."

How she's talking about my performance, her professional insight—it's a better compliment than anything I've heard before. I'm not just a good-looking face, another player to her.

She sees me. Really sees me—not just the captain everyone expects me to be, but the man I am.

And it's terrifying how much that means to me. How much *she* means to me.

Shit, Steele. You're skating back into dangerous territory again.

"Here." She hands me a set of headphones and I slide down next to her, our legs brushing. Lightning shoots up my thigh, straight to my dick, and I'm grateful it's dark in this room. Otherwise she'd see the way she's affecting me —there's certainly no hiding it.

Staring straight ahead at the monitor, I place the headphones over my ears as she rewinds the film. We watch in silence for a few minutes, and I try to focus on the interview—something, anything—other than the heat radiating off her body, her vanilla scent wrapping around me. Blood roars loud in my ears and I can't hear what I'm saying on the film, nor do I care. My entire body's humming, on high alert Harbor shifts in her chair and her knee falls against mine and that slight movement has my dick at full mast.

Fuck me.

She pulls her headphones down around her neck, smiling in the dark. "Fantastic, right? You were great, Weston."

I can't tear my gaze from her mouth, the pretty pink bow of her lips. I remember what she tastes like, feels like, and I want more.

Need more.

This is the moment. Deciding between what the team needs and the man wants.

I've spent my entire career making the right call, the safe play, the decision that protects everyone else.

Maybe it's time to make a decision just for me, just this once.

"Harbor…" My voice is gruff as her eyes flick to mine.

"Yes?"

The way she gazes up at me through that thick fringe of lashes tips me over the edge. I'm untethered, the rope that's been holding me together unraveling. I give into temptation, bending down and pressing my lips to hers.

Heaven.

She doesn't pull away. Instead, she leans in, her soft sigh a whisper in the darkness. Like she's giving in right along with me.

We're both surrendering and it feels so damn good.

I slip my tongue into her mouth and taste her. She's sweet, and warm, and slightly minty, and I don't think I'll ever get enough.

"Weston…" she moans, but she doesn't stop kissing me. She tangles her tongue with mine and slides closer, our bodies inches apart.

Taking the chance, I grip her hips and pull her onto my lap. She answers by winding her hands around my neck, her delicate fingers caressing the hairline and sending a delicious shiver rolling down my spine.

I want this woman.

Right the fuck now.

I don't want to waste another second. No more analyzing and second-guessing.

Moving my hand from her waist, I caress the round

peach of her ass, the fabric of her skirt silky smooth beneath my calloused palm. I want to feel her skin, the heat radiating from her body onto mine like rays from the sun.

"Harbor…"

She pauses and pulls away slightly. "Mmm…"

I run my thumb over her bottom lip, taking all of her in. "I want you. But I know there's a lot on the line—"

The tip of her tongue darts out, brushing the rough skin of my thumb.

Fuck me.

She gazes up at me, her pupils dark and wide, hair tousled and messy. No longer the composed PR professional, she's the picture of sultry innocence.

"I know. I want you too." Her voice is low and quiet as her palm flutters to my chest, resting over my stuttering heart. "I haven't stopped thinking about what happened in the locker room. About you."

We're really doing this. Crossing every line we set to keep things professional.

Risking everything we've both worked for.

"So what do we do about it?"

She hops up, plucking her heels off her feet. Hurrying over to the door, she shuts and locks it before spinning back around to face me, determination blazing in her eyes.

Game on.

We're past the point of no return now. And I don't want to go back anyway.

She smiles at me. "What happens in the film room, stays in the film room."

CHAPTER 18
HARBOR

can't believe I'm doing this.

Discipline over desire, Harbor. That's what it takes to win.

Maybe it's time I stopped playing by my father's rules.

Because I'm not walking away now.

Not with Weston freaking Steele, captain of the Coastal Crushers, staring at me like this. Like I'm the most gorgeous woman on the planet.

Even if this is a one-off thing.

Even if it proves my dad right about me.

Maybe I don't have the right mindset for a career in professional hockey.

But right now, all I care about is following my heart. For once in my life, I'm doing what I want.

Not what's expected of me, what I should do.

I'm choosing me over the Hayes's legacy.

Because I need to know. Know what his hands feel like on my bare skin, how his rock-hard body feels pressed against mine.

How he feels inside me.

I need him.

This is probably a terrible decision, and an even worse career move.

But still, I twist the lock, unbuttoning my blouse as I make my way back across the room.

Back to Weston and his piercing blue gaze.

Butterflies zoom around my belly as his eyes rake over me, assessing the situation.

I should probably feel self-conscious. The man's gorgeous, a professional hockey star. I'm sure he's seen his fair share of beautiful women.

But surprisingly, I'm not nervous or insecure.

All I feel is buzzy excitement.

This is really happening.

He reaches up, his large hands wrapping around my waist, pulling me into his lap again.

"Perfect," he murmurs, his fingers tickling my bare stomach. "So damn perfect. I've been wanting to see you like this."

"Like what? Naked?"

He chuckles, a low, throaty rumble sending a ripple of excitement zinging through me.

"Yes, that. But I was going to go with something more poetic. I was thinking more along the lines of undone."

"Oh." I lick my bottom lip, contemplating his answer. He's definitely deeper than I gave him credit for.

"And I wanted to be the one responsible for that. Maybe someplace a little more romantic than the video room, though." He traces his finger along my cheek, down my jawline to the divot in my neck.

I half-sigh, half-giggle as he undresses me slowly, so

slowly, my blouse slipping off my shoulders, my arms, until it pools on the floor in a silky puddle.

"This…" He drops his lips to my ear, heat rushing over me. "Right here. This freckle's been taunting me since I met you." His tongue darts out, licking the spot.

Cupping my cheek, he kisses me softly and I melt into him. He tastes so good, fresh and minty, his lips moving over mine. I open to him and his tongue slides in, exploring. Chill bumps rise on my skin as his hands tangle in my hair.

I could stay like this, locked away with Weston, forever.

So this is what it feels like to choose myself over other people's expectations. To prioritize my happiness over family reputation, personal desire over professional perfectionism.

My father would call it weakness. But it's the toughest thing I've ever done.

I feather my fingers over his strong pecs, his biceps. The man is ripped, his muscles visible even beneath his gray T-shirt.

Breaking our kiss, he reaches behind him and yanks his shirt off, dropping it to the floor next to mine.

Fuck me.

He's every bit as gorgeous as he was in the locker room. I didn't know there was such a thing as an eight-pack in real life, but he's got it. I trace the ridges of his abs, the deep V of his hips peeking out from the waistband of his shorts.

Sexy as hell.

I'm torn between savoring the moment and cutting straight to the chase, my pussy throbbing with desire.

Weston drops his lips to my chest, kissing the delicate skin peeking out of my bra. My nipples harden into sharp points as he thumbs them through the thin satin material. Reaching behind my back, he smoothly unhooks the lingerie, lowering the straps over my shoulders and freeing my breasts.

Cupping the tender flesh in his palms, his calloused fingers tickle my sensitive skin. Wetness floods my panties and a moan falls from my lips, loud in the quiet space.

"Fucking gorgeous, baby," he murmurs, bending down to lick and suck my nipples. "I've been dreaming of these perfect tits since the first press conference."

My entire body's hot and humming with desire as I straddle him, hitching my skirt up around my hips for better movement. He's fully aroused, his cock thick and hard against my belly through his shorts.

I need this man right now.

"Weston..." My eyes flutter closed as I get lost in the haze of him—the crisp scent of his cologne, his tender touch, the desire shimmering between us.

I can't think, can't second-guess. All I can do in this moment is feel and it's fucking magical.

"Harbor?" His deep voice brings me back to reality. "I'm only going to ask you this one more time. Now's your chance to bow out. Because once we do this, there's no going back."

No going back.

To the safety of professional distance, to my father's playbook of perfection.

The point of no return. Maybe it's exactly what I need to finally start living.

"Are you sure?" His gaze is steady on mine, pupils dark and wide.

I've never been more sure about anything in my whole damn life.

I nod. "Absolutely. I want you, Weston."

What I don't say—can't say—is: *I need you.*

Too much, too soon.

I'm borderline already going too far, but right now I don't care.

All I care about is the incessant pulsing between my thighs, the racing of my heart as he slips his hand between my legs.

"Yes…" I practically hiss the word, my hips moving all on their own. Wanting—needing—more.

Harder, faster.

He strokes the sensitive skin, teasing my swollen clit through the satin of my panties.

God, I need this man.

To show him how sure I am about this, I shimmy off his lap and slip my panties down my legs, losing the skirt in the process.

I'm fully naked in front of him and his lips break into a Cheshire cat grin.

"What?" I raise a brow, biting at the corner of my mouth.

"You're sexy as fuck, you know that?" He stands up, ripping his gym shorts off and freeing his cock. Fisting himself, he pumps a few times before rummaging through his bag and producing a condom.

"Wow. You're prepared. Was this on your to-do list today?"

"No. But I am the oldest child by five minutes. Preparedness is a byproduct of the position." He tears open the foil packet and rolls the rubber over his impressive length. Then he sinks back down onto the chair, pulling me toward him.

I drop down onto his lap, gliding my hand up and down his stiff shaft. He's big.

Like, really big.

I mean, proportional and everything. But the man's six-five. A giant to my five-foot-four stature.

"You still good?" Weston's hands still on the small of my back, eyes narrowed.

I swallow hard. "Yeah. It's just—you're really...big."

He laughs, his chest vibrating. "Don't worry, Hurricane. It'll fit. I won't break you. Promise."

His expression's so intense, so sincere, and my breath hitches in my throat.

I won't break you.

Promise.

I'm not sure that's a promise he can keep.

Choosing this moment, choosing him—that's shattering every wall I've carefully constructed around my heart.

Maybe it's time those walls finally come down.

CHAPTER 19
WESTON

Harbor's straddling me, her luscious tits pressed up against my bare chest, her scent filling my nose. The floral notes of her shampoo mix with the musky, heady smell of desire, and I'm a fucking goner.

I slide my fingers through her wetness, swirl the pad of my thumb over her swollen clit. Arousal coats my fingers as I slip inside her for the first time.

I'm positive it won't be the last.

She tenses around my hand as I move in and out, one finger, then two, her eyes fluttering closed as she gives into me.

She's so damn beautiful like this, her head tipped back slightly, exposing the long lines of her neck. Golden waves of hair flow over her bare shoulders, nipples tight and rosy.

Undone.

This is exactly how I pictured her in my fantasies, pretty pink lips curving into a slow smile as I work her hot, slick heat.

Mine.

The word pops into my head, echoing through my mind with each thrust of my hand.

Mine. Mine. Mine.

I've never been this possessive. Never wanted to claim someone as completely as I do her, desire overriding all rational thought.

The sort of thinking that destroys captains and their teams.

This could turn out very, very badly. For both of us.

She sighs, a happy little exhale, bringing me back to the present moment.

I'll stress about the million and one ways this thing could go sideways later. Right now, I need to focus on the goal—ruining Harbor for any other man.

Ever.

Easing my fingers from her body, I bring them to my lips. Her eyes pop open in surprise.

"What…" She gazes up at me with glassy eyes. "Why'd you stop?"

I suck my fingers, slurping her juices from my skin and never breaking eye contact.

"I needed to taste you."

"Oh." Her lips form a surprised little circle.

"Fucking divine. Addictive." I finish licking my fingers, then seize her mouth in a hot kiss. Sliding my tongue between her lips so she can taste herself.

Palming her ass, I lift her until her pussy hovers over my cock.

"I've been thinking about this way more than I'd like to admit," I murmur, inching the tip of my dick into her. "How tight and wet you'd be."

She opens her legs wider, taking more of me in. "And?"

"You're even better than I dreamed." I push further

inside, muscles tensing, then relaxing as I massage her ass. "That's good, baby. Breathe."

A tiny puff of air dusts my chest as she exhales, a pink blush coloring her cheeks.

"You're doing so well." I squeeze her ass, nipping at the delicate skin of her neck. She relaxes against me and I thrust all the way in until there's no space left between us.

"Oh my god, Weston…" she whispers, almost reverently, and I'm literally in heaven. Harbor's arms wrapped around me, my dick buried deep inside her.

Brushing a stray hair from her eyes, I touch my lips to hers. Soft at first, then harder and deeper. She squeezes my cock with her muscles and starts moving her hips, rocking against me.

Fuck, yeah.

I meet her thrust for thrust, matching her rhythm and pacing.

This woman's absolute perfection, riding my cock like she owns me.

Which, in this moment, she 100% does.

Hands fly, our skin slapping as she rides me in the dark media room.

Harbor fucking Hayes, coming undone on my lap like a rowdy cowgirl. Riding me like it's her motherfucking job.

I'm catapulting through space right now, white-hot sparks zinging through me, my balls tingling with the familiar pressure signaling a release.

Clutching her ass, I piston harder, faster, deeper, chasing the climax. I know she's close—her face and chest flushed, breathing ragged, a light sheen of sweat beading at her brow.

I brush my lips against the shell of her ear and whisper, "Come for me, Harbor. Let go and fucking come."

That's all it takes to rocket her over the edge, muscles spasming as she cries out. "Oh my god, oh my god, oh my god…"

I don't let up, even as her body shakes against my chest. Instead, I drive harder into her hot, tight pussy. Harder, faster, and deeper, her nails clawing at my lats. I'm going to have scratch marks—may even be bleeding—but it will be worth it.

"Fuck me…" I hiss, finally exploding my release.

I slump against the cool leather chair, spent and sated, panting like I just did sprints.

"That was fucking fantastic…" I close my eyes and try to catch my breath, spasms of pleasure rolling through me.

Harbor trails her fingers over my chest, my abs, her breathing still uneven. For a perfect moment, the world outside this room doesn't exist. No team, no cameras, no consequences.

I want to freeze time, hold her here. Just like this.

Her phone buzzes against the floor, shattering the spell. She stiffens against me, and the air around us shifts.

"That was…intense." She eases off my lap, being careful not to dislodge the condom.

The cool air of the room hits my skin and suddenly, I'm chilled. Chilled and hyperaware that I'm naked and alone as she snatches her bra and panties from the floor, hastily throwing the undergarments back on.

Covering herself.

And there it is, the walls going back up. Professional Harbor reasserting control over the woman who just came apart in my arms.

I recognize the pattern because I'm about to do the same damn thing.

I wanted to hold onto this, to her, to the possibility of us. Like it could change something. But it doesn't.

I'm still the captain trying to save his team. And she's still the PR consultant trying to prove herself.

But having tasted her, touched her—it makes leaving this media room and going back to how things were—that much harder.

"God, Weston. This complicates everything." Her eyes flash with conflict, desire warring with reality.

"It doesn't have to." I carefully roll the condom off my dick, wadding it in tissue to dispose of somewhere more private. Can't leave behind the evidence.

"It does. You know it does. No one can know about this." Her expression shifts as she steps into her skirt, pulls up the zipper.

I blink, fighting through the sex haze we created only a few seconds ago.

"What?"

"This—" She waves her hand through the air, motioning between us. "You and me. We probably shouldn't have done this."

An icy wave of regret washes over me, dampening the post-orgasmic high.

Harbor's already retreating. Erasing what happened before it can even matter.

Or she's doing what she's been taught to do. Flee before anyone gets hurt. Hide behind professional responsibilities and protect your heart.

When things get messy, when emotions threaten control, retreat to safety. Her dad's voice is probably echoing in her head the same way mine's telling me to protect the team at all costs.

This is my chance to say something meaningful, fight for the possibilities.

But I can't.

She's right. There's too much on the line. The team, her job.

We're doing the right thing. Protecting ourselves and our futures.

Even if it sucks.

I shrug. "You're right. We probably shouldn't have."

She pauses, her eyes wide for a long second, like she's stung. Then she slides her blouse over her shoulders, focusing on the neat row of buttons.

"So, one-time thing then?"

My gut tightens and sinks.

Fight for it, Weston. Don't let her walk away.

"Sure. One-time thing."

"Okay." She pulls her hair back into a ponytail, slipping her feet back into her stilettos. "That's the safest thing. For both of us. One time only, to get it out of our system. Deal?"

Harbor stares at me and I swallow back a grimace.

Now we're making a fucking deal? Might as well slap a contract on the desk and make it really fucking official.

Like what just happened between us was some kind of business transaction and not the most intense connection I've felt since…maybe ever.

I nod, taking in those hazel eyes still sparkly from the sex. Anything to avoid admitting that what just happened did, in fact, change everything between us.

"Deal."

"Great. Because we still have to be professional. We can't let whatever this was…" She waves her hand again and acid rises, burning the back of my throat. "Ruin our relationship. You know?"

I suck my teeth and nod. "Yeah. You're right."

Ducking down, I grab my shorts and T-shirt, shove the condom into my bag. I throw my clothes on as quickly as humanly possible. I have to get out of here, and fast.

"Alright then. I'll see you around."

Tossing my duffel over my shoulder, I hustle out of the media room without looking back. Dick deflated and ego bruised, wondering when the hell I became the guy who chooses being a good captain over being a man who goes after what he wants.

And why I keep letting the best things in my life slip away without a fight.

CHAPTER 20
HARBOR

hat the hell am I doing?

W I stare up at the smooth white ceiling in my hotel room, the AC blowing over my heated skin. I just had fantastic, mind-blowing sex with the most gorgeous man on the planet and proceeded to tell him it was a ONE-TIME THING.

Like, what in the actual fuck is wrong with me?

You're doing exactly what you always do—playing it safe.

Getting the jump, making sure you're the one who makes the call.

Dad trained you well.

Oh shit. That part stings.

Almost as much as hearing Weston readily agree that getting together was a mistake.

Even though I said it first, he didn't have to go along with it.

Seems like maybe you're both thinking about keeping your jobs—and your professional reputations.

I huff out a deep breath and roll over on the fluffy

white bed, gazing out into the chaotic waves of the Atlantic.

Why does everything always have to be so complicated?

Just once in my life, I want things to be easy, simple. Like they always are for Piper.

She would never let Weston walk away.

Never.

Piper would've locked him down the second his lips touched hers. They'd probably already be engaged.

And what did I do?

Turned him down. Multiple times. Then finally gave in, only to pull a quick 180 and tell him things between us are over before they've barely begun.

Good god, I'm an absolute head case.

I sit up and kick my shoes off, wiggling my toes, the shell-pink polish sparkling in the soft lamp light.

But I can't be the scandal. That's not what this team needs, what I need.

What I need is a win.

Pretty sure you just had one. An amazing, strong, beautiful man, with an equally amazing cock, fucking you into oblivion in the media room.

#winning.

But at what cost?

There it is again. My dad's voice, complete with hard, cold stare.

I thought you cared about the job. The family name. Our legacy.

Not just hooking up with a hockey player, chasing after some fleeting high with a man.

Fuck my life.

No matter how hard I try, I can't get away from my dad

and his sky-high—and frankly, unrealistic—expectations of me.

Maybe I need to book a virtual appointment with Dr. Martina to get my head back in the game.

Buzz, buzz.

Leaning over the bed, I fish my cell from my purse. Piper's name pops up on the screen. A video call from my sister's the next best thing, I suppose.

"Hello?"

"Whoa." She arches a brow, eyes narrowing. "You fucked him, didn't you? The captain?"

Cheeks burning, I shake my head in protest. "No! Why would you say that?"

"Oh, c'mon, Harbs. Don't play coy with me. You've got that just-fucked look going on. Messy hair, flushed face. And your blouse—the buttons are crooked."

I check my shirt.

Shit, she's right.

Tugging at the gauzy fabric, I quickly fix my shirt, avoiding my sister's pointed stare.

"Admit it. You got with the sexy hockey star. Good for you."

"Fine. You're right, I did."

"Yes!" Piper grins and pumps her fist in the air. "And? How was he? Huge? I heard hockey players have big dicks."

"Oh my gosh, Piper!" I giggle, blushing. Because she's not wrong. Weston is very well-endowed.

"He does, doesn't he? Look at you, down in Florida living your best life. When can I meet him?"

I exhale a heavy sigh. "Probably never. I told him it was a one-time thing."

"What? Are you mad, woman? You sleep with a hockey

star and then tell him it's over? What in the actual fuck, Harbor!"

"I know. Trust me, I know. But it's not like we can date. I'm trying to save the team from scandal. How does it look for the PR consultant to be hooking up with a player?"

"You're single. He's single. So who cares?"

"It's optics, Piper. The tabloids would be all over that."

"The tabloids or Dad?"

My gut clenches at the mention of our father. *How does Piper always know?*

I fidget with the bangles on my wrist. "This has nothing to do with Dad."

"I'm calling bullshit on that."

"Fine. Maybe it has a little bit to do with him. What would he say if he found out I banged the team captain in the film room?"

"Impressive…I didn't know you had something that kinky in you, big sis."

I roll my eyes at my sister, even as the corner of my mouth curves up in a smile. Straddling Weston in the dark, remembering how it felt to be pressed up against his strong chest, his hands caressing my ass.

"It was amazing. But it can't happen again." I run my fingers through my hair and try to sound convincing.

"Harbor, don't let Dad rule your life." Her voice is low and firm, her gaze serious. "Why do you care so much about what he thinks?"

Out of nowhere, tears spring to my eyes. "Because it's *Dad*. The great Coach Doug Hayes. Everybody knows him. So by extension, they know me. There's expectations, you know? I have to work harder, be better than everyone else."

"Well, you do work harder and you are better. So I'd

say your job is done. Now go out and live your damn life.
Fuck Dad. You deserve to be happy, Harbor."

I take a shaky breath, absorbing her words.

Maybe she's right. Maybe I should do what I want, let
go of expectations and choose myself for once.

Who am I kidding?

That's not in my DNA. I'm the daughter of the greatest
hockey coach of all time.

I have a legacy to protect. A team to rebuild. A championship to win.

Eyes on the prize, Harbor.

"No, I can't, Piper. It's too risky."

My sister presses her lips together and I feel her disappointment through the phone.

"I don't know why you bother going to therapy. Maybe
you should try to get a refund because it's obviously not
working."

Ouch.

"You don't understand. Your job is low-stakes, no
expectations. You don't know what it's like."

"Wow, okay. Thanks. Now you're sounding like Dad,
too." Piper's tone goes cold. "Do you hear yourself right
now? You just dismissed my entire career because there's
not crazy pressure tied to it, a championship trophy on the
line."

Her words sting because she's absolutely right. I *do*
sound like him. Dismissive. Elitist. Acting like only
winning matters.

"That's not what I meant—"

"It's exactly what you meant. And you know what's
really fucked up? You're using Dad's logic to justify
staying small. To avoid going after anything real. You're
trapped in his shadow, chasing after whatever you think

will make him happy—if he's even capable of that emotion. Jury's still out. But don't come crying to me when you're alone and miserable, with only your career to keep you company. Because that's what's going to happen." Her ponytail swishes behind her with each harsh word, a furrow etched in her brow.

"One day you'll wake up and everyone around you will be married with kids and you'll still be single. Trying to live up to someone's stupid expectations and falling short because no one—not even you, Harbor—is perfect."

Her words cut deep because they're true and I know it.

I've spent my entire life seeking my father's approval. And for what? A gold star he'll never give me? He's never satisfied, never happy or proud. Even when I land the biggest client of my career, it's not enough.

"But what if I fail, Piper?" My voice shakes, and I hate it. Hate how weak I sound, hate the constant self-doubt gnawing at me. "What if I prove him right, about everything?"

"Then you fail, Harbor. But at least you fucking tried to be yourself instead of his perfect little daughter."

With that, she disconnects and the screen goes black.

Super.

Somehow I managed to push Weston away and piss my sister off all in a few short hours.

Buzz, buzz.

Hoping Piper's calling me back to kiss and make up, I glance at my cell.

Dad: Saw the presser. Coach Keller has quite the reputation

Dad: Tough but good. Big step up from the dipshit they had before

Is my dad actually giving me positive feedback right now?

Mind blown.

> Dad: Don't think I would've hired a rookie.
> But probably the best they could get

There it is. The backhanded compliment I expected. Never simple praise. Always qualified, always second-guessing.

> Dad: Had dinner with Jarod from the
> Olympics committee. He has an open
> spot on his marketing team

For fuck's sake. The man never lets up. He can't acknowledge my success—it always comes with conditions, qualifications, immediate suggestions for something "better."

> Harbor: Thanks, but I'm good. The team's
> going to have a great season
>
> Harbor: They're championship material

Blue dots swirl, each spin adding another sharp twist to my gut, my anxiety peaking

> Dad: I'm not sure they have what it takes.
> So many distractions
>
> Dad: That's not how you win

And I'm one of the distractions.

The realization hits hard, sucking the air from my lungs.

I'm not just failing to maintain professional boundaries —I'm actively undermining everything I came here to achieve.

I can't be one of the reasons the team doesn't win. The Crushers deserve a PR consultant at the top of her game and a captain with singular focus.

Not someone who's distracted—and distracting.

My dad's right again.

And I fucking hate it.

CHAPTER 21
WESTON

t's been three days since Harbor and I had sex in the media room. Three days of silence fucking with my head worse than any hit I've taken. No call, no text. Like nothing happened between us.

And the quiet is killing me.

I can't stop thinking about her. The way she took control, locked the door and straddled me.

Honestly, she's hot as hell.

Every single thing about her.

The way we fit together, her pussy tight and slick as she rode my cock. Hard and fast, begging for more.

I'd love to give her more. Right the fuck now.

Unfortunately, she's avoiding me. It appears she's going to stick to the whole *one-time thing.*

"You done warming up there, Cap? Or do you need more groin stretching? You know, to be on the safe side?" Bennett snickers down at me as I move through my pre-workout stretch routine.

"Fuck off, Bennett. And yeah, I'm done." Gripping my stick, I ease off the ice as Coach Keller waves us over.

"Welcome to pre-season conditioning, boys. We're going to run drills and sprints old-school style today, so I hope you're nice and warm."

Bennett elbows me and I hold back an eye roll. I want to make a good first impression on Keller—I don't need any trouble with the new coach.

Digging my blade into the ice, I carve a small groove. A nervous habit I've had since youth hockey league. This is the first practice with a coach who doesn't know shit about my leadership style, and I'm already off-balance. Keller's the type who'll strip that 'C' right off my jersey without a second thought. No need to give him a reason.

"We'll start with blue line to blue line sprints. Captain, why don't you lead us off? Take Bennett and Morrison with you. Line two, be ready. You're up next." Coach pulls out his stopwatch, and my nerves fire up as I skate over to the line.

Which is stupid because this is pre-season conditioning. I've been skating since I was two years old and these are my teammates, not rivals.

Still, tension's thick, my muscles tightly coiled as I crouch down into position. Instinctively, I know I need to prove myself to Keller, and now's as good a time as any.

The whistle blows and I take off, ice flurrying around the blades of my skates as I sail across the smooth surface. Bennett and Morrison stay with me, all of us needing to impress the new coach, none of us wanting to come across the line last.

Chest heaving and arms pumping, I fly across the line a split second after my brother.

"Bennett, 3.04 seconds, Weston 3.12 seconds, Morrison,

3.22 seconds. Next." Keller calls out the times but doesn't offer any further commentary.

I skate around to the back of the group, trying to catch my breath and prepare for round two, ignoring Bennett's victorious smirk.

Little shit.

Rolling my shoulders, I suck in oxygen and focus on staying loose. Not letting my brother into my head.

It's crowded enough in there as is, what with Harbor's voice echoing through my mind every time I close my eyes.

Her laugh, her moans, the way she called my name when she came apart on my lap.

Offense line two takes off, the scratching of blades on the ice bringing me back to reality. Line three's up, then the defensemen, followed by the goalies, Callum and Klein.

"You ready, Cap?" Bennett shoots me a sideways glance and my jaw tightens.

"Of course I am."

Coach blows the whistle and we take off, my quads firing. The swoosh of blades digging into the ice ricochets around the rink as we turn. Bennett's right next to me, half an inch in the lead. I push harder, but he still outskates me.

"Fuck," I hiss under my breath, lungs burning.

In ten years of competitive hockey, no woman's made me lose my focus during practice. Not even Bee.

Dammit.

Harbor Hayes is rewiring my motherfucking brain.

"What's got you twisted, Cap? Usually takes a playoff loss to throw you off this bad," Bennett mocks, and my gut clenches.

I don't need my brother pointing out every tiny victory he manages to score.

"Letting you win." I scowl over at him, arms above my head to increase lung capacity.

"Uh-huh. Right." He skates away, seemingly unphased, and I squeeze my eyes shut.

Focus, Steele. You have to beat him this time.

Sucking in a deep breath, I visualize my blade crossing the finish line first.

I've totally got this.

Spinning around, I head to the back of the line. That's when I spot her.

Harbor, in dark jeans that hug every curve and a navy blazer, looking as fuckable as ever. She's standing behind the glass talking to Prince and a group of people, most likely community sponsors.

My chest tightens, and I square my shoulders, standing up taller. Not that it matters—she doesn't even glance this way.

"Line one, ready?" Keller's thumb hovers over his stopwatch and I hustle to the line, trying to get my head on straight.

I need to beat my brother. Now more than ever.

"And...go!"

I accelerate off the line, faster than the last two times. Body down, grinding, ice flying. Bennett's a blur in the corner of my eye, but I try to forget about him. My only goal is coming across that blue line first.

No matter what.

"Bennett, 3.01, Weston, 3.03, Morrison, 3.1 flat."

Fuck me.

I still didn't beat my brother.

Sneaking a peek over my shoulder, I'm bolstered by the fact that Harbor's not paying any attention to the ice.

"Cap, you gonna beat me today? Even once?" Bennett's voice tips up and I'm beyond irritated.

"Letting you have this one, Puck Bunny," I shoot back, although that's not the truth of the matter.

I'm off my game and I know it.

"Aww, where's the fun in that?" he taunts, ice spraying off his blades.

Doubling down, I suck in a deep breath.

You've got this, Steele.

Callum and Klein race and now I'm back on the blue line in position.

"And go!" Keller hits the stopwatch and I take off like a shot, wind cold on my face.

Arms pumping, I pivot and race back to the line.

"Bennett, 3 flat, Weston, 3.01, Morrison, 3.1."

Son of a bitch.

Shaking the sweat from my hair, I sneak another peek at Harbor. She's in her element, yapping with the sponsors and ignoring everything around her.

Thank god. Because right now, I'm a big fucking disappointment.

"One more shot, Cap." Bennett bends down, making a big show of stretching, and I push down all my feelings.

Now or never.

"Last round, Line One—" Keller hits the stopwatch, and I shove off the line a split second behind Bennett.

Not ideal.

I push as hard as I can, quads burning as I make the turn.

"Weston, 3 flat, Bennett 3.02, Morrison, 3.1. Good job, boys." Keller nods his approval as I suck in oxygen like it's my motherfucking job.

"Weston." Coach's voice stops me as I start to skate

away. "Nice finish. But you were sloppy on the first four. Whatever's going on in your head, get it sorted by tomorrow."

My heart thuds harder and ice runs through my veins.

Shit. I'm that fucking obvious.

"Yes, sir."

"Good. Because I need my captain locked in, not scattered." He moves away, leaving me with the clear message that I'm on thin ice.

Harbor's not just threatening my job. Now she's threatening my captaincy.

Bennett circles around me. "About fucking time, Cap. I was beginning to think you needed performance coaching off the ice too." Bennett slaps me on the back as I spin, arms resting on my head.

"Saved the best for last, Benny." I huff out the words, but Bennett's not buying it.

"Bullshit. You've been off for three days straight. Callum noticed too." He glances around, making sure Coach isn't listening. "Whatever's happening with PR Barbie's fucking with your game."

My jaw clenches. "Stop with that nickname, Bennett. It's derogatory and you know it. She deserves respect, like every other member of the team. Also, I don't know what you're talking about."

"Sure you don't. When's the last time I beat you in four straight sprints? Never, that's when." He leans closer, voice dropping. "Look, I don't care who you're banging. But if it's affecting your leadership, the team's gonna notice."

Fuck.

Because he's right. If Bennett can see it, everyone can.

"It's handled," I mutter.

"Is it? Because you just lost to me four times, bro. And

now you're eye-fucking the PR consultant during practice."

"Harbor?" Callum glides up next to us, water bottle in hand. He looks from me to Bennett, then back to me again. "That explains the shitty skating."

"Not you too," I growl.

"You know I don't get involved in your business, Wes. But when the distraction affects practice..." Callum shrugs. "Maybe talk to her instead of pretending she doesn't exist."

"She's the one avoiding me."

"Then stop letting her," Bennett says in a matter-of-fact tone. "You're the captain of a professional hockey team. Act like it."

With that advice drop, my brothers skate away, leaving me alone. Hands on my knees, I take in a deep breath and try to shake off my uneasiness. I glance around the rink, checking on the team. My gaze sweeps past the boards toward the sponsor area.

And there she is.

We lock eyes for a split second, her cheeks turning the same pink as when she was riding my cock. She tucks her hair behind her ear—her nervous tell—and for a quick moment, the rink disappears. Our connection's like a low magnetic hum across the ice, something only the two of us can sense.

Her lips part slightly, and I remember exactly how they felt on mine. Soft, warm. Perfect. How she tasted. How she whispered my name when she came.

For a heartbeat, the mask slips and I see her—the *real* her. Beautiful, vulnerable.

But then she straightens her blazer and the shield comes flying up, locking into place.

One-time thing.

Like hell.

I saw the look in her eyes, even from across the rink. Hunger. Desire.

Jaw tense, I press my lips together and skate back to practice.

Game on, Hurricane.

Because Harbor Hayes is about to find out just how persistent a captain can be.

CHAPTER 22
HARBOR

I successfully avoided Weston the last few days. Tough, but not impossible.

My streak ended this afternoon when I spotted him at practice.

And holy freaking hell.

He's hot as sin on the ice, in his element.

Having grown up around professional hockey, I'm not one to sit around and drool over the players. It's one of the reasons I'm effective at my job. I'm practically immune at this point.

Weston Steele's becoming the exception to this rule.

Professional women don't get distracted by players in this business, Harbor. You're either here to work or to chase men. Choose.

My dad's voice chides me and I bristle, straightening my shoulders.

I choose work. Every single time.

But watching Weston sprint, the sheer power and strength as he flew across the ice, had me clenching my thighs and losing my train of thought. I went breathless for a full second, my belly swooping when he locked his ocean blue eyes with me.

Not good.

How am I supposed to work with the man all season long? Knowing how his body feels against mine, the way he unraveled me with his mouth, his hands.

His amazing dick.

I stare at the text messages, my hand trembling slightly.

> **Weston:** Prince wants me, you, and Keller to do a local news spot during the youth hockey thing this weekend
>
> **Weston:** To kick off the Hockey with Heart initiative
>
> **Weston:** Meet at The Rusty Anchor to go over talking points? 8 PM

I kicked around five different ways to say 'no,' but none of them sounded compelling.

Sorry, I can't because you're too gorgeous and I don't trust myself with you

We'll probably end up naked and we can't go there again

Dr. Martina thinks I'm self-sabotaging my career

My dad reminded me not to distract you from winning

If I see you again, I'll fall even more and we really, really shouldn't be doing this

Yeah, no. I couldn't very well send any of those texts. Instead, I typed:

> **Harbor:** See you at 8

Now I'm standing outside the Rusty Anchor at exactly 7:59 PM with a yawning pit of anxiety in my stomach.

Stay strong. You've literally been single for years. Now's not the time to break your streak.

I shove through the doors and peer around the dim space, searching for Weston.

"Table for one?" The hostess grabs a sticky plastic menu, her jaw working hard on a massive pink wad of chewing gum.

"No. I'm meeting someone. Last name Steele."

"Oh." She gives me a quick once-over, taking in my light-yellow maxi dress and sandals, and my cheeks burn. After a long second, she spins and leads me through the restaurant. The bar's packed, every seat taken, and most of the tables are filled as well.

"Is it always this crowded?" I ask the hostess.

"During the summer, yeah. It's peak tourist season. Your date's outside."

"Oh. He's not...we're not on a date," I stammer as she pushes the patio door open, holding it for me.

"Uh-huh. Sure."

Shit. Even the hostess sees what I'm trying to deny. There's more to this than work, personal feelings mixed up with my professional reputation, and we both know it.

She points me across the cobblestone patio toward Weston, not bothering to leave the comfort of the restaurant's AC to take me all the way to the table.

My heart hammers hard, palms sweaty in the thick Florida humidity as I make my way over to him. String lights illuminate the space and the whole vibe is romantic.

Dammit.

This is supposed to be a work meeting, not a dinner

date. So why's my stomach churning with butterflies on speed as I slide into the metal chair across from Weston?

"Hey."

Fuck me.

He's gorgeous in the bright moonlight, jaw shadowed with dark stubble. Dressed casually, he's in a dark blue T-shirt that brings out the deep flecks of navy in his eyes.

"Hey." I swallow hard, throat suddenly dry.

"Thanks for coming." He tips his chin at me and my heart skips a beat.

Keep it professional, Harbor. A quick meeting, in and out.

"Sure. I want this charity rollout to go well, too."

His jaw ticks and disappointment flashes over his face, then disappears just as quickly.

"Same." His voice is gruff and low, blending with the distant crashing of waves on the beach.

I peer over my shoulder, noting all the empty tables around us. "I'm surprised no one's out on the patio tonight."

Weston shrugs. "I rented out the entire space."

"What? You did?" Shock rolls through me, my stomach doing a slow barrel roll. "Why?"

"Privacy, Harbor." He levels his gaze on me and suddenly I can't breathe, my pulse fluttering in my neck. "We need to talk."

I twirl the gold bangles on my wrist. "About the charity rollout? It's kind of hush-hush, but not a huge secret, Weston."

"That's not what we need to talk about."

"Yes, it is." I drop my voice to a whisper, leaning in closer to him. "What happened before, it can't happen again."

Even if you want it to.

I silence that voice and forge ahead. "We have too much to lose, Weston."

"You know how I got here, Harbor?"

I shake my head, blood whooshing loudly in my ears. "I mean, yeah. Hard work, dedication, sacrifice."

"All of that, sure. But also by taking risks." His hand inches across the table toward mine, our fingertips almost touching. "I want to take a risk with you, Harbor."

My pulse goes into overdrive, a hot flush creeping up my neck. "Weston..."

"I get that you're out here trying to prove something. To management, the team. Your father. Hell, maybe yourself. And I get it, believe me, I do. But I haven't clicked with anyone like this before. Ever." He licks his lips, and I try very hard not to stare at his mouth. "What happened the other day—I can't stop thinking about you." His fingertips brush mine and a heat blooms low in my belly.

I take a shaky breath.

"Me neither." I whisper the admission, face flaming. "But I don't want to be a distraction."

He trails his thumb over mine. "Too late for that."

The rough, calloused pad of his thumb on my skin sends sparks skittering up my arm and I'm hyperaware of everything. The way the humid air has my dress clinging to me, the soft glow of the twinkling lights reflecting in his eyes, the distant sound of waves in perfect sync with my heartbeat.

Even the warm metal of the chair beneath me feels charged with possibility.

Dammit.

How do I say no to him—to us—when every inch of my body's screaming 'yes'?

"Can I get y'all something to drink?" A waiter appears

out of nowhere, startling me. I pull my hand away from Weston's so fast I almost knock my water over.

"Uh, yeah. Sure. Thanks. I'll have a glass of pinot grigio." I stutter the order, pretending to scour the menu when really my mind's stuck on Weston.

Too late for that.

Is it possible he's as affected as I am?

"I'll take a draft beer. Thanks." Weston orders and the waiter disappears back into the bar.

"Do you think he saw anything?" I whisper.

"No. And I'll leave him a big tip to encourage discretion."

"Oh. Okay." I let out a tiny exhale of relief, my mind whirring.

Can we really do this? Am I going to give into temptation, risk everything for Weston?

His foot taps against mine beneath the table and I raise my eyes to his.

"What are you thinking, Harbor?"

I take a deep breath, bite at my lower lip. I'm torn between following my instincts or backing away and playing it safe.

"I don't know." I give him my honest answer and wait.

His hand finds my knee and a shiver of pleasure races up my thigh as he rubs my leg.

"Now you're playing dirty," I tease, and for the first time all night, a smile lights up his face as he laughs.

"Whatever it takes, Hurricane."

The waiter drops off our drinks and we decline his offer of food, wanting to be alone more than anything. A few seconds later, the waiter's gone.

"Well? Am I out of the penalty box yet?" One of Weston's dark brows arches high and I tip my head, debating.

I've never wanted to say yes to anything more in my life.

The lights sway in the gentle breeze, casting everything in a golden glow straight from a movie.

This can't be my life.

It's too romantic.

Too risky.

Champions make sacrifices, Harbor. They're laser-focused on the one thing that counts: winning.

Shoving my dad's voice out of my head, I give Weston a shy smile and pray I don't regret this moment.

The moment I took a leap, a chance.

"We need to set some ground rules."

CHAPTER 23
WESTON

"Ground rules, huh?" The corner of my lip quirks as I suppress a smile.

She didn't say no.

The white string lights illuminate the pulse fluttering in her neck, warm humidity hanging between us.

"Yes. Rules. To protect our jobs—and us." She tucks a golden lock of hair behind her ear and I can't wait to unravel her again. Tangle my fingers in her silky strands, her breath coming in quick, shallow pants as I kiss her and make her mine.

"Weston? Are you good with that?"

Even agreeing to rules feels like a victory when Harbor Hayes is involved.

"Rules?" I steeple my fingers, pretend to contemplate her proposal. Because right now I'm saying yes to anything she'll offer me. But I'm not about to admit that. "If that's what makes you feel better, Hurricane, sure."

"Okay." Her face breaks into a smile. "Good, we're on

the same page then. So rule number one: No one can know about this. Not even your brothers."

My gut twists into a tight knot and I huff out a slow breath, oxygen leaking from my lungs. "I won't offer the information up freely and I'll try to downplay as much as I can. But I'm pretty sure they're going to figure it out, Harbor. We're triplets. Practically inseparable from birth. Trust me—they'll know."

Especially since both Bennett and Callum already called me out.

"Plus, we're living together in the rental house Gia found for us. It's going to be damn near impossible to sneak around. Driftwood Cove's not Manhattan." I point out the obvious and she cringes, her face going pale at this reality check.

"Right. I suppose you're correct. Your brothers will most likely figure it out. What if they tell someone? What if Coach Keller finds out?" Her voice tips up with panic, her teeth worrying at the corner of her lip, and I'm drawn to her mouth. I'd rather be somewhere totally private, kissing her on those glossy lips, than establishing ground rules. But here we are.

Reaching across the table, I cover her small hand with mine. "They won't. And even if they did, I'd handle it. I won't give them details, okay? It's not my style anyway."

"That's fair."

"And I'll swear them to secrecy. No one else on the team will know."

"The team. That's rule number two. This thing between us can't affect the team. Not my work on the PR campaign or your performance on the ice. We both need to stay focused on winning."

"Obviously."

"I figured that was a given." She takes a quick sip of her wine, sets the glass down. "Rule number three: no talk about the future. Let's take this day by day and see what happens."

This last rule catches me off-guard, my chest squeezing. *No talk about the future.*

That cuts deeper than I expected. Not because I planned to propose or anything—but because part of me wanted to imagine something more to us than a casual day-to-day thing.

"I'm fine with that..." My voice fades out for a second as I process this last rule. "But what's your reasoning?"

Her smooth brow furrows for a quick second and she drops her gaze to the table, avoiding eye contact. She takes a shaky breath, her chest rising and falling. The sound of the waves crashing in the distance is loud in the yawning silence stretching between us.

Finally, her eyes flick back up to mine. "It's just safer that way. We don't know how the season's going to go, what the future holds for either of us. Let's stay focused on the present for now."

My gut churns, and I want to push back on this third rule. Call it out for the bullshit that it is.

Harbor's scared of getting hurt.

It's written all over her face—in the tightness of her jaw, the thin set of her lips. She's protecting herself, putting up walls before we've even started.

I recognize this play. It's the same defensive strategy I use when a season's not going as planned. Control what you can, avoid committing to outcomes you can't guarantee.

But relationships aren't hockey games. You can't play it

safe and expect to win. You need to put everything on the line.

I need to prove myself to her.

Show her this thing between us is real.

That we can go the distance.

"Okay. Live in the moment. Got it." I squeeze her hand, and her breath catches when my thumb traces across her knuckles. The simple touch sends heat shooting up my arm, the tension in her jaw loosening as she breaks into a slow smile bright as the fucking Florida sun. I'm grateful she's giving me a chance to knock down those brick walls she's so carefully built.

"Good. If we stick by those rules, we can definitely make this work."

"Why do I feel like you're going to make me sign a contract or something, Hurricane?"

She giggles, the light, tinkly sound floating on the wind, and my stomach unclenches.

"Not a half-bad idea, Steele. I can throw one together real quick."

My phone buzzes against the metal table—probably Bennett wondering where I disappeared to for the 'strategy meeting.' I don't even glance at it.

Harbor's eyes dart to the phone, surprise flickering across her face. "Aren't you going to get that?"

"Nothing's more important than this conversation."

She blushes and every muscle in my body tenses. I want—no, need—to get Harbor alone again. To be with her.

"I have a better idea. Let's seal the deal—in private." I shoot her a heated stare, and the pink of her cheeks deepens.

"I want you to know—I don't usually do this with hockey players." Her admission is shy, quiet.

"Good thing I don't usually lose." The way her lips part tells me she understands exactly what game we're playing.

"Walk me back?"

"Sure."

I toss a massive tip on the table, as promised, and we slip out the side exit, avoiding the crowd inside the Rusty Anchor.

I'll follow the rules. For now.

Harbor Hayes thinks she's protecting herself with the rules.

She has no idea she just handed me the playbook for winning her completely.

And I've never played a game I didn't plan to win.

CHAPTER 24
HARBOR

The door to my dark hotel room clicks shut behind us and before I can say anything, do anything, his mouth crashes into mine.

Hot. Possessive. Controlling.

Like he's been waiting a lifetime for this—and tonight the wait's finally over.

My back pushed up against the wall, his lips on mine, he manages to pull every thought out of my head. One by one, until the only thing left is him.

Weston Steele.

And it's fucking amazing.

My entire body shimmers, floating as he hitches up my dress, balling the fabric in his large palms.

"Harbor..." His voice low and gravelly. Dangerous in the best possible way.

"Weston..." I murmur into his open mouth, slipping my tongue inside and tasting him. He's slightly salty and hoppy from the beer, fingers tangling in my hair.

"You have no idea what you do to me, Hurricane."

God, I want this man.

More than I've ever wanted anyone in my entire life.

I want his hands on me, everywhere. His mouth, his naked body on top of mine. His glorious dick drilling into me. Taking charge, owning me.

"I want…" My voice catches as he nips at my lower lip, sending a sharp bolt of desire straight to my clit.

"Yeah?" He doesn't stop his assault on my mouth, driving his tongue in deeper. Taking my breath away.

After a few long minutes of kissing, he pulls away. "What do you want, Harbor? Tell me."

He stares down at me, his dark pupils wide. My core throbs, his hard body pressed against mine, pinning me to the wall.

I want to stay like this forever.

But I can't say that.

Shit. I'm already breaking the rules.

"I want…you." I finish the sentence simply, leaving everything else unsaid.

A growl vibrates deep in his throat as his hand drops from my hip down to my panties. He caresses me through the silky fabric, finding my already swollen clit and circling the sensitive spot with his thumb. A bolt of pleasure shoots up and down my body and I'm hot all over.

"Are you attached to these?" he murmurs, toying with the lacy edge of my thong and trailing soft kisses up and down the tender skin of my neck.

I'm breathless, shaking my head 'no.' With a quick tug, he rips the panties from my body. The sound tears through the air, sharp and final, like the last thread of restraint snapping. He tosses the flimsy undergarment to the floor.

"I was hoping you'd say that."

Dropping down to his knees, his face is inches from my

bare pussy. "I've been wanting to do this since the first day we met."

Without another word, he dips down, licking me all the way from back to front. His tongue teasing me, my legs trembling with pleasure.

"Oh…" I moan into the quiet darkness, threading my fingers through his hair. He hitches his arms behind my thighs, supporting me and diving deeper into my wet heat.

"Fucking delicious." He eats me out like a starving man enjoying his last meal, waves of pleasure rolling through me. I'm glad he's holding me up—otherwise I'd melt into a puddle of lusty desire right here on the hotel room floor.

Swirling his tongue around my clit, he gently sucks the sensitive skin into his mouth and my body shakes. The familiar tingle builds low in my center and I'm close, so freaking close, to coming.

"Weston—" I bite back a scream as my thighs tremble, an intense orgasm crashing through me. Hands flying to grip his shoulders, I dig into the thick cords of muscle and hold on for dear life as he continues to lap and suck at my pussy.

After several long seconds, I sink back against the wall. "Wow. That was…amazing."

He swipes at his mouth, grinning up at me. "A fucking delicious warm-up."

Rising, he winds his hand around my neck and pulls me in close, kissing me. I'm acutely aware of my scent on him, my arousal coating his lips.

"You taste like mine." His voice is low, rough against my skin. "And after tonight, you won't forget it."

Despite what I said back at the restaurant—all the talk about rules—his words send a thrill shooting through me.

Mine.

After tonight, you won't forget it.

I doubt it's possible to forget anything about Weston Steele at this point. And certainly not when it comes to sex.

The man's as good in the bedroom as he is on the ice.

"Come here." Taking hold of my hand, he pulls me gently toward the bed. "I want to see you. All of you."

Stepping in closer, he inches my dress up slowly, so slowly, lifting the fabric up and over my head. Cool air hits the exposed skin, chill bumps rising in the wake of the smooth fabric.

His fingers trail up my thighs, over my belly, all the way to my breasts.

Caressing.

Reverent.

"I love your tits." He thumbs my nipples through the thin satin bra, drawing them into diamond-sharp points. "So fucking perfect."

Reaching around, he unhooks my bra and lets it fall to the ground.

Leaving me naked, exposed.

More vulnerable than ever before.

Weston cups both my breasts in his large hands, massaging them. Dropping his head, he sucks one nipple, then the other into his mouth.

I close my eyes and give into the sensation, pleasure rippling through me.

Giving into him.

I'm tired of thinking, then overthinking. Right now, all I want to do is feel. Let Weston take the lead and just be.

Here, in the moment, with him.

He eases me down onto the bed, then grabs the back of his T-shirt and rips it over his head.

Abs for fucking days.

And I am *so* here for it.

Reaching out, I tiptoe my fingers over the ridges of his abdominals. Making my way down to his belt, pulling the supple leather from the metal buckle, the loops. Unbuttoning his jeans, my mouth salivating.

This man is literal perfection, rivaling any sculpted Greek statue sitting in the Louvre.

"You've officially ruined me for all other men." I trace the deep V of his hips, yanking at his pants.

He stills, eyes darkening. Leaning down, his mouth brushes mine. "Good." His voice rumbles, deep and thick. "And I'm not done yet."

Kicking out of his jeans, he crawls onto the bed with me, pushing me back against the pillows. Cupping my cheek, he touches his lips to mine in a soft, slow kiss. Sliding his tongue in, swirling around, taking his time.

Leaving me panting and needy. Wetness pools between my legs and I arch against him, desperate for friction.

"Aww, Hurricane—what's the rush? We have all night," he teases, his hand finding my core.

"You have morning practice tomorrow, right? I can't keep you out past your bedtime."

"I'm a big boy, baby. You don't have to worry about that." He spreads my legs, trailing his fingers through my wetness.

"What we do can't affect the team. Your performance—"

He presses a finger to my lips. "Sshh. I'm zero percent worried about my performance right now."

Brushing his thumb over my lower lip, I suck it into my mouth and his pupils dilate wider still.

"God, you're fucking sexy, Hurricane." He slides a

third finger inside me, curving up to find my G-spot. I swallow down a moan, his lips tipping up into a grin.

"She likes that." He drives in harder and my hips arch of their own accord, wanting more.

"Weston—" My eyes flutter closed as he works my pussy, edging me closer to the brink.

Then he slows and I whimper, thighs clenching.

"Eyes on me, Harbor. I want to watch you come all over my fingers."

His dirty words turn me on even more, my pussy spasming around his hand.

"Don't stop, Weston. Please—don't stop." My voice is breathy, pleading.

I'm fucking begging at this point, and I don't even care.

"Such a pretty little pussy," he murmurs, finger fucking me hard and fast. "Mine."

The declaration's so simple, yet so determined.

Like he's never letting me go.

That's what rockets me over the edge, my body convulsing as I shatter around his hand.

"Yes…yes…yes…" I pant the words, Weston wringing every last drop of orgasm from me. A light sheen of sweat slicks my skin and I'm burning all over.

For him.

"You begged so sweet, Hurricane." A smile dances on his lips, a dark glint in his eyes. "And I'm not even done yet."

Taking both my wrists in his hand, he eases my arms above my head.

"Right there, just like that, baby. Hands above your head. Just for me."

Breath hitching, I swallow hard as he pulls down his

boxer briefs and kicks them off. Nothing's between us now. No clothing, no pretense.

It's just me and Weston in this moment.

"God, you're stunning." He stares down at me, at my breasts arching up toward him due to the position, my rosy nipples.

Licking his lips, he drops to my nipple, sucking the sharp point into his warm mouth. Pleasure rolls down my spine, my pussy throbbing with each swirl of his tongue.

"Say you're mine, Harbor." The words a whisper on the heated skin of my breast, he flicks my nipple with his tongue, then grazes the tender bud with his teeth.

"I'm yours, Weston." My voice is high-pitched, breathy and needy.

"Good girl." His praise oozes over me like warm maple syrup, filling my chest with a lightness. "That's a good fucking girl," he murmurs, nipping at my other breast. "So fucking perfect for me."

I let out a strangled moan, another orgasm already building, and he hasn't even penetrated me yet.

"Fuck me, Weston. Please," I beg, desperate for him.

Every single perfect inch of him.

"I love how needy you are, Hurricane. I like making you come undone." He plays with my clit and I arch up against his palm, circling my hips to get more of his touch.

"I want you inside me." I practically keen the words, and he shoots me a sheepish grin.

"Then spread those legs, Harbor. Because I'm about to fuck you like you're mine."

Gripping my thighs, he drags me down to the edge of the bed. He grabs a condom and rolls it on, then thrusts deep inside me in one smooth, perfect motion.

"So fucking perfect, Harbor." His voice is strained,

reverent, as he moves inside me. Filling me all the way up. I've never felt so full, stretched in all the right ways.

Keeping my wrists pinned above my head, he drives into me again and again. Our hips moving in sync, no space between us at all.

"That's a good girl, Harbor. Take it, all of it. Let me fill you all the way up, baby."

Weston pistons in and out, faster and faster, my heart hammering so hard I feel like I might explode. Black dots dance in my peripheral vision and my muscles spasm.

"Come for me, Harbor. Come all over me, gorgeous. I want to feel you lose it around my cock."

That's all it takes to unravel me fully and completely. I fracture around him, crying out and shuddering.

"Weston!"

He slams his mouth to mine, swallowing my cries with a possessive kiss. Keeping up the rhythm, he chases his own release. A few thrusts later, he explodes inside me.

His body finally stills, but he doesn't move. He stays buried inside me, his forehead pressed against mine.

"I don't want to be anywhere else but inside you." His fingers trace light circles over my belly and I sigh, content for the first time in as long as I can remember.

"Same." I trace the outline of his cheek, his jaw. "Which is a real problem—because you've got hockey to play, and I've got a team to save."

CHAPTER 25
WESTON

oly hell.

Fucking Harbor Hayes was life changing.

The way her eyes flutter shut when she's close to unraveling. The flush across her chest, her breath catching.

The way she takes my cock—every last inch of it—squeezing and milking me until I'm more wrung out than after a game.

And the best part? The way she's mine.

All her moans, every inch of her luscious body.

Mine.

But it's more than that. The way she looked at me when she said she was mine—like she meant it and it scared the hell out of her. That look's going to keep me awake for the next decade.

I want her all over again and I only left her hotel room fifteen minutes ago. Sneaking out like some damn rookie trying to dodge curfew.

Except now there's more—so much more—on the line.

I didn't mean for this to get so tangled. It wasn't supposed to be complicated.

But it is.

And those rules we set? I already know they're going to be shot to hell.

Starting with rule #1—no one can know.

Uh-huh, sure. Because there's no fucking way Callum and Bennett aren't going to sniff this one out. They'll probably piece things together by the end of the week, knowing my nosy-ass brothers.

As quietly as possible, I creep into the foyer of the rental house using my phone as a flashlight. I'm dehydrated as hell, which—coupled with the lack of sleep—is gonna make practice significantly more painful tomorrow. I need water before I hit the sack for the few remaining hours of the night.

"Strategy meeting went long, huh?"

Fuck my life.

Callum's standing in the glow of the pendant light, shirtless in joggers at the kitchen island, chugging a pink electrolyte drink.

I scrub my hand across the back of my neck and do my best to look innocent.

"Uh, yeah. Late night."

He stares at me for a long second, dark brows knitted.

Finally, he breaks the awkward silence. "Be careful, Weston."

It's not a warning. Just a quiet reminder of everything that's at stake.

He tosses his drink into the trash. "I've watched the fallout when captains lose focus. And I've never seen you look at anyone the way you looked at her during practice."

I frown. "You were watching me during practice?"

"Everyone was watching you during practice. Including Coach." He shoves past me and heads upstairs, leaving me to contemplate my life choices.

I lean against the cool marble counter and huff out a deep breath. I meant for this thing to stay easy, physical. No expectations, no fallout.

But Harbor Hayes isn't the kind of woman you touch and forget. And now that I've had her, I don't know how the hell I'm supposed to go back to the way things were.

The moment I kissed her, I was a fucking goner.

I just hope it's not going to bite me in the ass.

And if it does? I'll deserve every damn bite.

Because there's no way in hell I'm walking away from her now.

——————

Although I'm working on four hours of sleep, two cups of coffee, and sheer adrenaline, I somehow manage to have the best practice I've had in weeks.

"Nice play, Weston!" Coach Keller yells from the bench as I slap another puck deep into the goal.

About fucking time.

My game's back—and it's better than ever. I haven't been this locked in since playoffs two seasons ago. Every pass is crisp, every shot finds its mark. Even Bennett can't get under my skin today because my body's still humming with satisfaction from last night.

"Looks like Cap's got his shine again." Bennett circles around me, a shit-eating grin on his face. "Must have been a helluva PR session last night."

He winks, and I resist the urge to shove him into the boards.

"Fuck off, Benny. All the training in the gym's paying off is all." I keep my tone neutral, eyes locked on the puck, careful not to give anything away.

"Right, right, that's what we're calling it these days," he snickers, twirling his stick in his hands like he's got all the time in the world. Then he leans in, dropping his voice. "Hope she gave you lots of talking points."

I scowl. "Bro. Grow up. We had drinks and talked about the charity thing. That's it."

"Sure." He pushes off, skating backward. "Just saying. If this is your new pre-game ritual? Keep it up. You haven't looked this sharp in weeks."

"Weston! Word in my office?" Keller tips his chin at me, motioning me over.

Fuck.

There's no way he knows.

We've been careful. Benny and Callum might suspect, but I haven't breathed a word to anyone.

Coach can't know.

"Sure." I skate over to the bench, plopping down and unlacing my skates. My mind whirs, running through all the possible reasons Coach could possibly want to talk privately.

None of them are good.

Rising, I follow Keller into the tunnel, weaving through the concrete maze of the arena. We pass the locker room, the gym, the training room, empty conference rooms until we finally come to his office. He unlocks the door and flicks on the light, tossing his clipboard onto his tidy desk.

His office is sparsely furnished, only a desk, a few chairs, and a computer monitor. No photos, no homey touches.

"Haven't had a chance to decorate yet?" I glance

around at the bare walls and he shrugs, sinking down into his chair.

"I'm not too concerned with my office decor. What matters to me right now is performance—specifically, getting everyone into peak shape before the season starts."

I swallow hard, swiping my sweaty palms down my thighs. "Yes, sir. I understand."

"You were locked in out there today. Your drills were faster, stick skills sharp—keep it up."

"Yes, sir."

"Today you embodied what a captain of a pro hockey team should be—determined, focused, on point. The guys are watching you and gauging your reaction to this reloca-tion. I've seen how you interact with your teammates. You're calm, no drama or bullshit. I like your style, Weston."

"Thank you, Coach." I roll my shoulders, wondering where he's going with this little speech.

"I know Prince has you doing a lot of the song-and-dance shit with the PR consultant and the rebranding campaign."

My stomach twists into a tight knot at the mention of anything to do with Harbor.

"I'm not in a position to stop the owner of the team from using you however he sees fit. That being said, if the PR crap gets to be too big of a distraction, let me know. Our goal is to win games. It's fine and good to lob an assist every once in a while, but I don't want my captain losing sight of what matters." He locks his gaze with mine and my mouth goes dry. "Winning."

I nod. "Yes, Coach. Understood. So far, Prince hasn't thrown me anything I can't handle."

Keller steeples his fingers together, gazing across the desk at me. "Good."

He pauses for a long second, the air conditioning humming behind me. Even with the AC cranking, I'm sweating beneath my jersey.

"You and Harbor seem to work well together."

My throat constricts and I practically choke on air. Hearing her name roll off Coach's lips sends a sharp bolt of anxiety ripping through me.

"We do, yeah."

"Keep it that way, Steele. Because the second I see your performance slip, or the team dynamic falter, I'll know where to locate the source. My number one priority is protecting this team's chances this season—at all costs." He leaves the rest unsaid, the unspoken words hanging heavy between us.

No distractions.

No feelings.

Eye on the prize.

"That's all. Have a great strength training session."

With that, he swivels to his computer and starts typing. Effectively dismissing me.

I stand and walk out of the office, more on edge than before our little chat.

It's unclear if Coach suspects anything. But he's definitely watching—and that worries me almost as much.

Because I've never wanted anything as bad as a win this season.

Until her.

Now I've got both in my hands—Harbor and hockey—and I'm teetering on a razor-thin line.

One wrong move and I lose everything.

And the worst part?

I'm not sure which loss would wreck me more.

Losing hockey would gut my identity, everything I've worked for my entire life.

But losing Harbor?

That would gut my soul.

I've made hockey my mission, careful never to let anything compete.

Now? I'm fucking terrified to find out what wins if I'm forced to choose.

CHAPTER 26
HARBOR

t's been over forty-eight hours since Weston slipped out of my hotel room, and I still feel the whisper of him everywhere.

His hands, his mouth, his body.

Touching me, holding me, kissing me.

I can't get him out of my mind.

Don't want to get him out.

But there's no room for that today.

Today's all team polos, smiling for the cameras, and pretending like nothing's happening between us.

This morning, it's all about Hockey with Heart—not the man who's starting to take up too much space in mine.

"Harbor! Where do you want this banner?" One of the admins holds up the new Hockey with Heart banner I designed, shaking the white-and-blue fabric.

"Hanging over there." I point to the center wall of the rink.

"On it." She scurries away, and I take a deep, cleansing breath.

In less than an hour, Driftwood Cove's youth hockey league will be here for the clinic hosted by the Coastal Crushers. Every player's involved, plus the new coach. And of course, Mr. Prince will be standing on the sideline watching my every move.

Somehow, this event feels more monumental than any presser we've had so far. All eyes will be on me—and Weston.

The thought's not comforting.

"Hello, hello." Mr. Prince squeezes my shoulder from behind, startling me. I jump about a foot in the air—thank god I'm not wearing heels, or I would've definitely face-planted.

"Hi. Everything's all set up for the clinic." I gesture to the ice, at the orange cones and small extra goals I requested for the occasion. "I asked Coach Keller to have the team show up about thirty minutes beforehand so I could give them a few pointers on dealing with the kids and the media. And they have sufficient warm-up time, of course."

"Super." Prince shoots me a wide grin, clearly pleased. "I'm loving the direction this rebrand is heading. The sponsors are happy—early ticket sales are on track to keep pace with last season. A big feat, considering we relocated to a much smaller market. Well done."

Warm happiness seeps through me, loosening some of the built-up tension.

"I'm so glad to hear. After today, I anticipate merch sales going up as well. Having the new mascots, Riptide and Lil Rip, at the clinic today is going to drive those sales. Couple that with gifting every youth player a T-shirt, plus tickets to Family Night. We're building the fanbase, starting now."

"No—we've already started. The ESPN interview with Weston was so strong, I had other owners calling and asking how I did it. And I have you to thank for that, Harbor. You've taken a bad situation and managed to turn things around."

My cheeks heat at his praise and a rush of relief rolls through me.

Good first period. But you haven't won the game yet.

Of course my father's voice intrudes on my happiness. Always reminding me I'm not good enough.

"Thanks, Mr. Prince. Still work to be done, though." I smile and try to ignore the nagging feeling of not doing enough, being enough.

Players begin rolling into the arena, laughing and talking to each other.

And there's Weston, suited up in his gear, helmet in hand. Looking as gorgeous as ever.

He glances over at me and my breath hitches under his heated gaze. A stare so intense I almost stop breathing, my heart pounding a mile a minute.

With a quick inhale I hope Mr. Prince doesn't notice, I try to get my swirling emotions under control.

It's really damn hard when Weston's staring at me like that. All primal and possessive, his jaw set, lips slightly parted.

Like he's ready to set the world on fire and burn everything down for me.

I fidget with my bracelets, the jingling snapping me back down to Earth.

"Excuse me for a moment, Mr. Prince. I need to go check on the camera crew and make sure they're ready to roll."

"For sure. No problem. And Harbor?" He reaches out, gripping my elbow.

"Hmmm?"

"Keep up the good work. Your dedication to the team's second to none." He shoots me a wink and I flash him a tight smile.

If only he knew how dedicated you were the other night...

Shoving that voice out of my head, I hustle out to the lobby. Mainly to get away from the watchful eye of Prince and the rest of the team. I need one minute to collect myself before going back into the arena.

"Hey."

I clock the now-familiar deep voice without turning around, the husky tone sending a thrill through me.

Spinning, I smile at Weston, pulse racing.

"Hey. Everything good? You ready to skate with some tiny people?" I joke, tucking a loose strand of hair behind my ear.

"Yeah, I am. How are you?"

The way he asks the question—eyes flickering over my face, watching for my genuine reaction like he actually gives a damn—I've never felt so seen in my entire life.

"I'm good. A little nervous about the rollout, truthfully." I surprise myself with the honest answer.

A rarity in the PR world.

"Really? Why? Everything looks great."

I gnaw my bottom lip, contemplating how much to say. "Kids are a wild card. You never know what to expect with those little guys. One wrong move by a player, one slipped swear word, and all the good mojo flies out the window."

"Right." Weston nods, his expression serious. "How about this?"

He takes a step forward, the crisp scent of his cologne curling around me, his fingers lightly touching my arm.

"We go in, smile, and don't swear. I'll keep it PG—even if you keep gazing at me like that."

He winks and I blink up at him, warmth creeping up my neck.

Damn.

He's too good at this—steadying me and unraveling me in the same breath.

I'm in very dangerous territory right now, every single rule on the verge of being broken.

Champions stick to the playbook. They don't go off-script.

"Excuse me?" A brunette in tight jeans, a crisp white button down, and stilettos—with scarlet red lips and black sunglasses slung on top of her head—interrupts us. For the second time today, I jump, backing away from Weston as fast as I possibly can.

"Yes?" I swivel to the woman, plastering a tight smile on my face and praying my cheeks aren't as red as they feel. "Are you with the youth league?"

A half-snort echoes loudly through the empty space. "Um, no. I'm looking for my father, Max Prince."

"Oh. He's inside the arena." I point over my shoulder. "I'm Harbor Hayes, the PR consultant."

"Victoria Prince. His daughter." She offers her hand and I shake it politely, noticing she doesn't bother checking out Weston at all.

Clearly not affected by hockey players.

I recognize her type immediately—sharp, polished, probably has an MBA from some impressive Ivy League school. She's giving big city vibes all the way, making me feel underdressed in the team polo, jeans, and sneakers. The kind of professional woman who doesn't mind taking up space, making tough decisions. Everything I've tried to be, but somehow she makes it look effortless.

"Well, I'll let you two get back to whatever you were doing." Her eyes cut from me to Weston, giving us both an appraising stare. "Nice to meet you, Harbor."

She clicks her way into the arena, the door whooshing closed behind her.

"Oh my god, you don't think she saw anything, do you?" I fan my face, trying to keep any hint of sweat at bay. I don't have time to redo my makeup.

"Saw what? Us talking? Totally innocent. Also practical, seeing as how we're interviewing together after the clinic. Don't worry about her." Weston brushes off the exchange like it's nothing, but anxiety still pings through me.

"Do you know her? She didn't even acknowledge you."

He shrugs. "Met her once or twice. She has a real reputation for being an ice queen. Pun fully intended."

I giggle. "The nickname fits. Wonder why she's here?"

"Don't know. Don't care. Not my business."

"Probably a good way to operate."

The outside doors to the arena fly open again, and this time a flood of excited children pile into the building.

"That's my cue. Gotta jet. Relax, Hurricane. You've got this." He winks at me and jogs away to prepare for the clinic.

And just like that, he's gone. Leaving me alone in a room full of kids and chaos, which has absolutely nothing on the storm raging inside my head.

———

I stand behind the glass, marveling at the magic of the youth hockey clinic.

Weston's in his element, smiling and laughing with the kids, coaching them. I had nothing to worry about there— the man's a natural.

He's got 'Future Coach' written all over him.

And future daddy.

Oh my gosh.

Rule #3—no talk about the future.

So why in the hell did I feel myself ovulate just then, when Weston knelt down to the little boy's level, coaching him on holding his stick?

Not good.

Every single rule's in jeopardy—and that's not on Weston.

It's on me.

Because you want to say fuck the rules.

Be bold for once in your life.

I grip the wall, knuckles white.

I can't.

I could lose everything. And so could he.

"He's great with kids, huh?" The local reporter gazes out at Weston on the ice and a sharp pang of jealousy stabs me straight in the chest.

"He is." My tone's careful, measured. I'm holding back so much, fearful of giving anything away.

"Is he single?" She twirls her hair, practically salivating.

Shit.

I desperately want to say no, but I'm afraid that will be too obvious.

Instead, I shrug. "I don't think so."

Vague, non-committal. Hopefully enough to shut her down.

"I'm definitely going to find out." Her eyes widen as Weston grins at the blonde boy, giving him a high-five. "He's yummy."

Oh, for fuck's sake.

"So, the post-clinic interview. Should we set up on the side of the rink? Weston stays in skates, Coach Keller, you, and me on the side?" I shift the focus back to work quickly.

The reporter breaks out of her Weston trance, checking her notes. "Sure, that works."

The clinic winds down, Coach Keller and the team leading the kids in a cheer. Riptide and Lil Rip skate onto the ice for photo ops with the kids and players, the photographers catching it all on camera.

Perfect.

Exactly the picture we want to paint. Pro hockey team engaging with the local youth, boosting community spirit, giving back.

My heart soars, my vision coming alive.

"Ready for the interview?" The reporter taps her headset, ready for her five minutes to shine with Weston.

"Sure."

Together, we head to the side of the rink and I wave Weston and Coach Keller over.

"You made a lot of kids happy today, Captain." The reporter bats her long lashes at Weston, and I try to bury my aggravation.

Weston gives her a tight smile. "I hope so. Youth hockey's such a critical part of the game. Happy to give back."

The tension in my shoulders loosens at his words.

Great response.

Even better, he seems unphased by her flirtatious charm.

"Coach, what's your vision for the upcoming season?

New locale, new-to-you team looking to rebuild after a disastrous—and scandalous—end to last season..." Her voice trails off, the words hanging in the air for a second before Coach Keller responds.

"We're aiming for the Cup. Each game better than the last. And we want Driftwood Cove with us every step of the way."

Damn.

Another perfect answer.

"Ms. Hayes, you're the new face of the Coastal Crushers administrative team. But you're in no way new to the game. Your father's the legendary Coach Doug Hayes. How does it feel to be embroiled in the professional game of hockey yourself, with that mantle resting heavy on your shoulders?"

Of course my question's difficult—and personal. Not the easy shots both the guys had.

I smooth my hair over my shoulder, standing tall. "It feels amazing, actually. I love hockey—always have. The transition's been seamless and I look forward to a fantastic season with this stellar team in this amazing town."

Too many superlatives, Harbor. Overcompensating.

"I mean, who could blame you? This team is amazing. So talented." The reporter fawns over Weston, and I swallow down a little bit of vomit.

"Yes, they are. The team's committed to the local community and we're excited to invite every Driftwood Cove family to Opening Night!" I beam at the camera, praying the interview's almost over.

Mercifully, Riptide and Lil Rip skate over and ham it up. The cameras cut to the mascots, and the reporter follows close behind.

"Thanks, guys." I turn to Coach Keller and Weston. "I appreciate the help with the local media."

"Sure, no problem." Weston rakes his hand through his hair, relaxed and smiling.

"Glad this worked out. An event like this during pre-season's fine. Once we get rolling, we'll have to keep the distractions to a minimum." Keller's tone is gruff and no-nonsense as he flicks his eyes to mine, then Weston's.

"Right." I nod, trying not to spiral. *Is he talking about the clinic? The interview?*

Or is this a veiled warning?

"Well, thanks again, Coach. Looking forward to a fantastic season."

He tips his chin at me and stalks away without another word, leaving me and Weston alone together.

Dropping my voice to a whisper, I hiss, "Do you think he knows anything? Was that a threat?"

Weston shakes his head, careful not to look at me while the cameras roll. "No. He's focused on winning. Don't worry, Hurricane."

Despite his reassurances, I am worried.

Really fucking worried.

I've dealt with a lot of scandals in my career, but none have felt quite this personal.

Because this time, my life's on the line—and I've never had so much at stake.

CHAPTER 27
WESTON

'll admit it—the hockey clinic was actually kind of fun. Much as I bitched about it, I enjoyed watching the kids faces light up when I taught them a new stick skill or they connected with the puck.

Hell, maybe one day I'll be coaching my own kids.

My mind instantly flashes to Harbor. I have to give her credit. The whole Hockey with Heart thing is her vision—and it seems to be working. Everyone in town's excited about the upcoming season and they love the hammerhead shark mascots, Riptide and Lil Rip. She managed to nail the right blend of intimidating and family-friendly—not the easiest task in the world.

The woman's damn good at her job.

She's good at a lot of things.

Scrubbing a hand over my face, I grab my phone from the nightstand.

Weston: You up?

I blink at the bright screen in the dark. It's after 10 PM and today was a long day for her. She's probably already asleep.

Hurricane: Yes

Heart hammering, I text back.

Weston: Can I see you?

Hurricane: Like Facetime?

Weston: I was thinking more like beach walk

Probably a violation of rule #1, but right now I don't care. I want to be with her.

Hurricane: You think anyone will spot us?

Weston: I'm not too worried about the sea turtles turning us in. It's 10 PM. Beach will be empty

Hurricane: I'm in

Weston: I'll meet you at the dunes behind the Inn

Hopping out of bed, I pull on a pair of running shorts and a T-shirt. Then I tiptoe down the stairs, carefully avoiding the living room where Bennett's shouting obscenities at *Call of Duty*. Headphones on, he's fully immersed in battle. I'm sure he doesn't notice me sneak out, and Callum's been in his room since eight.

I duck out through the side door of the garage. Not

wanting to risk being spotted in the Porsche, I jog down the pathway to the beach and walk along the shoreline toward the hotel. The moon's full, silver slashes of light slanting across the white sand beach. I inhale the salty air, the humidity wrapping around me.

I'm closing in on the Driftwood Inn, the soft, golden glow of the hotel spilling into the night. Just beyond the dunes, I lean on the railing and wait for Harbor, the waves crashing on the shore. The sound's rhythmic, peaceful, and I'm instantly more relaxed.

I could get used to this.

Back in Manhattan, I rarely left my apartment at night. Too loud, too crowded. Paparazzi hung out on every corner, waiting to catch you doing something, anything. Even a trip to the bodega for a protein shake was an opportunity to get snapped.

I don't miss that at all. For the most part, the locals are friendly and welcoming. Excited we're in town, but they leave us alone and respect our privacy.

Driftwood Cove could actually work out, assuming we have a good season. Only time will tell there.

I'm surprised I haven't hated it more.

Might have something to do with the woman on the boardwalk.

Harbor's walking toward me, her hair loose and blowing behind her in the gentle breeze. The dimmed lobby lights of the Inn illuminate her curves, her bright smile when she spots me at the dunes.

I'm never getting over this girl.

This is more—so much more—than sex or lust. We have a connection. The kind that's so powerful, so special it takes your breath away.

The kind worth fighting for.

"Hey, handsome." Her voice is soft, floating on the wind to me.

"Hey."

Grabbing her hand, I pull her behind the grassy dunes and press my mouth to hers. Soft, warm, receptive. She tastes like forever. I wrap my arms around her, resting my hands on her perfect peach of an ass.

"I missed you," I murmur and she giggles, the sound sweet and tinkly.

"Me too. I'm glad you called. I couldn't sleep."

I tip back, gazing down at her. "Why?"

"Too keyed up from today. Sometimes when an event's really big or stressful, it takes me a minute to decompress, you know?"

I nod. "Yeah. Same thing happens to me after a game. I have a whole post-game meditation ritual. I can share it with you if you want."

"Really? That'd be great." She beams up at me like I'm the brightest, most amazing man in the world and my chest cracks open.

I'm falling in love with this woman.

Voices carry across the sand from the Inn patio and Harbor stills in my arms, a flash of worry dancing across her face.

"Let's walk." Touching only her pinky finger, I lead her away from the potential prying eyes at the hotel. We walk down the beach, away from the main hotel and condo area, toward the private residences. Most porch lights are off, the inhabitants asleep.

"So…" I glance over at her, noticing her face is already more relaxed. "I hesitate to tell you this…but I had fun at the clinic today."

"Really?"

"Yep. I liked working with the kids. Seeing the joy on their faces when they hit the puck was really cool."

"You're a natural."

I shrug. "I don't know about all that."

"No, you are. All of you guys were great, but I heard a lot of moms bring up your name after the clinic. You better be careful or you're going to get recruited as a coach during the off-season."

"I wouldn't mind if I have the time."

"You were great with the kids. Not to get too personal, but do you want to have children of your own?"

Direct violation of rule #3.

But I don't bring it up.

"I think so. Once hockey settles down a little bit. I want to be able to spend time with my kids, you know? My dad wasn't around much when we were growing up—first, he was playing hockey, then he was busy impressing Prissy."

Harbor grabs my hand, lacing her fingers with mine and squeezing. "That must have been hard."

"It wasn't optimal. I swore to myself I wouldn't be like that with my own kids. So I've put off relationships and stuff for hockey."

Until now.

I leave the words unsaid, pulling Harbor down to the shoreline. The waves lap at our feet and I trace her soft, smooth cheek.

"You're so damn beautiful, Hurricane. You're turning me inside out, making me think about things I never thought could be mine."

"Weston…" She rests her face in my palm and I want to stay like this, out on the beach with Harbor, forever.

No team, no rules, no expectations.

Just the two of us.

Being real and raw.

"Say you feel the same way. Please." I work to keep the pleading tone out of my voice, not wanting to come off desperate.

Even though I totally fucking am.

I need her to be mine.

"You know I do. I've never felt this way about anyone..." She inhales a shaky breath, blinking, the moonlight shimmering in her eyes. "It scares me."

Instead of delivering some hollow speech, I cup her face in my hands and kiss her. Soft and deep, making her believe in me.

In us.

After a long minute, I whisper, "Don't be scared, Harbor. I wish I could tell you everything will work out. But I can't. All I can promise is I won't hurt you."

"I want to believe you, Weston..."

Tipping her chin up, I lock eyes with her. "I've got you, Hurricane. Trust me."

She blinks up at me through the dark fringe of her lashes. "I do trust you."

"Then take the shot, Harbor."

She lifts up on tiptoe and kisses me like I'm the only game she's ever wanted to win.

CHAPTER 28
HARBOR

After the success of the Hockey with Heart clinic, Prince demands I take the next day off.

It's been so long since I've had a vacation day, I'm not even sure what to do. I'm lounging by the hotel pool under a big yellow-and-white striped umbrella and trying to relax, when my cell buzzes, vibrating my chaise.

Thank god.

Something—anything—to get my mind off Weston and our situationship.

Piper: I'm in the lobby of your hotel

Wha-what?!? My sister's here, in Driftwood Cove?

Harbor: Shut up!

Piper: No, for real

I swivel my head toward the tapping noise behind me.

My sister's grinning at me through the large glass lobby window.

Jumping up from the chair, I hurriedly tie on my sarong and race inside to greet her.

"Piper! What are you doing here?" Throwing my arms around her, happiness bubbles inside me. I hadn't realized how much I missed my sister until now.

"Geesh, Harbs, you're crushing me..." She squirms in my tight grip, giggling. "I told you I'd come see you. My assignment got pushed up a few weeks, so here I am."

"Amazing! I can't believe you're really here. You brought your swimsuit, right? Let's take your stuff up and then head back to the pool."

We haul her suitcase upstairs, and she changes while I yap her ear off.

"Can you believe he said that, Pipes? He literally said the word *mine*."

Piper pops her head out of the bathroom. "Really? But did he growl it, like the heroes always do in romance books?"

I throw my head back, laughing. "Now that you mention it, yes. Yes he did. It was most definitely a growl."

"You lucky bitch." Piper scrunches her nose up. "You found yourself a real-life book boyfriend. Weston sounds amazing."

I collapse back on the white fluffy duvet and close my eyes, flashing back to the other night. Weston's hands all over my naked body, his warm lips on mine.

Making me feel something I've never felt before.

Something dangerously close to love.

"He is, Pipes. So amazing. He's strong and dedicated, determined. An amazing listener who always knows just the right thing to say. Also freakishly tall and gorgeous." A full-body shiver rips through me, remembering how his touch made me come undone.

"Oh my god."

My eyes fly open. Piper's standing over me, her green eyes narrowed. "You're in love with him."

"What? No," I protest, scrambling to sit up. I don't like the way my sister's lording over me right now.

And I really don't like the way she's calling me out. Like she's my damn therapist.

"You are!" She points at my chest, a deep, red flush creeping over my skin like a snaking vine, giving me away.

"I am not. We're not even official." I smooth my hand over my ponytail.

"Sure, right," Piper tuts, pulling on her sandals. "So if he asked to put a ring on it tomorrow you'd say no?"

I bite down on my lip, my heart pounding double-time.

How does my sister always know things?

"I didn't say that..." My voice trails off, my mind skipping to the wedding. The white satin dress, tiki torches on the beach, Weston in a tux.

Of course I'd say yes.

A shot of panic bursts through me.

I'd say yes.

So what about this job, my career? His career?

Instead of making the predicament clearer, my sister's muddled me up even more. I don't know what to do about anything.

Piper sinks down next to me on the bed and wraps her arm around me. With a shuddery sigh, I lay my head on her shoulder and huff out a breath.

"I'm sorry I said those things to you before. About your

job and pressure and expectations. I didn't mean to hurt you."

"I know, Harbor." She rubs my arm and I feel a touch lighter. "It's okay. And you don't have to always choose work, you know."

My stomach clenches and knots, her words hitting me hard in the chest.

"I know," I whisper the lie, so softly I know there's no chance Piper believes me.

Her fingers tickle my skin and I focus on the tiny circles, going round and round.

Just like me and Weston.

Skating around each other, stuck in this weird, twisted dance. Getting close, then pushing away. Again and again.

Deep-down, I know it's only partly because of the job.

Another part of me is absolutely terrified of getting my heart broken.

Because that's what happens to women who fall for pro hockey stars.

Even ones as perfect as Weston.

Happily Ever Afters don't exist in real life. Not really.

It's a story old as time.

One my father's been reminding me about since before I could read.

Don't get involved with the players, Harbor. Nothing good will come from that. Stick to the sidelines. It's safer there.

But what if my dad's wrong? What if this thing between me and Weston is real?

Sometimes you have to take a risk, Harbor.

Take the risk.

My father's voice is replaced by Weston's in my head and the heaviness in my chest eases, oxygen filling up my lungs.

Maybe we can make this work.

"Go for it, Harbor. Choose love this time." Piper gives my arm a reassuring squeeze, her words ringing like a mantra in my head.

Choose love.

For once in my life, I'm going to follow my heart.

Weston Steele's worth the risk.

————

Piper and I are having drinks at the lobby bar when my phone rings. I glance down and Weston's name flashes on the screen.

"Answer it." Piper nudges my elbow, raising her eyebrows.

"No. I'll call him back."

"Answer it! Or I will..." She grabs for my cell on the teak bar, so I preemptively click Accept.

"Hello?" I'm breathless, having just beat my sister out for the phone.

"Hey, Hurricane. You thinking about me?" There's a playful smirk in his voice, and I can't help but smile.

"Maybe..." I play coy, pretending that Piper and I haven't been talking about him since she got to Driftwood Cove.

"Hopefully all good things."

"Absolutely."

"Great. That's what I wanted to hear. What are you doing this weekend?"

My stomach flip-flops with nerves and excitement. Because of course I want to see Weston and introduce him to my sister.

"Not exactly sure. My sister's in town unexpectedly.

She wants to meet you." The words tumble out of my mouth before I can stop them and Piper's lips curve up in a huge, wicked smile. She takes a sip of her dirty martini and leans in closer to the cell, hoping to overhear more of our convo.

"That works out then. Bennett's throwing a little team house party, and I want you to come."

Breath hitches in my throat. Those aren't the weekend plans I hoped he'd suggest.

"I don't know, Weston...we're trying to keep a low profile. Do you really think that's the best idea?" I run my finger along the rim of my glass, the smooth surface cool and wet on my skin.

"Probably not. But it'll be more obvious if you don't show."

He has a point. Bennett and Callum will definitely know something's up, if they don't already. From there, it's only a matter of time until the entire team finds us out.

"C'mon, Hurricane. What do you say? My house, Saturday night? I promise not to take your clothes off."

Damn.

"Oh, in that case, I'm definitely not showing up," I tease, clenching my thighs at the mere mention of potential nudity with Weston.

"Or I can. Whatever makes you happy, baby."

I try not to visibly swoon at his words. Not when Piper's watching my face like an FBI interrogator ready to pounce.

"Fine. We'll be there. But I'm serious about keeping things chill. Remember rules one and two?"

"Like I could forget." His tone's serious, a sharper edge to his voice.

At least he remembers all that's at stake.

"I'll act like we're at the rink. We're colleagues in public. No one will be the wiser." He tries to reassure me, but vodka churns in my stomach.

"Okay."

"Okay?"

"We'll be there. And Weston?"

"Yeah?"

"Remind your brother to keep this get-together quiet. The team doesn't need every puck girl in town crashing the party."

"Got it. I'll pass that along. Can't wait to meet your sister. And see you again, Hurricane. Bye."

He disconnects and I stare at the cell in my hand, the L-word hovering on my lips.

"Say it," Piper leans in and whispers with a smirk. "Just say it."

But I don't. Not yet.

Because I know once I do, everything changes.

CHAPTER 29
WESTON

t's an hour until puck drop—if the puck were a house party and the stakes were my personal life imploding in front of the entire fucking team.

I don't know why I agreed to this party in the first damn place. The whole thing's got bad idea written all over it.

After all, it was a Bennett plan and he's not exactly known for his great judgment.

But it's too late now.

I hold the back door open for my brother as he rolls the keg into the yard.

"You think this is a good spot?" Bennett points at a patch of lawn, and I shrug.

"Sure. Good enough."

If we're having a keg at all.

Which doesn't seem like the best plan, all things considered. I don't bother reminding him that the pre-season starts in a little over a month and we're supposed to be toeing the line. Training harder than ever before.

Focused solely on winning the Cup and establishing a winning franchise.

All of those words would fall on deaf ears. Bennett's sole goal right now is having a lit-as-hell party and probably getting laid. He's had a rough time with the move, tougher than he lets on.

I know he misses the city—the girls, the parties, the vibrant night life. Callum's adjusted fine, never big on that scene in the first place. And Driftwood Cove is perfectly fine with me, now that I'm with Harbor.

But Bennett's been riding the struggle bus hard. This party was the compromise. Better he misbehaves at home, where I can supervise him. I'd much rather he be in our backyard than at some club off A1A, throwing hundreds at strippers. At least here I can lock him in his room if he misbehaves.

"Bro—is Harbor gonna make it?" Bennett whacks my shoulder, one brow arched. "You gonna get a little action tonight?" He rocks his hips back and forth in a lewd humping gesture, and I bite the inside of my cheek so hard I taste the tang of blood.

"Shut the hell up, Benny. And yeah, she's coming to the party with her sister. Keep your hands off the sister." I let the action comment slide, not wanting to straight-up lie to my brother's face.

"A sister, huh? That could be fun. A little threesome action?" He waggles his brows, and my fingers curl into fists. He's one minute away from getting punched out.

Lucky for Bennett, Callum sticks his head out the back door. "Did you order twenty-five pizzas, Bennett?"

"Sure did. People are gonna be hungry."

A warning bell clangs loudly in my head.

"Fuck. This is a team party, Benny. That's a shit ton of pizza."

Bennett shoots me a sly smile. "I may or may not have mentioned the party on my socials..."

Double fuck.

This is exactly what Harbor's worried about, second only to keeping our relationship a secret. Making sure the team stays out of trouble is a screaming priority. For both of us.

Callum doesn't say a word, letting the porch door slam as he retreats into the house. Dude knows when things are about to go south.

Although I would have appreciated the back up.

"Bennett, don't you remember the reason we're all down here instead of still in New York?"

He stares at me from across the yard, folding his arms across his meaty chest.

"Yeah. Because Coach Evans screwed Prince's wife. What's that got to do with the party?"

"Big picture, bro. Keller wants us to stay out of trouble. The only reason I agreed to this party was because you promised it'd be small. 'Just the team.'" I throw my fingers into the air, quoting my brother. "Now you're telling me you posted about the party on Instagram?"

Bennett shrugs. "Yeah. And Facebook. What's the big deal, Wes? You're such a killjoy these days."

I stalk across the grass, closing the distance between me and my brother. "The big deal, Bennett, is that we're supposed to be staying out of trouble. Not inviting it to our fucking house." I spit out the words, my jaw clenched so tight my molars ache.

"Chill, dude. It'll be fine. You'll see. It's gonna be low-key."

The loud thump of bass shakes the ground, the top of a huge party bus visible over the privacy fence. The high-pitched squeal of laughter spills into the air and my stomach sinks.

"Low-key, huh?"

"That'll be the DJ."

I stare up at the sky and wonder for the thousandth time how I'm related to this guy. We're literally nothing alike.

He jogs past me, smacking me hard on the back. "Relax, Cap. I've got it all under control."

"Uh-huh," I mutter at his retreating backside, dread rolling through me.

Because Bennett's idea of under control is a helluva lot different than mine.

Pulling my cell from my pocket, I debate texting Harbor and telling her not to come. This party's starting to feel like a landmine, and I don't want to be the one responsible for blowing everything up.

But then I remember the way she stared up at me the other night, her cheeks a soft pink and her eyes glowing. Gazing at me like I was someone she could trust, count on to protect her.

I shove my phone back into my pocket.

You've got this, Steele.

The worst that can happen is too many people show up and we shut the party down early. No biggie.

I hurry into the house to change before more people show up, every nerve firing in anticipation of seeing Harbor again.

———

By sunset, the party's in full swing. Most of the team's here, sitting around the yard eating pizza and drinking beer. The DJ's playing music at a perfectly acceptable volume, and we've had zero neighbor complaints.

So far, so good.

"Yo, Cap. The PR girl's here," Morrison shouts across the yard and heat creeps up my neck.

Awesome.

Nothing like calling attention to me and Harbor before she's even walked through the door.

"Thanks." I keep my tone neutral, acting casual as I stride across the grass. Not too fast—I don't want to appear overeager.

But you totally fucking are.

Truthfully, I've been counting down the minutes until her arrival. I hope I can get her alone for at least a few minutes tonight. I'm dying to kiss her, taste her again.

Weaving through the crowd of people in the kitchen, I hurry to the entryway.

And there she is, looking beyond fuckable in a little black dress and heels way too high for a house party. Standing next to her is a tall brunette in a slightly longer red mini dress.

Shit.

Mental note to keep the sister as far away from Bennett as humanly possible. She's right up his alley—but then again, most females with a pulse typically are. Bennett's not overly selective in that department. Prides himself on being equal opportunity, in fact.

"Hey, Harbor." I head over to the sisters, then pause awkwardly. I'm dying to bend down and brush my lips over hers, but that move's out for obvious reasons. A hug even feels too intimate, with everyone watching.

I settle on a hybrid side hug, a pink blush coloring Harbor's cheeks.

Fucking gorgeous.

"And you must be the sister."

"Correct. I'm Piper."

"Weston. Nice to meet you. You two want something to drink?"

"That'd be fantastic. I'm dying of thirst," Piper says.

"Cool. Kitchen's this way." I lead them through the crowd, a few players saying hello to Harbor as she passes. I notice several heads turn, checking out her ass as she sashays by, and I try to tamp down my annoyance.

I can't very well put my arm around her and declare she's mine. Not here, not in this crowd.

But you want to.

Shoving the thought aside, I offer beverages to Harbor and Piper. Both of them take a Solo cup of wine, then we weave out to the backyard.

"Wow—nice place. Gia did right by you." Harbor motions at the glowing pool, the spacious backyard.

"It's good, yeah. Plus, it's a three bedroom. I'm way too old to be sharing a room with my brothers. Bad enough we're living together again." I take a slug of my beer, the music cranking up a bit louder.

Piper giggles, and I'm struck by how similar her laugh is to Harbor's. Although she's a brunette and Harbor's a blonde, I see the resemblance between them. They have the same high cheekbones, the same bow lips. She's taller than Harbor, with a darker complexion, but it's obvious they're sisters.

Piper moves in closer to me, dropping her voice low so only the three of us can hear.

"So, Weston—how do you feel about my sister?" She pins her gaze on mine, and I choke on my beer.

Harbor slugs her sister. "Pipes…"

"Um…she's great." I stammer the response, my gut tight and face burning.

Nothing like getting grilled.

"She is, isn't she?" Piper throws her arm around Harbor's bare shoulders, narrowing her eyes at me. "If you do anything to hurt her, I will mess you up. And I mean it."

Somehow, I don't think she's joking.

"Heard. Loud and clear."

"Hey, hey…" Bennett strolls up, breaking the tension. "You must be Harbor's sister. I'm Bennett. The cooler, more fun triplet. Also, better looking." He shoots Piper a cheeky wink, and my stomach rolls.

Piper laughs, flipping her hair over her shoulder, and I wonder if I should be worried about the two of them. I bet they could get into a lot of trouble together.

"He's mostly harmless." I wave Callum over, wanting a back-up chaperone for Bennett. "And this is Callum, the goalie. Our other brother."

"Oh, the goalie. Always very serious." Piper purses her lips together, and Bennett snorts.

"Damn. She knows her positions," he smirks, shooting her a flirtatious once-over.

Piper snorts at the double entendre and Harbor elbows her sister, a subtle warning.

"I'm not that serious. I prefer driven." Callum tips his beer back, takes a long slug.

"I don't think I need to ask who the fun one is here," Piper says, staring directly at Bennett.

Shit.

I didn't anticipate Harbor's sister being a firecracker.

"I resent that. I'm extremely fun," Callum says, his voice gruff.

"Prove it," Bennett challenges. "Game of ping-pong, me vs you. Loser cannonballs into the pool. Clothing optional."

"You're on." Callum sets his empty beer bottle on the closest table and takes off toward the game room, Bennett and Piper right behind.

"You okay leaving your sister alone with those two knuckleheads?" I ask, inching closer to Harbor.

"Sure. Callum's there—he won't let anything happen."

"Good, I was hoping you'd say that." I lean in, my lips hovering at the shell of her ear. Her sweet perfume tickles my nostrils and all I can think about is getting her upstairs, alone.

It's reckless. Stupid, even. One wrong look from the wrong person and the whole season could blow up in our faces.

But fuck it—I need her.

"Let me give you a tour of the rest of the house."

Her lips tip up in a slow smile and she nods, following me inside. I'm careful not to touch her, even though my fingers burn with the desire to press against the small of her back, lead her up the stairs.

Instead, I keep a respectful distance between us. Pretending we're colleagues, just short of friends.

Eyes darting around the room, I duck upstairs with Harbor right behind. We tiptoe up the wooden steps, and I'm suddenly glad Bennett hired a DJ. The music's so loud no one hears us, plus there's tons of distractions. No one will even notice we're gone.

Turning the knob to my room, I grab Harbor's wrist

and pull her inside. Spinning around, I box her in with my arms, our faces inches apart.

"Hi."

"Hi." Her voice is quiet, barely above a whisper. But there's a sultriness, a longing there, sending all my blood rushing straight to my cock.

"I missed you, Hurricane."

"So did I." She winds her arms around my neck and then we're kissing, the bass from the music outside vibrating the floor.

She tastes like wine, a slight hint of vanilla on her lips as I slip my tongue into her mouth.

"God, I've been waiting to do this," I murmur, sliding my hands down to her hips and pulling her closer to me. Inhaling her floral scent, getting lost in her. "This is all I've been wanting to do."

I palm her ass cheeks, squeezing, and she giggles.

"Weston…"

"I want you. You're prancing around in this tiny slip of a dress, and all I can think about is taking it off."

"We can't," she breathes into my open mouth.

"We can." I press down on the lock, the click snicking behind us. "See? Privacy."

"You're a bad boy, Weston Steele. What would HR think about this?"

"Probably nothing good. How about we don't tell them?" I drop my lips to the tender skin of her neck, nipping and sucking. "They don't need to know about this…" I glide my hand up her thigh, bunching the fabric of her dress in my hand. "Or this." Sliding her panties to the side, I trail my fingers through her wetness. "Such a good girl, soaking and ready for me."

She exhales a soft, breathy moan as I sink two fingers

into her tight pussy. Moving in and out, conscious of the time constraint. Her muscles contract around my fingers, nipples peaking through the thin material of her dress.

"You're fucking glorious, Harbor, you know that?"

Her lips curve into a smile beneath mine and my cock lengthens and hardens in my pants.

I want this woman.

Need her, like I need air to breathe.

In this moment, the only thing on my mind is fucking Harbor. Making her come all over my cock, unraveling for me and only me.

"Lose your panties." My voice is husky with desire as I issue the command.

She doesn't hesitate, gripping my shoulder for balance and stepping carefully out of her panties.

"Perfect." I slide another finger into her, flicking my thumb against her clit. She writhes against the door, her head thrown back.

"You like that, baby? Just like that?" I press on the sensitive bud and she squirms under my touch.

"Weston…" She moans my name and I unzip my pants, pulling out my cock. I'm hard and ready to go.

"Shit—condom," I mutter, pulling my fingers out of her pussy.

"It's fine. I'm on birth control and I trust you."

I pause. "You sure?"

She gazes up at me, eyes hazy with lust. "Yes, I'm sure. Fuck me, Weston. Bare. Nothing between us. I want you to be my first."

My heart stutters in my chest.

Harbor's never been with someone like this.

The vulnerability, the way she trusts me—she's giving me something real. Something I don't want to fuck up.

I press my forehead to hers. Because this isn't just sex. Not with her. Not now.

Pumping my cock a few times, I line up with her entrance and slide in.

Fucking heaven.

Tight and wet and hot, and I sink in like I'm home.

"Fuck..." I hiss, gripping her hip and pulling her closer. "You're so fucking tight, baby. Perfect for me."

"Yes..." she moans, grinding against me.

Our bodies move together, frantically seeking more. More friction, more heat, more of each other.

"You feel that, baby? How fucking deep I am? That's what you do to me, Hurricane—turn me into a damn animal."

She arches into me, our bodies slapping together. "God, yes. Weston...don't stop. I want all of you. Every filthy, perfect inch."

Hearing her dirty words, I drive into her. Fierce and deep. I want Harbor to remember me and my cock every time she takes a motherfucking step. To feel me inside her still, deep and aching. Pushing her over the edge.

"Harbor..." I kiss her hard on the lips, my tongue tangling with hers. Wrapping my hand around the delicate column of her neck, I squeeze lightly, testing. She doesn't flinch, doesn't pull away. "Come for me, baby."

I press on her neck, pistoning into her hard. The door rattles, but I'm not concerned about the noise. Everyone's downstairs, dancing and drinking.

Harbor unravels in my arms, her body convulsing. I loosen my fingers around her neck and she sucks in a desperate breath as I drive into her. A few thrusts later, I explode, the hot pulse of my release mixing with hers.

Pressing her body to mine, I kiss her—hard and deep—my hands stroking her hair, her face.

"God, baby. You're so fucking perfect." I hold her to me, heart still racing, sweat cooling on our heated skin. She's trembling and flushed, wrecked and radiant—and mine.

All mine.

I know—right here, right now—I'd burn down everything in my whole damn life to keep her.

We stay still for a moment longer, wrapped up in silence and sweat and the illusion that this bubble won't burst. But we've already been gone too long.

"Guess we have to go back out there…" I adjust my shirt, tucking away my cock.

"Sadly. I don't want to leave Piper alone too long though."

"Hold on, stay still." I duck into my bathroom, returning with a warm washcloth. Gently, I wipe between Harbor's legs, washing away all the traces of us and tossing the cloth into my hamper.

We redress quickly, and I crack open the door, checking both directions.

"Coast is clear."

Harbor slips into the hallway first, smoothing her hair down and trying to pretend we didn't break every rule we made. I follow behind her.

"Damn, Cap. Hope you stretched first."

One of our defensemen—Ford, a solid D-man with a dry sense of humor and zero filter—is leaning against the wall, arms crossed and eyes narrowed. His gaze flicks to Harbor's tousled hair and swollen lips, then back to me.

My stomach drops.

Shit.

CHAPTER 30
HARBOR

O h fuck.

Fuckity, fuck, fuck.

Face flaming, I race through all the possible reasons I could be up here, with Weston up in his bedroom.

None of them seem remotely believable. Not the way his teammate's staring at us right now.

"Hey, Ford. You lost?" Weston answers smoothly, his tone calm and controlled. "Party's downstairs, man."

"Coulda fooled me." The guy—Ford—shoves off the wall with a smirk.

"We were just talking about the youth clinic. Great job with the kids out on the ice!" I flash him a bright smile, my voice high-pitched and overly enthusiastic.

"Sure." Ford's eyes flick between me and Weston. Then he leans into Weston and points at his zipper. "Your fly's down, bro."

Oh god.

He totally knows.

FUCK.

Rule #1 blown to smithereens. Rule #2's probably right behind.

And if Keller finds out? It's over, for both of us. Weston could be benched—or worse—cut from the team. And I'm done. Cooked. My chances of proving I belong here gone, in one stupid second.

Red-hot panic pumps through my veins, my heart beating triple time. I'm probably in the cardiac danger zone right now, on the verge of a heart attack.

Weston nonchalantly pulls up his zipper. "Thanks. Hate when that happens."

The bass ramps up and people cheer from the yard, and Weston nods his head toward the stairs.

"Shall we?"

Without a word, I move down the stairs, taking one careful step at a time. I do not need to trip on top of everything else.

At the bottom of the staircase, Weston pulls Ford to the side. They're a few feet away from me, not fully within earshot. But I'm able to make out a few words from the conversation, the most important ones being *Keep it between us.*

I bounce from foot to foot, trying to remain calm. Inside though, I'm an absolute wreck.

Ford could go straight to Keller. Or Prince. He could out us to the entire freaking locker room and there's not a damn thing we can do about it, other than deny, deny, deny.

A solid PR strategy, and one I'm not above using. Desperate times call for desperate measures.

But that would chip away at the team morale and put Weston in a terrible position.

Dammit.

Why does this have to be so freaking complicated?

Exactly why you weren't supposed to get involved in the first place.

Winners don't get distracted, Harbor.

I don't need my dad's voice in my head right now. I feel bad enough as it is, watching Weston navigate the sticky situation with his teammate.

Spinning my bracelets on my wrist, I bite the inside of my cheek and shove down the flutters of panic rising in my chest.

Stay calm. Freaking out isn't helpful to anyone.

Weston strides over, a hand shoved in his pocket, and Ford goes the other direction.

"Shit…" I whisper as soon as Weston's by my side. His jaw's tense, worry lines furrowing his brow.

"It's handled. He won't say anything." He doesn't reach out to touch me and I feel the absence acutely.

I hate this.

"I'm sorry." I press my lips together, regret rolling through me.

"Harbor, this isn't your fault. And it's going to be fine. Trust me." His deep blue eyes meet mine and he's so sincere, I almost believe him.

Almost.

But now we have to go back out there and pretend nothing happened. Smile. Laugh. Act like my career's not hanging by a thread that could snap at any second.

"Harbor! There you are—I've been looking all over for you!" Piper rushes up to me, glowing. Cheeks rosy, she's definitely had more than one drink. Bennett's right behind her, grinning.

"Hey, guys. Party's bumping now. Let's dance." He

hooks his thumb at the patio door and Piper claps her hands together like a high school cheerleader.

"Yessss! I love dancing."

Grabbing Bennett's hand, the two of them bolt outside. Weston and I exchange a wary glance and follow.

The night keeps getting better.

The DJ's pumping hip hop, so loud my eardrums ring the second I step outside. The night air's warm and humid, my skin instantly sticky. Bennett and Piper grind together, dancing in the center of a much larger, drunker crowd than before Weston and I went upstairs.

Weston leans down, his lips inches from my ear so I can hear him over the music.

"Want me to break that up?"

"No, it's fine. Piper's a big girl. She can handle herself."

"Okay. Say the word and I'll stop him."

I can't worry about my sister right now. All I'm thinking about is Ford and what he saw upstairs. What he's going to say to his teammates, the coach.

Sure, Weston said he handled it. But did he really?

Only time will tell—and I hate leaving things to chance.

"Harbor, right?"

There's a tap on my arm and I spin toward the voice.

Wonderful.

Victoria Prince. The Ice Queen herself. Here, at the party that's going very wrong, very fast.

FUCK, FUCK, FUCK!

"Hey! Yeah, it's Harbor. How are you, Victoria?" I force my lips into a smile, my face so tight there's little chance I'm coming off as sincere.

Thank god it's dark.

"Please, call me Tori. I heard about the little get-together. Thought I'd pop by and see what's going on."

She casts her eyes around the lawn, taking in the keg, the DJ, the growing crowd. "Good times."

She sounds less than amused.

"Bennett doesn't doing anything small." Weston stares at his brother swaying with Piper in the middle of the crowd, his hands on her narrow hips.

"I heard about him." Tori stares at Bennett, gyrating with my sister, and a cold sweat breaks out on the small of my back.

"He's the fun one." Weston scrubs a hand over the back of his neck, a vein popping in his thick neck.

"Hmmm." Tori's tone's non-committal, like she's sizing up Bennett—and the entire situation.

"Want something to drink, Tori?" Weston gestures to a nearby cooler, and she nods.

"Sure, I'll take a water. If you have that." Her tone's borderline snarky, and I wonder why, exactly, she's here.

Did Prince send her to check up on the team?

Or me specifically?

I fidget with my bracelets and pray Weston returns with the drinks sooner rather than later.

"The rebrand's going well." Tori floats the compliment, not taking her eyes off the dancing.

"Thanks. It's been intense, but I'm happy with how things are going."

"Daddy's been pleased."

"Wonderful."

"Listen—can I give you a little advice? Hockey daughter to hockey daughter?" She cuts her eyes at me and a prickly tingle skates down my arms, every single nerve in my body on edge.

"Sure." I play it cool, even as the tiny hairs on the back of my neck rise.

"You're doing great work. But the lines between personal and professional are starting to blur—people notice. And when Daddy's investors notice, contracts get reevaluated. Quickly."

My stomach clenches and my chest tightens, forcing most of the oxygen from my lungs. Suddenly, I'm struggling to breathe.

Victoria Prince is warning me.

Away from Weston.

FUCK.

Weston sidles up with the drinks and I fight back the panicky sensation rushing over me.

Breathe.

No one *knows* anything.

Plausible deniability.

We still have a loophole, an out.

"Thank you." I take the drink from Weston, resisting the urge to chug the entire Solo cup of wine in one long gulp. "And thanks, Tori. For the advice. Would you excuse me a moment? Ladies' room."

Pretending I have to pee, I hurry away. I feel badly leaving Weston alone with Tori, but I'm sure he can handle her. I need a second to pull myself together. Between Ford and Tori, I'm about to burst.

"Whoa, little lady—" A sweaty palm darts out, grabbing my arm. I stagger on my heels and try to steady myself, tottering. "Where are you running off to in such a hurry?" The man leers at me, his words slightly slurred.

I vaguely recognize him from all my community outreach. The reddish beard and shocking jade green eyes jog my memory—he owns the Rusty Anchor.

"You're that PR lady, right? The eye candy the hockey team hired to get their franchise out of the shitter."

I bristle, his hand still clutching my arm. "Harbor Hayes. And I wouldn't say the franchise is 'in the shitter,' as you so eloquently put it."

"Well, everyone knows the old coach threw the season. It's gonna take more than a move down to Florida for them to prove they have what it takes to win. Know what I mean?"

He's louder now, his voice carrying over the music. A few people glance our direction, including Weston and Tori. A couple phones lift, filming without subtlety.

"They do have what it takes. But thanks for your input. I'll be sure to pass it on." I rip my hand out of his grip and his drink splashes on me, cold and strong.

"Damn, now you spilled my drink. You're a feisty one." He grabs at the hem of my dress and yanks me forward. More of his drink sloshes out of his cup, this time landing on my chest.

My brain blanks and my limbs don't work. I'm frozen, caught between instinct and panic.

"Get your hands off her." Weston's deep voice booms over the music, and now there's a crowd of people around us.

"Easy, dude. We were just chatting about how this hot piece of ass is going to save the team with her *skills*. Bet you know all about that."

A streak of tanned muscle flies close to my face, then the man's stumbling backward, both his hands cupped over his nose. Blood streams through his fingers and flashes of light blind me as people capture the moment. Multiple phones are recording, the red dots blinking like predator eyes. Someone's frantically typing—probably uploading to TikTok before the blood's wiped from

Bennett's knuckles. Bennett's reared back, ready to take another swing at the guy.

"Bennett, no—" Callum snags the back of Bennett's shirt, pulling him away.

"Get this animal off me!" the man cries, cowering. Tori races over, helping Callum and Weston with Bennett.

I stand there, gaping and in shock.

"Don't you ever touch her, you fucking hear me, you piece of shit!" Bennett screams, his face red and twisted with rage.

"Go inside," Tori shouts, shoving the Steele brothers toward the door. "Party's over!"

Tears threaten at the corners of my eyes as I stare in horror at the scene, all the people talking and filming.

"Harbor, let's go." Piper's arm wraps around me as she drags me across the lawn toward the house.

My entire body's numb, fear and dread mixing into a nauseous cocktail in my gut.

"This is going to go viral," I whisper. "There's no way I can stop this from leaking."

"It's okay, it's okay." Piper's fingers trace calming circles on my damp, sticky shoulder, but I don't feel any better.

I'll handle it.

Weston's strong, steady voice rings in my head.

He can't handle this.

And I'm afraid I won't be able to either.

CHAPTER 31
HARBOR

M y phone's blowing up in my bag before Piper and I even get into the Uber. I'm shaking so badly my teeth click together and my breathing's shallow and uneven.

"Breathe, babe. It's going to be okay. Everything's fine." Piper strokes my arm as the car pulls away from the house.

"Oh my god. Cops." I stare out the window in horror at the police cars flying down the street, red and blue lights flashing.

I don't have time to fall apart now. Right now, I have to do my job. The job Prince is paying me big bucks for.

With trembling hands, I text Weston.

> Harbor: Tell Bennett to get a lawyer
>
> Harbor: Be cooperative, but don't answer anything without representation

Mercifully, he texts me back immediately.

Weston: They're taking B and that asshole down to the station

Weston: That dude's gonna press charges

Shit.

And there's video footage of the fight, probably circulating as we speak.

Harbor: Call your lawyer and agent

Harbor: I'll loop management in

Weston: Tori already called Prince

Fu-u-u-ck.

Of course she called Daddy.

My cell vibrates with an alert.

Bile rises in my throat as I read the words: *Coastal Crushers player Bennett Steele's on thin ice*

Oh. My. God.

I click into the TikTok video and there I am, front and center. That creep pawing at me. Then Weston's next to me, his hand on my back. There's a flash of light, the camera shakes. Loud noises and screaming as Bennett pummels the guy.

Blood. Tons of blood.

Callum and Weston pulling Bennett off the man, Tori's arms waving at the DJ and telling him to shut it down.

I play the video again, then again. Zooming in, pausing, searching for angles.

Watch myself looking disoriented as that asshole grabs at me. Then Weston's suddenly there. Too close, too intimate. Looking very much like a possessive boyfriend. The optics are career-destroying: the PR consultant drunk and getting groped at a team party, the captain swooping in.

"It's going to come down to optics," I mutter. "Bennett looks like the aggressor on the video—and defense of others only works if the response wasn't excessive. He snapped. That's what people will see."

The sound quality's not good enough to hear what the creepy guy's saying to me, not close enough to catch how he pulled me up against him.

Dammit.

This is bad. Very, very bad.

"That's not good." Piper's quiet, watching the video over my shoulder.

"No, Pipes. It's really not."

"But Bennett was protecting you."

"I know. He can explain everything to the cops, and hopefully the guy won't press charges. Plus, there were witnesses. Maybe no one else caught everything on camera. But surely people saw and heard what happened."

"Shit, what a mess," Piper mumbles.

"Shit is right."

The Uber stops in front of the Inn, and Piper and I climb out. Everything's normal here, calm, a sharp contrast to the chaos we left behind at the party.

"Now what?" Piper glances at me, her brows knit with worry.

"Now I do damage control. Try to spin this the best I can. Come on."

We hurry into the lobby, going past the bar to head upstairs. As we walk by, I catch a glimpse of the TV behind the bar.

"Oh fuck…" I mutter, frozen as I stare up at the screen. The bright red ticker tape on the 10' o clock news alerting everyone to a breaking story involving the Coastal Crushers.

Scandal.

Exactly what the team's supposed to be avoiding.

My bag vibrates and I break out of my trance. I need to get my head in the game here.

Pulling out my cell, my stomach sinks.

Piper touches me lightly on the arm. "You don't have to take that."

"I do."

Answering, I hurry back outside. Trying to get away from the crowd, anyone who may overhear.

"Hi, Dad."

"What in the actual fuck did I just see?" My dad's angry voice bellows through the speaker, my eardrum ringing from the intensity.

"You saw the video."

"Me and everyone in America, Harbor. My daughter, the PR rep, at some booze-fueled frat party. A player draped all over you, while another player beats the hell out of some drunk. I saw you dragging the Hayes name into the gutter."

My voice tightens, along with my chest. "Bennett was protecting me, Dad. That man touched me—"

"You think that matters? That any team owner or GM in the league gives a fuck about why it happened, Harbor? Stop playing the victim. You're an embarrassment. You were supposed to be better than this."

Tears well in my eyes. From his harsh words—and because he's speaking the truth.

I let everyone down tonight.

"I was doing my job, Dad."

"Your job? Your job's to stay clean, above reproach.

Fucking invisible. Not be in the video. The star of the motherfucking show, at the center of the storm. PR has one job, Harbor: to control the narrative. Now you *are* the narrative. Well done." His tone's low and derisive, disappointment leaking down the line.

A tear escapes, sliding down my cheek.

He's right. I failed tonight.

"You'll never have your own legacy. And now you're fucking up mine. All because you can't separate your personal shit from the real work. The Hayes name means something in this industry, and you're destroying it."

"Dad—"

He cuts me off. "You were never built for this game. Not like I was. I warned you, Harbor. Told you time and again—stay out of the big leagues. Now hang up, get out, and let the professionals fix what you broke."

The line clicks and I stare down at the phone, hot tears streaking down my face. My chest heaves as I hyperventilate, my worst nightmare coming true.

Let the professionals fix what you broke.

Tipping my head back, I swipe at my wet cheeks and stare up at the twinkling stars in the inky night sky. Take a few deep breaths, letting the sound of the ocean waves wash over me.

All the late nights and stressful moments, the press releases and creative spins roll through my mind. The people I've helped, the careers I've saved.

I've come too far to let some drunk asshole derail me. This isn't how I'm going to go out.

I won't give up now. Can't give up now.

Wiping away running mascara and tears, I take a long, deep breath of the salt air.

I can do this.

Regaining my composure, I march back into the hotel lobby and grab my sister's arm.

"How'd that go?" She's half-jogging to keep pace with me.

"Terrible, as always. I have a job to do, though. Can't worry about Dad right now."

Two minutes later, we're back in the room. Piper heads straight for the shower, and I crash into the desk chair.

It's going to be a long night.

Firing up my laptop, I start crafting a holding statement while simultaneously speed-dialing Prince. I'm positive he's already heard about the incident, but I still need to call.

"Harbor—tell me you have a handle on this thing." Prince answers before there's even a ring on my end.

I blow out a breath. Desperately wanting to say yes and reassure him, but knowing that's a lie.

"Working on it, sir. Have you seen the video?"

"Fuck, there's video?"

"Unfortunately, yes. Probably multiple. We need legal involved ASAP."

"I'm on it. Messaging now."

There's tapping in the background as Prince writes to the legal team.

"There's something you should know, sir."

"That doesn't sound good."

"I'm in the video."

"What?"

"It's not what it looked like, sir. Unfortunately, Beau, the Rusty Anchor owner, was drunk and being inappropriate. With me. Bennett saw and reacted."

"Tori told me he flew off the handle. Someone called the police."

"He was protecting me, sir."

"Great. So now one of my superstar wingers is most likely facing assault charges. Fucking terrific." He huffs out a loud, aggravated breath. "We just cleaned up the last mess and now this?"

"I know, sir. And I'm very sorry. About all of it." I hesitate, try to get control over my shaky voice. "I'm drafting a statement. It's…PR-world accurate."

"We don't need PR-world accurate. We need real-world accurate. Clean it up. Now."

I bite the inside of my cheek, force myself not to react.

"Chad from legal will be in touch. He'll want to review the statement and brief you before you talk to anyone— press, police, sponsors. Anyone."

"Understood."

"No posts, no comments, no off-the-record bullshit. Keep your mouth shut until we say otherwise."

"I wasn't planning to say a word."

"Good. Because the next thing you say could cost us the season."

My stomach rolls with dread and anxiety, hands sweating.

"I'll have that first draft to your inbox in twenty."

"Harbor—" There's a long pause and I twirl the bangles on my wrist, my gut twisting. "I think you need to take a step back. You're involved in this mess. It's not good for the team to have you front and center right now."

"What? No. I can't step back now. The team needs me now more than ever."

"You're a liability, Harbor."

"I'll be an asset, sir. Promise."

Another long pause and I bite my lip, waiting. This

can't be it. I can't walk away now—there's too much work to be done.

"I know the ins and outs of the team, Mr. Prince. Plus, every detail from tonight. I'm the best person for the job."

More silence. This is it. I'm getting fired.

"Fine. Last chance, Harbor. You're on thin ice. I'll be waiting on that statement."

He clicks off and I sink back into the chair, staring at the blinking cursor on the screen.

Last chance.

I need to fix this.

Bennett's freedom, Weston's captaincy, the team's season, my entire fucking career.

Everything I care about hangs in the balance—and I'm the only one who can prevent total destruction.

CHAPTER 32
WESTON

don't sleep. Not a single minute. Between the cops, lawyers, and back-to-back calls with Prince and the GM, I don't even see my bed until 4 AM.

By this point, sleep is a lost fucking cause.

Besides, every time I close my eyes, the image of Harbor getting groped by that Beau Lawson guy haunts me.

His hands on her, the way she froze in fear.

I can't get that picture out of my mind.

My beautiful girl, panicked.

When the sun rises, I give up and head to the rink. A solo morning skate session is about the only thing that can center me right now.

That, and talking to Harbor.

But she's not answering my calls. I tried her last night when I left the station, then again once I get home.

I texted her, too.

Weston: You okay?

Nothing.

Silence.

I know she's fine—Prince told me he talked to her, then rattled off the plan of attack. Signature Harbor Hayes material.

Say nothing.

Admit nothing.

No comment.

Still, not talking to her is tearing me up. I need to hear her voice, see for myself that she's okay.

She always picks up.

Or she used to.

Without thinking, I jerk the wheel hard and steer in the direction of the Driftwood Inn. The rink can wait—I need to see Harbor. Touch her, reassure her.

Pink rays of sunlight break through the dusky gray morning, puffy cotton candy clouds billowing in the sky as I stride through the parking lot of the Inn.

Everything's going to be okay.

We can weather this storm.

Together.

I head through the lobby, baseball cap pulled low on my forehead as I make my way to the elevator.

No one's inside and the hallway's empty when I step out.

I rap lightly on Harbor's hotel room door. Once, twice.

She cracks the door open on the third knock.

"Weston…" Her voice is soft with sleep. "You shouldn't be here."

"I had to see you. Make sure you're okay."

"Come in." Grabbing my wrist, she pulls me into the dark room, slamming the door behind us. She drags me across the floor, into the bathroom, and clicks the lock.

"Why would you risk coming here?" She folds her arms across her stomach and blinks up at me, still adjusting to the light.

"I told you. I had to see you." I step toward her, smooth her golden hair from her face. Dark circles rim her bloodshot eyes, physical evidence that she's barely holding herself together.

She sighs, biting her lip. "You shouldn't have come. The media's all over this, and we both have targets on our backs."

"I don't care. Are you okay?"

Her chest shudders as she breaks eye contact, staring at the sink.

"Yes." She's quiet and unconvincing.

"Harbor—" I stroke her cheek and she leans into my touch. "I'm sorry about all this. I wish I stopped that Lawson jerk off before he touched you."

"It's not your fault, Weston. And I'm glad you didn't get tangled up in this mess. How's Bennett?"

"Fine. It's not his first run-in. My brother's well-versed in bar fights. Pretty sure legal will be able to mount a good defense. But Prince is talking to the league today. He's probably getting suspended for at least a game or two."

And that's on me. I was five feet away. I should've seen it coming. Stopped things before it all blew up.

Her hands ball into fists at her side. "Suspended. Dammit. I'm sorry."

Worry swims in her hazel eyes and I run my thumb over her bottom lip. "Sshhh. Not your fault. My brother made his own choices."

"Because of me."

"Hurricane, he's okay. Trust me—Bennett doesn't mind trending on social media."

"Oh god, tell me he's not commenting on anything."

"He's not. But he's low-key loving the hashtag #*Steelefist*."

She giggles, her lips curving into a hint of a smile, and for the first time since last night, my chest loosens. I take a chance, dropping my lips to hers. After a second, she relaxes in my arms. Soft and warm, she kisses me back and some of the tension from last night slips away.

We're going to be okay.

We have to be.

"I love you." The words escape before I can stop them, raw and desperate in the small space. I don't regret them, needing her to know how I feel. That I'm not going anywhere.

Harbor's eyes widen, her lips parting in surprise.

"I know that's a violation of rule #3, no future talk. But fuck the rules. I love you, Hurricane. Whatever comes next, I need you to know that."

A buzz interrupts the moment, vibrating my pocket. I pull out my cell with trepidation.

"Shit. Team meeting at ten. Mandatory."

Harbor nods. "I know. I'll be there."

I want to say more, to talk about us. But Harbor's already switching to work-mode, her expression serious. Any trace of a smile's now gone and I can practically hear the clock ticking.

Still, cold dread's replaced by a whisper of relief. With Harbor on deck, the situation will be managed, contained. I'm sure of it.

"I better go. Need to get ice time in before the meeting."

I kiss her one last time, trying to convince myself everything's fine. Then I tiptoe out of the room for practice, leaving Harbor perched on the side of the bathtub. Typing away on her phone, screen glowing in her hand.

———

Stepping off the ice after my solo practice, I'm sweaty and exhausted. The events of the last twenty-four hours are starting to catch up, the adrenaline waning. I could go for a nice, long nap right about now.

"Steele. My office. Now." Coach's voice catches me off-guard. I hadn't realized he was watching.

Anxiety snakes through my veins, each breath another flick of tension licking my insides. I follow Coach Keller through the tunnel and try not to panic. But judging by his ramrod posture and tense shoulders, I'm betting this isn't gonna be a pep talk.

"Sit." Coach practically barks the command and I bristle as I sink into the chair across from him.

He crosses his thick arms over his chest and stares at me for a long beat that feels like fucking eternity.

Finally, he shakes his head. "What in the actual fuck, Captain? A team kegger at your house with the mother-fucking locals? Where the hell's your head at, son?"

His brows crush together in a deep frown and my stomach bottoms out.

No sense sugarcoating the situation.

"Not my shining moment, sir."

"I'll fucking say. Remember that speech about keeping our heads down and staying out of trouble? I expected more from you, Steele."

Those words hit hard.

I expected more.

So did I, and the crashing realization that I let everyone

down—Coach, the team, Bennett, Harbor—steals my breath away, tight pressure building up in my chest.

"I know and I'm sorry."

"Sorry, Captain? You're fucking *sorry*? What good does sorry do? Bennett's benched indefinitely until the legal issues are cleared up. He's facing possible team and league fines. The press is climbing up my ass, demanding interviews. We're trending on fucking social media. And you're *sorry*?"

I hang my head in shame, shoulders slumping. I should have stopped this. The party, the fight. This is on me.

"You're distracted, Steele. I've seen it since we got here. I have half a mind to rip that C right off your motherfucking jersey myself."

A sharp blow to the solar plexus, all the air knocks from my lungs.

I'm going to lose my position.

What's worse, I deserve to.

I take a shallow, shuddery breath. "I haven't been the leader this team deserves, Coach. And I own that."

"Fan-fucking-tastic." Coach leans back in his chair, slinging one foot over his knee.

"Go ahead and fine me. Bench me. Take the C. I deserve it."

There's a long, painful silence, the wall clock ticking like a time bomb behind me as I await my fate.

"I should do every single one of those things, Steele. You let things get out of control when you should have stepped up and taken the lead." He rakes a hand through his short hair. "But I'm not gonna do that. Now's not the fucking time to replace the team captain, even if you're doing a lousy damn job."

My eyes jerk up, locking with his.

"Step the fuck up, Weston. Get your head out of your damn ass. Stop getting distracted by Harbor Hayes. I don't care if you're in love, in lust, or planning a fucking wedding. You're the captain of this team first, everything else second. Choose, Steele. Now get the hell out." He tips his head at the door and I jump up, eager to escape.

Racing to the locker room, I try to process what just happened. I'm not benched. Not fined or suspended.

I'm still the captain of the Coastal Crushers.

But he definitely knows about me and Harbor—and I don't know what to do about that. He's not just threatening my position—he's forcing me to choose between Harbor and everything I've worked for since I was seven years old. The captaincy isn't just a letter on my jersey. It's who I am. But losing Harbor? That would destroy who I want to become.

She's the one thing I'm not willing to give up.

Not now, not ever.

CHAPTER 33
HARBOR

've walked into press rooms full of angry reporters. Handled playoff scandals, trade leaks—even the time a player 'accidentally' stole a golf cart. But nothing's ever rattled me like this team meeting.

This time, it's not just the team's reputation on the line —it's mine too.

Typically, I'm calm. Polished. The woman with a plan.

But not today.

Not after staying up all night, drafting holding statements, press releases, managing the buzzy onslaught of social media.

And especially not after Weston sidelined me with his declaration this morning.

I love you, Hurricane.

Hearing him say those words left me reeling.

Not because I don't love him back.

I do, with every fiber of my being. But it all feels so risky, with everything on the line.

His voice echoes through my head as I walk into the

chilly conference room. Worried eyes trained on me, waiting for my personal brand of slick PR advice. I take my seat toward the front as Coach Keller commands the podium.

"As you all have most likely heard, Bennett Steele's benched until the legal charges are sorted and the league decides what action, if any, they'll be taking. None of that's under my purview, nor my jurisdiction. I'm here to coach the team and win games. We'll be resuming business as usual, starting with practice Monday morning. Stay focused on training and stay out of trouble."

With that, he stalks back to his seat and Prince takes the floor.

"The last twenty-four hours have been a whirlwind." His eyes scour the room, fast and frantic. Like he's had three too many cups of coffee. "We're working on holding things together, clearing Bennett's name, and making sure justice prevails. Harbor?"

Prince waves me up to the podium and I rise on shaky legs, trying to hide the tremor in my hands.

You don't have what it takes to be in this world, Harbor. Get out and let the professionals handle it.

I shove that thought down and step up to the podium, clearing my throat. My vision blurs for a terrifying second and I panic. Everyone's watching, waiting. My dad's voice screams in my head. Weston's love swirls around me, hanging in the air.

What if I screw this up? What if this is the moment everyone realizes I'm a fraud and I don't belong here?

I blink hard. Once, twice.

"Morning." I glance around the room at the faces of the team I so desperately believe in and want to save.

The team I royally fucked over last night.

By being in that video in the first place. Being a PR consultant who became the scandal instead of managing it.

I can't meet Weston's eye. The way he's gazing at me from across the room, like I hung the damn moon and polished the freaking stars. When we both know that's so far from the truth it's comical.

You're ruining the Hayes name.

Setting my notes on the conference table, I stare straight ahead and deliver the speech I practiced thirty-four times in my hotel room.

"I know this week's been a lot. From the successful youth clinic to the events of the weekend. There's been noise, speculation, and a few headlines we didn't ask for."

I take a breath, scanning the room. Prince thrums his fingers on the table and Coach Keller's scowling at me like I'm a wad of gum stuck to the bottom of his sneaker.

"I won't sugarcoat it. The footage looks bad. But what's in the video doesn't tell the whole story, and I have faith the truth will prevail. We're working with legal to make certain the context is fully understood.

"What I need from all of you right now is simple: silence. Stay focused. Stay professional. Don't post, don't share, don't comment. If the media asks you any questions, your answer is 'We're focused on hockey and supporting our teammates.' Full stop."

Ford locks eyes with me and I swallow hard over the lump in my throat before continuing.

"No one wants distractions. Least of all me. My job is to protect this team's reputation. And that hasn't changed— not after this weekend, not ever. You've worked your asses off this off-season. Let's not let thirty seconds of negative viral video derail months of preparation."

Someone in the back mutters, "PR spin."

Just loud enough for me to hear. A few heads nod, and my stomach turns. These are my guys—the ones I've been working my ass off to protect—and they're questioning whether I'm the liability Prince warned me about.

"I was there. I saw what happened. I know things got heated, and I know how fast the internet jumps to conclusions. But we're not going to play that game. We're going to control the story—not react to it."

A few of the guys nod, their faces relaxing. Prince stops thrumming and Coach Keller shifts in his seat.

Everything's under control.

"Questions?" I glance around the room, every eye pinned on me.

Morrison raises his hand. "So what do I tell my sponsors? One of them DM'd me this morning. Do we just act like nothing happened?"

"Great question..." I pause, twisting my bracelets. "You can tell them the matter's being handled. Nothing to worry about."

"Cool." He tips his chin at me, and I shove down the sick feeling in my stomach.

None of these guys deserve this. They're out there busting their asses and one stupid video could tank everything for them. Their sponsors, their livelihood.

"Anything else?" I glance around the room, checking for questions. No one else raises their hand, so I step away from the podium and Keller takes my spot.

"Practice Monday morning, seven sharp. Don't be late." Then he stalks out of the conference room without another word.

Players file out, some of them in hushed conversation. No one stops to talk to me, a few shooting me sideways glances.

Cheeks burning, I act like I don't notice.

"Harbor—" Tori's at my side, her French-manicured hand on my elbow. My mouth goes dry, pulse rate instantly skyrocketing.

"Hey…"

"Are you okay?"

Her eyes search mine. Woman to woman, for one brief second, and I nod.

"I'm fine."

"Good. You did your job. But there's more to the clean-up, as I'm sure you know."

I swallow, my lips pinched in a tight line.

"Sponsors are asking Daddy pointed questions. About team leadership and whether management can control the situation. I'd hate to see careers destroyed over poor judgment."

Straightening my shoulders, I resist the urge to crumple under her pointed stare.

"Understood."

"Have a great day."

Then she spins and exits the room, her stilettos clicking on the linoleum floor.

Right behind her is Prince.

"Good speech. Now let's deliver."

His tone's firm, clipped. And I've never felt more judged in my entire life.

"Absolutely, sir. I'm on it."

He smacks my shoulder, shooting me a tight smile. "You're a Hayes. I'm sure you are."

I try not to flinch as he brings up my father.

You're not worthy of the Hayes name.

Once the room's clear, I gather my notes and bolt for the safety of my office. Anywhere but here.

"Harbor..."

Weston's leaning against the wall in the hallway. His deep voice echoes off the cinder block walls, stopping me in my tracks. I tighten my grip on the papers in my hand.

"You were incredible in there." His ocean blue eyes flick over me and my throat constricts.

"Thanks."

Reaching out, he grips my elbow and I shrink away. I don't need anyone seeing us like this.

Too close.

Compromised.

"You sure you're okay? You don't have to carry all of it alone, you know." Small crinkles of worry crease around his eyes, and my chest aches. I want to tell him the truth, but there's too much on the line.

"Yeah. I'm fine. Talk later."

The lie burns like acid in my mouth. Hurt flashes across his face and my heart aches. I want to be honest with him. To tell him how I feel, that I'm crazy about him.

But I know that's the best way to burn both of our worlds down to the ground.

Instead, I lock my lips together and stride away.

I've already fucked up too many lives as it is. I can't drag him down with me—not when I'm drowning.

Because the problem with spin is, eventually, it spirals out of control.

CHAPTER 34
HARBOR

Miraculously, I keep the train on the rails for a few more weeks. We're closing in on the first preseason game, and the party incident is in the rearview.

Beau Lawson officially dropped the charges two days ago, thanks to the efforts of legal.

Bennett's still benched for the first two games of the season until the league closes their investigation. But he swears it's good for his aura and not to worry about it.

Piper flew out to her next assignment last week, and her absence left a gaping hole in my life. I miss her now more than ever. Especially since I'm keeping my distance from Weston.

I'm not what he needs right now, and we both know it.

We've texted and Facetimed a lot, and he's snuck over to the hotel a couple of times since Piper left.

But seeing him in public is too risky.

Even kissing in my hotel room feels dangerous.

Once the season kicks off, we'll reassess. Revisit the rules. Maybe make new ones.

Until then, we're trapped in the neutral zone—no shots, no movement, just waiting.

I hate it.

But I can't blow up his life. Not any more than I already have.

So I do what I've always done—throw myself into my job. I line up a dozen community events, visit local charities and meet the people in charge. I schedule player media days, coach the rookie on handling the press, process media credentials.

The best part? I get to a zero inbox.

#goals.

Life's not exactly great, but it's manageable. Doable. Livable.

I'm at the office sipping my first cup of coffee and flipping through photos from last night's practice to be used in the pre-game montage. I linger on the photo of Weston —he's crouched down over the puck, sweat beading on his brow. Intensity radiates off the screen and I click the box to select the image.

A knock on my door jerks me out of my trance.

"Come in." I don't bother turning around, still buried under a stack of player bios demanding the perfect image.

"Harbor, you're going to want to see this."

Julianne, one of the PR assistants, hands me her cell. Her voice is oddly flat. Off. My stomach clenches, the coffee swirling.

I glance at the screen and my blood runs ice-cold.

A video thumbnail, frozen.

Me and Weston.

He's leaning in, hand on my waist, forehead nearly

touching mine. I'm gazing up at him, lips parted, dress sliding off my shoulder.

The hallway behind us is Weston's house. That same night. Right after we slipped out of his bedroom.

Different angle, even worse optics.

We never saw a camera, didn't think to confiscate cell phones.

I swallow hard, my vision tunneling.

Because that caption? Already viral.

Turns out the team's biggest distraction was in-house.

#Steelescandal #CrushersCrisis #offside #fraternizingmuch

Vomit rises in my throat and I lean over, retching into the trash can next to my desk. Waves of nausea roll through me and sweat beads at the nape of my neck.

No.

No, no, no.

Not after everything we just went through. We weathered the storm, things were practically back to normal. The season's locked and loaded.

And now this.

Julianne rubs my back, her light touch a physical reminder she's still here, watching me unravel.

I've never lost my grip like this before.

You've never been personally involved before.

In love with the captain of the team.

Swiping at the corner of my mouth, acid burning my throat, I sit up. Black dots dance at the corner of my vision and I'm hot and dizzy.

"Harbor…" Julianne's voice is quiet and far away. The room spins and I close my eyes, praying this is a nightmare. Soon, very soon, I'll wake up and this will all be over.

"Harbor!" She shakes my shoulder and I come to, jerking in the chair. "I'm calling the trainer."

"No. Please don't." My voice is a harsh whisper.

"Let me at least get you some water."

I nod weakly. "Thanks."

She scurries out of the room and I hunch over, head in hands. Hot tears prick my eyes, escaping down onto my cheeks.

I'm so fucked.

You'll never have what it takes, Harbor.

My father was right.

I don't have what it takes to be in professional hockey, to win. I let my personal desires come before my professional duties and look what happened.

My whole world's burning down.

And Weston's caught in the blaze.

The incessant buzz of my cell tells me everything I need to know.

The whole world knows about my illicit relationship with Weston Steele.

And I can't spin this.

No matter how hard I try—what I say or do—it's going to come off as disingenuous. Like a giant cover-up.

My credibility is shot to hell.

I stare at the photo of Weston on my computer screen and my chest cracks wide open. Aching.

For what we had, what could have been.

I wonder if he's seen it. If he knows I'm the reason his cell won't stop buzzing. I hope he hates me for it.

This would be easier if he did.

I know what I need to do.

And it's the hardest fucking thing I've ever had to do in my entire life.

The sharp trill of my cell ringing shocks me from my pity party.

"Harbor. My office. Now," Prince barks down the line, solidifying my decision.

With a deep, shuddery breath, I stand up and the world tilts on its axis for a second time. I grab the edge of my desk and steady myself.

You can do hard things, Harbor.

Repeating the mantra over and over again, I make my way through the maze of hallways to Prince's office. I rap on the door and wait.

"Come in."

He's pacing his office, ESPN playing on the TV mounted in the corner. I catch a glimpse of the headline ticker rolling across the screen and force down another round of nausea: **CRUSHERS IN CRISIS AGAIN: PLAYER ROMANCE LEAKED AHEAD OF SEASON OPENER**

FUCK.

My entire body burns with humiliation as the words scroll past.

I thought I could handle this, all of it.

I was so, so wrong.

"Close the door behind you." His voice is cold, all traces of the friendly boss gone.

I shut the heavy door and take the seat he offers.

"I don't need to explain to you how bad this is."

Resisting the urge to scrunch my eyes shut, I shake my head. "No, sir. You do not."

"To say I'm disappointed is the biggest understatement of the year. All I want—all I ever wanted—was a winning fucking season. Clean, scandal-free. What I got was this circus. And from Coach Doug Hayes's daughter, no less.

My PR consultant sleeping with the captain of my team."
He frowns, and my stomach knots so tight it hurts.

He holds up his hands. "Don't deny nor confirm that statement. Plausible deniability. I don't want to know."

The truth burns like poison as I simmer in my shame and regret. Prince folds his arms over his starched dress shirt, his frown lines deeper than ever.

"This has gone beyond distraction, Harbor. I can't have—"

I feel the words hovering in the air, the finality in his tone.

"You don't need to say it." I swallow over the lump in my throat, my breath catching as I fight back tears.

The team needs a clean slate. Weston needs a chance to be the captain without scandal hanging over him. This isn't just about preserving my dignity—I need to save Weston's career from the wreckage I created.

Prince blinks at me as I rise, straightening my shoulders.

"I'll resign, effectively immediately. But please let me tell the team. I owe them that much."

He huffs out a sigh. "Fine. Draft a statement to the press, while you're at it. Get it to me within the hour."

"Will do." Twisting my bracelets, I walk over to the door with as much dignity as I can muster.

"Harbor—"

I pause at the door. "You did good work. But sometimes that's not enough."

Biting my lip, I nod. "It's not about the work anymore."

Then I leave before he can say anything else.

CHAPTER 35
WESTON

'm running drills at practice with Morrison when I spot Prince talking to Keller at the boards. I pause for a beat, caught off-guard, and the puck whizzes past me into the net.

"Goal!" Ford pumps a fist in the air, and I curse under my breath.

Distracted.

I've been distracted the entire off-season. Ever since Harbor rolled onto the scene.

All I think about is her.

Where hockey used to take up 95% of my brain, now it's Harbor Hayes.

Her smile, her smell, the way she moans my name when she comes.

How she's all business—until she's not. Sliding up and down my cock, her luscious tits bouncing against my chest.

"Yo, Steele! You skating today or what?" Ford arches a brow and I shake my head, digging into the ice.

Like I said, distracted.

I need to get my mind back on the game. But with everything that's gone down, it's difficult.

The fight at the party, Bennett getting benched.

The video everyone in the motherfucking universe saw.

The aftermath's been the worst part.

I put my heart on the line—told Harbor I loved her. But after that night, she's been distant.

I get it. Both our jobs are on the line.

But I hate living like this. Never knowing when I'll see her again, if we'll have a moment of alone time.

I'm ready to say screw it and own up to the relationship with Coach. But I'm pretty sure Harbor's not on board with that plan.

So instead, I'm surviving on Facetime calls and solo hand jobs.

Not optimal.

"Steele!" Keller shouts across the ice, waving me over.

Bracing myself for a lecture about discipline, I skate in his direction. Keller and Prince are still talking, and Prince is waving his hands wildly, shaking his head. The man's clearly drinking too much caffeine.

A few guys snicker as I pass by and agitation churns in my gut. I hate being off my game and that's exactly how I feel right now.

I push my emotions down and unhook my helmet, running a hand through my sweaty hair.

"What's up, Coach?"

"This is what's up." Prince holds his cell out to me and my stomach plummets like a rocket falling through the atmosphere.

It's me and Harbor, the night of the party. I'm leaning

in for a kiss, hand on her waist, and she has that just-fucked look.

Shit.

And the comments section? Fucking brutal. *#PRPuck-bunny* is trending right alongside *#SteeleScandal.* Every amateur sports blogger in America's dissecting our body language, analyzing what this means. For me. For the team.

Forty-seven thousand views and climbing.

Harbor's professional death, monetized by the algorithm.

My mouth goes dry.

It's mid-morning. Harbor had to know this was out there.

As good as she is at her job, she must have.

Why didn't she warn me?

"Care to explain?" Prince's tone is low and menacing as he scowls at me.

I shrug, ready to take the hit. "Not particularly. It wasn't on company time."

I say this more in an effort to protect Harbor than myself.

Because obviously it's a big fucking deal to the team owner, given the fact that he interrupted practice to address the situation.

"Doesn't matter, Weston. It's all over the internet. I'm getting calls from the media. Sponsors will be next. This is the very thing we moved down here to avoid. Scandal. I gave this team one directive—stay out of trouble. Why can't anyone do that?" His voice is loud now, and guys are stopping drills to stare.

Next time I'm ripping that C off your motherfucking jersey myself.

My face burns, muscles firing with the fight-or-flight response.

Guess I'm a Steele through and through because that fight response is strong AF.

"Yeah, I kissed her. In my own damn house. And I'd do it again."

I pause, enjoying the look of shock on Prince's face.

"The only thing I'm sorry about is that some asshole took a video of me in my *private home* and then uploaded the damn thing to social media. But the rest? I don't regret any of it."

Most of that's true.

I don't regret her.

But I sure as hell regret the way this is going down right now.

How it's breaking us in slow motion—and I can't do a damn thing to stop it.

"Weston—" Keller's voice is even, controlled. His face more concerned than angry.

Like a father scolding a misbehaving child, urging him to apologize and make nice.

I hold up my hands. "I'll do what's best for the team. You wanna bench me for kissing Harbor? Do it. Trade me? Wouldn't be thrilled, but I get it. What I won't stand for is management telling me who I can and cannot date. Because that's not in my contract."

Prince glares at me, a vein throbbing at his temple. Keller stays calm, but I catch a slight twitch of his right eye.

"Hit the showers, Steele. Team meeting in an hour. We'll figure out the next steps and let you know." Prince dismisses me and I storm off the ice, throwing my blade guards on and grabbing my gear bag.

I'm in the tunnel when my phone rings. I pick up the phone, noting I have about fifteen missed calls—three of them from Harbor. And double that many text messages.

"Hey, Harbor."

"Hey. We need to talk." Her voice is tight, clipped. Not cold—more hollow. "Meet me in my office?"

"Sure. Give me ten."

I disconnect and toss the phone into my bag.

I don't know what Harbor's going to say, but I'm guessing it isn't going to be good.

———

I take the world's fastest shower, tossing on a T-shirt and joggers, and head to Harbor's office. A nervous dread slithers through me and pools low in my gut as I hustle past offices. I'm on edge, my world collapsing around me, a strange contrast to the bright white fluorescent lights of the hallway.

The captaincy's all but lost.

I may be benched. Or traded.

Coach doesn't trust me and Prince hates my fucking guts.

But the worst part of it all? Harbor's collateral damage.

The one person I want to protect the most is taking the brunt of the fall—and there's nothing I can do to shield her.

I raise my hand to knock and that's when the first blow lands solid on my chest.

Her nameplate's off the door.

Harbor's leaving.

Air whooshes from my lungs and I suck in a deep breath, trying to get a hold of myself.

This isn't happening.

I push through, ready for a fight.

She's sitting at her desk, perfectly still, fingers poised over her keyboard. The cursor blinks on the blank screen and the clock ticks on the wall. Marking the seconds until my universe shatters.

"Harbor—" My voice is guttural, the sound loud in the near-silent office.

She spins around so slowly I wonder if I'm in a time warp.

"I'm resigning."

The words I never wanted to hear float across the room in slow motion and my chest cracks all the way open.

"No. We can fix this. I'd rather lose hockey than you. I'll take a trade, get benched, give up the captaincy—I don't care. Not anymore. Don't ask me to pretend you don't matter more than all of it combined."

Her eyes fill with tears and for a quick second, the mask slips away completely.

"Don't you think I want that, Weston?" Her voice breaks on the words and she bites her lip, cutting her eyes to the floor. "But I can't let you destroy everything you've worked for since you were a kid. Not for me. I won't be the reason you lose your team, your captaincy, your dreams."

She swipes at a tear, the stack of gold bracelets tinkling on her wrist. "You say I matter more than hockey. But hockey is who you are, Weston. And I love you too much to let you forget that."

"No." I stride across the room, making it to her desk in three huge steps. She's so small and fragile in her office chair, a shell of her usual self. Dark circles rim her bloodshot eyes, and her hands shake slightly as she grips the edge of her desk. This is what defeat looks like on the strongest woman I know.

"I'll leave. I can make a trade."

"What? No. That's crazy. This is your team. You're the captain, the leader. They need you, Weston. Now more than ever. The season's about to start."

I huff out a breath, raking my hand through my damp hair.

"Doubt I still have that C on my jersey."

"What?"

"Prince is pretty pissed."

"Once I go, things will get back to how they were before."

Another sucker punch to the gut, and I feel sick to my stomach.

"I don't want to go back to how things were."

She blinks up at me, her expression neutral.

And that hurts the most, cutting me to the core.

"It's already sorted out, Weston. This is the only way to keep your career safe. Prove you're not distracted by me being here."

I want to fight. To yell and scream, get angry.

Even more—I want her to fight.

For us.

But she only stares up at me with defeat swimming in her red-rimmed eyes.

Broken.

So many things tumble through my head, things I should say.

But I can't. There's a hard knot lodged in my throat and my mind's spinning.

"I'm leaving tonight. And I'm not coming back."

"So this is good-bye then?"

She nods, her eyes glistening, and a swell of emotions

bubbles inside me. Anger, rage. Love, lust, longing. Agony and defeat.

I say nothing.

The silence stretches between us like a chasm I can't cross. She's three feet away, but she may as well be on another planet. I want to fight for us, but she's already gone.

Spinning, I stride across the room and yank open the door. I need to get out of here. Away from the arena, Coach, Prince.

Away from hockey.

But most of all, away from her.

Glancing over my shoulder one last time, I try to memorize the high curve of her cheeks, the way her hair falls in golden waves down her back.

"For the record, Hurricane, you were never the distraction. You were the reason I gave a shit in the first place."

CHAPTER 36
WESTON

peel out of the arena parking lot and speed through town, rock music blaring so loudly I'm surprised I don't immediately get a citation for noise violation.

Harbor's leaving.

By tomorrow, she'll be gone.

Where will she go? What will she do?

Because her career's tanked after this. She'll be blacklisted from hockey. No team owner will risk hiring the PR consultant who became the scandal she was supposed to prevent.

What's worse is she's not trying to spin anything anymore—she's just accepting her fate.

And it's all because of me.

She warned me, but I didn't listen. Wouldn't take no for an answer.

Because you love her.

Yeah, but at what cost? Because now she has nothing.

The way she looked in her office—defeated, broken—

those wide hazel eyes filled with pain. The hollow note in her voice.

I'm resigning.

Her father's going to eviscerate her. She's told me enough about him that I know she'll never live this down.

Coach Hayes makes my father look like Dad of the fucking Year.

The irony of all this is I'm the one who crossed the line. Yet I'll be fine.

Sure, I'll likely lose the captaincy. And that sucks. It's gonna be hard for me to take a step back from the position, to transition from being the leader to the led.

But at least I'll keep my job, my career.

None of it means anything without her.

Pain radiates through my chest, pumping through my veins with each beat of my heart.

For the first time in years, I let myself feel something again. I let her in—to my life, my heart—and it felt good. Right.

She's the only person I've ever connected with like this.

I thought we were forever. The real deal.

And now it's done. Over.

I'm leaving.

Pulling into my driveway, I cut the engine and rest my head on the smooth leather wheel. I close my eyes, pain and sadness washing over me in heavy waves, one rolling after the other.

I'm drowning, gasping for air, my chest tight.

So fucking tight.

I can't do this without her.

I've only felt like this—this crushing grief—one other time in my life.

When my mom died.

Harbor's so much like her. Calm, centered, focused. Fun and relaxed once you get to know her. Smart and sweet, full of light and love.

Another wave of misery sweeps over me and I vaguely wonder how I'm going to survive this.

Body heavy, I haul myself into the house. Bennett's on the couch playing *Call of Duty*, not a care in the world.

I try to dodge him, but he catches sight of me out of the corner of his eye. Yanking his headphones off, he gives me a quick once over.

"Bro, who died?"

"Not now, Bennett." My voice is harsh and ragged.

"Whoa." He holds up his palms. "I'd ask if you're okay, but I don't fucking need to. What the hell happened?"

"Harbor's leaving."

"What? Why?"

"I take it you haven't checked social media today."

He shakes his head, hair flopping on his forehead. "Nope. Phone's dead. Didn't charge last night."

I click on a text message and the video pops up.

Bennett hits play, his brows furrowing as he takes in the scene. "Shit."

"Yeah, Prince is pissed. Keller's upset, too. The whole damn thing's a mess."

"So Harbor got fired?"

I shake my head. "No, she resigned. Said it's the best thing for the team…" My heart pounds hard, remembering her words. "And for me."

Bennett kicks the coffee table with his bare foot, a loud thud echoing through the living room. "That's bullshit, man. And you know it."

"I do, yeah. She's always had the team's best interest at heart."

"And she's damn good at her job. Between her and legal, I'm pretty much off the hook. She even talked to one of my sponsors and convinced them not to void my contract."

"She did?"

"Yeah. She's a keeper, man."

I sink down next to my brother on the couch, holding my head in my hands to stop the incessant throbbing. "I don't know if I can go through this again. I don't want to lose her."

"So don't."

He says it like it's easy, simple.

So don't.

"She resigned, Bennett."

"Then stop her."

"I tried. But she won't listen. She's throwing herself on the sword at the team meeting—to save me and my career."

"Don't let her."

"What?"

"If you love her—and I know you fucking do, you sap—stop her at that meeting. Don't let her walk out like this. If you do, you'll regret it the rest of your life."

Something flickers inside me, and it feels a helluva lot like hope.

Damn, my brother's right.

Now's not the time to sit around and wallow. I have to show up to that meeting ready to fight.

For Harbor's job.

And for us.

Hopping up from the couch, a surge of energy roars through me.

I need to get back to the rink.

I have a relationship to save.

CHAPTER 37
HARBOR

I hide in my office until it's time for the team meeting.

Ashamed, embarrassed.

Deeply mortified to be part of the very thing I was hired to avoid.

#SteeleScandal is trending, hitting over 100,000 views in less than twenty-four hours. I can't stop scrolling with trembling hands, reading the vicious comments:

Nepotism at its finest.

This gives *taking one for the team* a whole new meaning.

Hayes always was good at scoring. Guess it runs in the family

And my personal favorite—*#PuckSlut.*

Hopefully, my father, the great Coach Hayes, doesn't see that one. Not that it matters—I already know I'm never living this down. At this point, he's probably disowning me. And why should I care? He's not there for me anyway, not really.

Not when it counts.

I declined his calls all morning, then threw my phone

on Silent and shoved the stupid thing into my desk drawer after his barrage of nasty texts.

Dad: Are you kidding me, Harbor?

Dad: You're SLEEPING with the team captain?

Dad: HAVE YOU LOST YOUR MOTHERFUCKING MIND?!?!

Dad: I raised you better than this

I've had more than enough of his bullshit. Lived my entire life trying to please him, measure up to his impossible standards.

But I'll never be enough for him, no matter what I do.

I get it. I let everyone down—Prince, the team, my father.

Weston.

Myself.

I'm ruined.

Toast.

Damaged goods.

I doubt Prince will give me a glowing recommendation, and even if he does, it's not like his words will hold much weight. My next employer would have to be clueless and desperate to hire me.

All of that's bad, sure. But the thing that scares me—really shakes me to the core—is I don't care.

None of this matters.

I'm losing Weston.

The man I'm wildly in love with.

And I never even told him. What's the point now? It's too late.

My chest constricts at the futility of our situation.

I've been in this business a long time, covered more than my fair share of shitstorms. I can spin worst case scenarios into bright spots in my freaking sleep.

But I can't spin this. This is different—and so much worse.

This is personal *and* professional.

Exactly what I wanted to avoid.

Never mix business with pleasure, Harbor.

"Harbor, you ready?" Julianne raps lightly on the door, and I close my laptop, rising from this desk for the last time.

"Yes." I force my legs to move. Across the room, down the hall, into the conference room where most of the team's already seated.

I step to the podium, scanning the familiar faces. Prince, scowling. Tori next to him, her scarlet lips pressed together in a tight line. Coach Keller, arms folded and brows pinched, looking aggravated to be here.

Ford and Morrison, Isaacson and Dupont.

Callum, his mouth turned down. Reserved.

Bennett's here, fists clenched and forehead furrowed. I'm assuming he's seen the headlines. Maybe even spoke to Weston.

Weston.

He's the only person not in the room.

Probably decided it's better not to be in attendance, given his starring role in the video.

I don't blame him.

Hopefully, he'll get to keep his captaincy and come out unscathed.

Gripping the edges of the podium, I ground myself in

the wood grain. Trying to hold on for a few more minutes before walking away with my head held high-ish.

But the room's too bright, too quiet. Too full of people I've let down.

I want to sink into a pit in the carpeted floor and cry myself to sleep. Instead, I clear my throat and forge ahead.

"Thank you for coming. I apologize for the extra meeting—I know how busy the team is as we gear up for the first preseason game. But I wanted to address the recent headlines with you all in person. As you may have heard by now, a second video of the team party held a few weeks ago has leaked."

A murmur trickles through the room, and I pause, waiting for the side conversations to fade. Pressure builds in my chest, but I push past the tension. The quicker I get through this, the sooner I can escape.

I swallow hard, take a quick sip of air. "Unfortunately, I'm in the video. Again."

More chattering, a few gasps, and heat creeps up my neck. "Although the video's innocuous and everything's speculation, it's better for the team and the brand if I resign. As of today, I'm no longer working for the Coastal Crushers."

My voice doesn't crack, but it should. Numbness has a way of icing even the most brutal goodbyes.

"No." Weston's deep voice booms behind me, shattering the silence. Heads swivel, all eyes suddenly on him.

I spin around to face him, his broad chest heaving like he sprinted here. His hair's disheveled, wind-blown, and his jaw's set with determination.

"If anyone should step away from this team, it's me." He's strong and firm, hard resolve etched on his face.

"I'm the one who broke the rules. I'm the one who couldn't stay away. And I won't apologize for that."

Stepping forward, he locks his eyes on Prince, then Keller.

"She was doing her job. I was the one pursuing her. Every time. So if someone's getting benched for this, it should be me."

My heartrate skyrockets as the entire room glances between me and Weston. My body burns, hands shaking. I've never been more grateful to be standing behind a podium in my life. At least the rest of the room can't see the full-body tremors.

Prince's furrow deepens and he opens his mouth to speak, but Weston cuts him off.

"Let's not pretend this is about professionalism. If that were true, both of us would be on the line. Harbor's the scapegoat here, and that's not fair. This woman—" He cuts his deep blue eyes to mine, and my stomach flip-flops the same way it always does under his gaze. "Cleaned up our messes, protected us and our image. She kept the Crushers out of the news when Bennett got in the fight. She cares more about the team than herself. That's why she's willing to take the fall for this."

He steps toward me. Only half an inch, but it feels like a mile.

"She doesn't deserve the humiliation she's enduring. All for falling for someone." His voice is softer now, his eyes only on mine. "Falling for me."

My breath hitches in my throat, and I want to run to him. Throw my arms around his neck and seal our love with a kiss.

But I can't.

"I won't let her stand up here and pretend she did

something wrong just so the rest of us can feel good about ourselves." Weston scans the room, his gaze lingering on Prince and Keller. "Every crisis, every mess, every scandal —Harbor's held the line. She's the reason we got to focus on hockey. And now we're going to let a fifteen-second video undo all that?"

His eyes flick to mine, burning with an intensity I've never seen.

"I won't let that happen. Trade me instead."

A loud thud reverberates on the conference table and Coach Keller stands. "Enough. The two of you, sit the hell down. There's no way in hell I'm trading my captain two days before the first preseason game. Not over some stupid viral video."

He sits back down, steepling his fingers and glaring at Prince and Tori. Prince licks his bottom lip, contemplating his position. Tori bristles but says nothing.

After a long minute, Prince squares his shoulders. "Well, we have the media to deal with now, Mike. The team's trending for all the wrong reasons."

"Yeah, I get it. Probably not a smart decision to let the consultant who pulled you out of a hole walk away. Maybe we should let her do her job, so I can do mine. What I don't want is more disruption to this team. We need to focus on winning. And that happens on the ice. I personally don't give a shit what happens outside of this arena, as long as we win hockey games. Now's not the time to lose another player. We're already down one Steele—I can't lose another."

"Agreed…" Prince's voice trails off as he steeples his fingers, glaring at first me, then Weston. "We would be two men down…"

Ford of all people raises his hand, and inwardly I

cringe. He could stand up and tell everyone the truth right now.

He clears his throat. "For what it's worth, Mr. Prince, Coach—I wondered why Weston's been stronger and faster than ever out on the ice. I think maybe I have the answer to his improved performance." Staring straight at me, I blush under his gaze.

A few of the guys nod, shaking their heads. Bennett raises his hand to speak.

"I hesitate to let you say anything, Bennett, since you're on probation. But what do you have to add?" Prince gestures at Bennett.

"I second what Ford said. I've never seen my brother more locked in. You'd be making a huge mistake letting Harbor go. You wanna see someone spiral? Cut her loose."

Prince frowns, his brows scrunched together as he contemplates my fate, the fate of the team.

"Damn it. The two of you put me in a real predicament here. I don't like it one little bit. But after hearing all this, perhaps I was too hasty in my judgment. Harbor, go back to your office and figure out how to make this shine. Weston, stay focused out on the ice and winning the damn Cup this season. The rest of you—stay the hell out trouble and don't make me regret this decision."

With that, he rises and stomps out of the room, Tori trailing behind in her stilettos. Keller follows and the rest of the room bursts into conversation.

But honestly, none of that matters to me.

"Weston—" My voice is breathy, lightness filling my chest.

He says nothing, instead taking one long stride toward me. Hand on my hip, he leans down and presses his lips to mine.

Right here in the conference room, in front of the entire team.

"I love you," I murmur, gazing up at him. The tension vanishes from his face and he breaks into a wide smile, arms wrapping around my waist. Fingers gripping his T-shirt, I melt into his strong body as he holds me tight against him.

Everything about this feels right.

"I love you, Hurricane. And I meant what I said. You mean everything to me."

There's a bright flash, followed by the sound of clapping. I pull away slightly and glance at the circle of guys around us.

Callum, Bennett, Morrison. Even Ford, his lips curving into a smug smile.

"Love looks good on you, Weston." Callum claps Weston on the back and shoots me a shy smile. "Congrats, you two."

"Yeah, congrats, Cap," Morrison says, with Ford right behind.

Members of the team file by, offering their congratulations and saying nice things about me and my work.

The entire time, Weston's arms hold me close, like it's the most natural thing in the world.

He leans in and gives me another long kiss and my heart soars.

"Okay, okay, break it up." Bennett nudges Weston. "We get it, you're officially the Crushers hottest PR nightmare—and our favorite power couple. Want me to post this photo with a hashtag?" He wiggles his brows. "#SteeletheDeal?"

CHAPTER 38
HARBOR

Tonight's the first preseason game, the semi-official kickoff to the season. Despite switching to green tea mid-afternoon, I'm still a bundle of jumpy nerves as I hustle through the tunnel of the arena. Loud music blares, hyping up the crowd during the second intermission. Riptide and Lil Rip skate around the rink, waving to excited children and their families, while the players take a quick break.

I've spent most of the game running around, making sure every last detail is perfect and tonight goes off without a hitch. I managed to catch glimpses of the game here and there. Weston's playing better than ever, scoring one of the team's goals so far. We're beating Portland 2-1 and there's only one period left.

Everything comes down to this moment.

"Harbor, final numbers are in. We hit max capacity in the arena." Julianne's voice crackles through my walkie-talkie, and I heave a sigh of relief.

Driftwood Cove showed up for the Coastal Crushers, even after the leaked videos.

Thank God.

Prince will be happy about that, another great talking point for sponsors.

I depress the side button on the walkie. "Wonderful. Be sure to keep track of all merch sales tonight."

"On it."

"Harbor…" Prince's voice echoes through the tunnel and I spin on my heels to face him, smoothing my hair over my shoulder. Tension's been thick between us since the leaked videos—I need everything to go perfectly tonight.

"Hello. Everything's looking good so far. We're at max capacity."

"So I heard. Good work. At least the local community's showing up."

We stare out at the crowd, a dark blue sea of Coastal Crushers jerseys, and pride surges through me. That's my design the fans are wearing, my mascot the kids love.

"I anticipate strong merch sales tonight, too. And post-game interviews are lined up."

"Fantastic." He bobs his head, the corners of his mouth relaxing. "Seems like we got everything together here at the last minute."

My stomach tightens and I swallow hard, knowing I'm lucky to still be here at all. Weston and Coach Keller saved my job, with a little help from the team.

Prince wanted me gone.

He turns to face me, all business in his suit and tie. "You did good work, Harbor."

Smiling, I adjust the bangles on my wrist, the tension bleeding from my body. Then he nods toward the ice.

"C'mon, let's catch the last period from the glass."

I fall into step behind Prince, the knot in my stomach finally loosening as we step out of the tunnel.

It's more than a seat—it's a statement. A sign of acceptance. Acknowledgment of my place on this team.

A quiet, public nod that I belong. Here, out in the open, where everyone can see.

We slide into our seats behind the glass as the lights flash and the team skates back onto the ice. The crowd roars, a wall of sound, and excitement vibrates through the arena.

Weston skates out last, eyes scanning the rink. Sharp. Searching.

Then he sees me.

His deep blue gaze locks on mine, a slow smile spreading across his face as he glides past and taps the glass twice with his stick.

My breath hitches, heart skipping in my chest.

Weston's mine.

And I am his.

And now the entire world knows it.

No more hiding, no sneaking around.

Weston Steele declared to everyone tonight that we're a couple—and he doesn't care who knows it.

The buzzer blares and the puck flies across the ice. Prince clenches his hands, his whole body swaying in the direction of the black disc with every drive toward the net.

Portland takes a shot and Callum gets wide, his huge body covering most of the goal. He snags the puck in his right glove, making the save.

"Yes!" I cheer along with the crowd.

Both teams play great defense and the score's still 2-1 after eighteen intense minutes.

Then Portland pulls their goalie with one minute left.

Six skaters crash into our zone, passing fast and pressing hard. I glance up at the bright time clock.

Ten seconds. Nine, eight…

A rebound bounces wide, straight toward the corner. Straight toward Weston.

Seven, six…

He snatches the puck, wheeling around and taking off down the ice.

All power and speed, and my heart pounds hard.

Five seconds, four…

He crosses the blue line and flips the puck toward the empty net.

Graceful, effortless.

I hold my breath as the puck slides in just as the buzzer sounds.

The Crushers win and the crowd explodes, blue and white lights flashing.

Weston lifts his stick high in the air and his teammates swarm him. Clapping his back, hugging, and fist bumping, together they celebrate the win. Callum skates out of the goal and bumps Weston's helmet, then embraces his brother in a fierce hug.

Happy tears prick at the corner of my eyes and I blink hard to keep them at bay.

Then Weston glances over at me. Our eyes lock across the rink and my pulse stutters.

The crowd's still on their feet when Weston breaks away from the pack and skates straight toward the bench. My breath hitches as he moves across the ice, never veering.

He skids to a halt in front of the glass, tapping his stick once, twice.

"Get down here," he mouths, and my entire body burns knowing all eyes are on us.

I race toward the gate, heart slamming against my ribs. Before I even make it to the boards, he's reaching over and tugging me onto the ice.

"Weston—"

Dropping his stick, he cups my face in his hands and kisses me like he's been waiting for me his entire life. And he doesn't care who's watching.

Rough. Raw. Real.

The arena erupts. A wolf whistle breaks through the noise, loud and unapologetic.

But we keep kissing, no longer caring.

After a long moment, Weston pulls away and presses his forehead to mine.

"Guess the secret's out," I whisper, breathless.

He grins down at me. "Good. I want everyone to know you're mine." Brushing his thumb lightly across my cheek, he shoots me a wink. "And if anyone has a problem with that, they can take it up with the captain."

CHAPTER 39
BENNETT

oly shit.

I never thought I'd see the day Weston went soft. But here it fucking is.

My brother, the grumpy team captain and the most driven, responsible guy on the planet, pulling his PR hottie onto the ice and kissing her under the bright lights of the arena.

Honestly, it's kinda great.

Almost gives me the warm fuzzies.

If you're into that kind of lovey-dovey bullshit. Which, for the record, I'm definitely not.

"You two getting a room or something?" I tease, elbowing Weston in the tunnel after the game.

Even though I'm still benched, Coach made me sit next to him the entire game in my freaking suit and tie.

At least we won.

"Go away, Puck Bunny," he growls out of the corner of his mouth, mid-lip lock with Harbor.

I chuckle, loosening my tie as I sidle down the long tunnel. Back to *Call of Duty* and my professional exile until the league decides my fate.

Coach Keller doesn't think it'll be too bad—probably only a one or two-game suspension. No biggie.

In the meantime, I'm racking up kills like nobody's business.

"Bennett. My office." Prince pounces on me the second I step foot in the hallway.

My muscles tense, but I play it cool, shoving a hand in my pocket.

"Did you hear from the league?" I match him stride for stride, taking quick steps to keep pace. Despite being at least five inches shorter than me, the man's clearly on a mission.

"No, not yet."

Shit.

If this isn't about the suspension, what the hell does the owner want to talk to me for?

"Uh, okay. What's this about?" I cut my eyes at him, trying to read his expression. All I get is a deep scowl of irritation.

Instead of answering, he holds his office door open and gestures for me to take a seat at his desk.

Right next to his daughter, Tori Prince. The Ice Queen herself, in her signature black blazer and white blouse. Long dark hair and even darker eyes, with those deep scarlet lips.

She'd be a real knockout if she wasn't such an uptight bitch.

This should be fun.

I swagger in, folding my large frame down into the dark leather chair and stretching my long legs out in front of me. Tori scoots away, attempting to put space between us. But she's effectively trapped between the desk and the wall, with nowhere to go.

Glowering at my thick thighs, her eyes flit to mine.

"Do you mind?" She waves her hand over my legs, her smooth voice dripping with disgust.

"Not at all." I shoot her a cheeky grin and don't budge an inch.

"Ugh." She shoves at my knee with her perfectly manicured hand, and I chuckle. Tightening my quad, my leg's basically immobile.

"Neanderthal…" she mutters under her breath.

Prince takes his seat behind the desk and stares at the two of us, hands folded in front of him.

"I can't take much more stress. My cardiologist increased my blood pressure medicine and I'm so fucking wound up I can't sleep."

Now that he mentions it, I do see the slight twitch of his right eye. I chalked it up to a nervous tick, but maybe it's from stress.

"Daddy—" Tori's sympathetic, reaching across the desk and folding her hand over her father's.

"I'd hoped the move down here would be good, calming. Being near the ocean, a fresh start, a new coach. One who isn't fucking my wife." His eyes drift shut for a second, and my knee jiggles up and down.

This is awkward AF.

Not sure why I'm here for all the family bullshit.

Prince sighs, opening his eyes and pinning his cold gaze on me.

"Then we get to Driftwood Cove and Rocky here decides to host fight night and TKO the local bar owner."

"Hey—" I hold my palms up. "It was in defense of our

PR consultant. I'm a hero. I averted an attempted sexual assault."

"Sure." Prince presses his lips together so tightly they turn white. "And now this latest bombshell with the second video."

"I know, Daddy. It's been a rough off-season." Tori bobs her head, managing to at least sound sympathetic to her father's problems.

"Damn right it has. Like I said in the meeting—I can't have any more trouble on this team."

"Agreed, sir." I nod, wanting to seem like a team player.

Because I really need this job and this whole conversation's starting to feel a little like a suspension talk.

Or worse—a trade talk.

That wouldn't be terrible news. Driftwood Cove's kinda boring. But I've never played hockey without Weston and Callum by my side. And I don't particularly want to start now.

"Super. That's why I called you in. Both of you."

I shoot Prince a quizzical look and Tori's dark brows inch up her smooth forehead.

"What are you talking about, Daddy?"

"Starting today, Tori's going to be looking after you, Bennett."

I guffaw and Tori makes a weird, strangled choking sound.

"Excuse me?" I cock my right brow. "With all due respect, sir, I don't need a keeper."

Tori snorts, and I glare over at her.

"What? I don't. I can handle myself."

"Uh-huh. Just like you did at the party? With a sharp left hook to the nose?"

"He deserved it and you know it." I fold my arms across my chest, knowing I'm fully vindicated in that matter. The courts fucking said so.

"Enough." Prince slams his palm on the desk, the sharp sound commanding our silence. "Bennett, you'll be moving into the condos. Everything's arranged. Your condo's directly next to Tori's, so she'll be able to keep tabs on you 24-7."

"What?" Both of our voices rise in unison. Hot panic floods my system, an adrenaline boost I wasn't looking for this afternoon.

"Daddy, I'm going back to New York. We talked about this. Everything's on track here and I need to focus on the business…"

Prince waves his hand through the air, cutting her off. "No, someone else can handle that. I need you here. Now. Protecting our investment." He tips his chin at me. "Someone has to keep an eye on him."

Tori shakes her head, her long, dark hair swishing across the smooth fabric of her blazer.

"No, thanks. Besides, I'm sure his brothers can watch him."

"Are you kidding me? Did you miss the whole captain – PR consultant mess?"

She blows out a breath, then scowls at me. "I haven't babysat since I was twelve."

"Well, good news then. I don't need a damn babysitter." I sit up straight, cracking my knuckles.

"The matter's settled. Tori, here are the keys to Bennett's new apartment. Curfew's nine PM. Every night of the week, except game days." Prince dangles a set of keys, holding them out to his daughter.

"You're joking." My jaw tenses, a vein throbbing at my

temple. Blood roars in my ears and I want to scream. "I'm on fucking lockdown now? You can't do this!"

"If you want to keep your contract, these are the terms, Steele. Take 'em or leave 'em."

I slide my cell from my pocket, scrolling through my contacts. "I'm calling my agent. This is nuts."

"Go ahead. Call. But it's in his best interest for you to be focused on your job—playing hockey. This new living arrangement does just that." Prince's lips curve into an almost-smile and nausea rolls through me.

The Ice Queen's my new damn babysitter.

Could have been a hot scenario when I was thirteen.

Now it's just kinda fucking annoying.

I swallow down the acid rising up my throat and cross my arms over my chest. "Fine. I'll agree to this bogus deal. But only until the league clears me to play."

"No. No way. This arrangement stands until you prove yourself to me—and to Tori. She'll be debriefing me daily. Toe the line and maybe I'll let you out of the penalty box."

I grind my molars, fury simmering in my gut.

"But I wouldn't count on it." Prince sits back, looking smug. Like he just solved a quantum physics problem or some shit.

"Daddy. I have things to do in Manhattan. I can't stay here and run surveillance on this." She waves her hand over me in a large circle, leaving a trail of expensive-smelling floral perfume in her wake.

I snicker. "You're right—I am a lot to handle. Probably above your pay grade."

She sneers at me. "Typical athlete. So full of himself."

"Okay, the two of you can bicker on your own time. You'll be spending a lot of it together."

With a dismissive wave, he shoos us out of his office.

I stand and stalk out, rage bubbling low in my gut.

He can't fucking do this.

I'm a grown man. A professional hockey player.

"I don't need a fucking babysitter," I growl the second we're out of earshot. "Hand over the keys, Princess."

Shoving my palm out, I wait.

Tori glowers at me, her long arms folded across her jacket.

"Not a chance in hell, Steele."

"What? You just said you don't babysit."

She dangles the keys in front of me, inches from my face.

"You're right, I don't. Consider me your warden until further notice."

Then she jerks the keys away and shoves them into her pocket, a sly grin pulling up her lips. "If I'm forced to do this, I'm going to at least elicit the maximum amount of pain."

Spinning on her stilettos, she click-clacks down the hallway, her tight little ass swaying side to side.

If I wasn't so pissed off, I'd maybe consider checking her out.

But not now.

Not with my blood boiling, fists balling at my side.

She thinks she can handle me?

She has no idea she just invited the fire in.

Because if I'm stuck with the Ice Queen...I'm not just gonna melt her down.

I'm gonna make her beg for the burn.

Game on, Princess.

. . .

Pre-order BAD BOY BREAKAWAY now!

Want an invitation to Weston and Harbor's wedding? Sign up for my newsletter to get the bonus scene!

All caught up on Driftwood Cove?
Check out the Peachtree Grove series!

CHAPTER ONE

Bree

Pacing the terrazzo floor of Terminal Three at LAX, I scowled with annoyance at my silent phone.

Crickets.

Pax, my soon-to-be-ex-boyfriend, was ignoring my barrage of angry texts.

Two days ago I'd seen a suspicious tweet from a twit named Keely: *Had the best night w/ @PaxJones!* But my breaking point was an Instagram pic of Pax kissing a rando girl smack on the lips.

It could have been a scene from his upcoming movie,

but I didn't think so. He'd told me he was in Montana, filming scenes for his next big film, a Western flick starring him as a gorgeous-but-lonely cowboy. But the background in the photo appeared to be the Pacific Ocean, and even though I'd never been to Montana, I was pretty certain that's NOT what it looked like.

I immediately did some digging and sure enough, that asshole was in Laguna Beach, staying at the Ritz. And he definitely wasn't alone, judging by the amount of Veuve and spa treatments charged to his room.

"Final boarding call for Flight 4356 to Atlanta, GA. All remaining passengers should board at this time."

I hesitated, took a deep breath. If I was going to flee LA and the paparazzi, I had to get on this plane. Any second now, the disastrous headlines could hit:

Relationship expert Bree Hart is no 'expert' when it comes to her own love life

Superstar Paxton Jones leaves so-called 'dating doctor' for B-list actress

Relationship guru Bree Hart left brokenhearted by actor Paxton Jones

Gah. I so did *not* want those headlines to hit. My dating podcast was finally trending, and I'd just made it into the Top 25 in the Relationship Category. This could devastate my career. Never mind my heart—Pax had already broken that several times.

I'd been trying (unsuccessfully) to dump Pax for the last 24 hours. Timing was everything and I wanted to break up with him before the media got wind of a cheating scandal. Then I'd disappear for a bit, under the guise of visiting my sister. Pax could step out with someone new, and I'd fade into the background, yesterday's news.

But, per the usual, Pax was even making breaking up

difficult. He wasn't answering my texts or calls, probably because he was too busy with his new sidepiece.

"Seriously. This is the last and final boarding call." The ticketing agent shot me a pointed look. I was the only person still standing at the gate.

Taking the not-so-subtle hint, I wheeled my suitcase over to the kiosk and presented my ticket.

"Have a safe flight."

"Thanks," I said, juggling my shoulder bag and luggage.

As I made my way down the ramp, my shoulder vibrated. Crap. That could be Pax, finally calling me back. I rooted through my bag and managed to fish out my phone.

"Hello? Hello?"

Silence. I checked the screen. One missed call and it was from Pax.

"Damn it!" I immediately hit his name, calling him back. One ring, two rings, three, four. Pax's voice came on the line, *"You know what to do. Leave me a message."*

"Hey, Pax, it's me, Bree. So, I saw your Instagram and it looks like you're with someone else. Not going to lie, I'm pretty upset and it's really uncool that you're not even answering my texts. But whatever. Obviously, you've moved on. I'm not going to stall here or anything, I'm just going to come right out and say it. We're—"

"Good-bye."

Seriously? Even Pax's *voicemail* was too busy for me. I dialed him back. I needed to get this off my chest this instant, so I could move on with my life and avert career disaster.

Ring, ring, ring. *Beep. "Sorry, but the voicemail box is full.*

Call back later." And with that, I was automatically disconnected.

"Ugh!" I cried, shaking my phone. "All I want to do is dump you!"

I slammed my phone back into my purse and looked up. Two flight attendants flanked the doorway to the plane and they were both staring at me.

"Boyfriend problems," I explained, a hot blush creeping over my face. They both nodded knowingly.

"Girl, who doesn't?" The attendants whispered something to each other, then glanced back at me. The one on the right ushered me over and checked my ticket.

"You're in Seat 2B now," she said, winking as she took my ticket. "We ladies need to stick together. Enjoy your flight."

"Thanks," I said, smiling in gratitude. "I will."

Breaking up with Pax would have to wait until I landed. I intended to take full advantage of first class while I had the chance.

———

As soon as the plane touched down in Atlanta, I powered up my phone to a string of missed texts from Pax:

"Babe. It's not what you think w/ Keely. But if you want to pump the brakes, that's cool."

"Life is too short to be unhappy."

And my personal fave:

"Could you still pick my laundry up at the cleaners? Thx."

Asshole, I thought, collecting my rollaboard and deplaning. *What did I ever see in that jerk? He couldn't even bother to call, just left me a bunch of texts, like a freaking middle schooler.*

I sighed and shook my head, exasperated at my terrible choice in men. Like most of my clients, I blamed it on my parents. If my dad hadn't skipped out on us when I was only eight, maybe I'd be better at this relationship thing. Probably not, but maybe.

Making my way over to the rental car area, I signed my life away for the opportunity to motor around the greater Atlanta area in a mid-sized Chevy Malibu. I collected the keys, dashed off a quick text to my sister, Brooklyn, and hit I-85, happy to be away from the prying eyes of the paparazzi.

———

Three minutes after I arrived at my sister's, she tasked me with afternoon chauffeur duty for my niece. Destination: Pee Wee football practice. Fine by me—it kept me busy and, frankly, I didn't have much else to do.

"Alexa, do you have your mouthguard? Water bottle?" I asked, popping the car door open for her.

"Yes, Aunt Bee, see?" She held up her pink mouthguard and water bottle as proof.

"Great. Then let's go." I shoved her mouthguard into my handbag and clicked the lock button on my key fob, although I highly doubted anyone would steal my car.

After all, we *were* in Peachtree Grove, Georgia. AKA, Smalltown, USA, home of the Peach Cobbler Festival and approximately 10,000 people, most of whom were born and would die in Peachtree Grove. My sister and her husband were two of the few "newcomers," meaning they'd only lived here for the last five or so years. (They wouldn't be considered "locals" until Alexa had children, probably.) Brooks moved when Alexa was a baby so her husband, Dr. Craig Williams, could be closer to the hospital at Emory, where he was both a prominent doctor and a professor. When she'd first described Peachtree Grove to me, I thought she was exaggerating, but then I came to visit. It was definitely a shock to my jaded LA system. No flashy cars or movie stars here. Just high school football. Which, by the way, is an actual, legitimate season. Seriously. It's *printed on calendars*, like the 4th of July and Easter. In Peachtree Grove, Friday is for football, Saturday is for football, and Sunday is for church and football. Weekdays are for work and football practice. Rinse and repeat.

Which I guess is why my niece loves football. And why I now found myself standing on a plushy field with tons of other pee wee players and their parents, looking for the head coach of the—what did Brooks say the name of Alex's team was?—oh yes, the Lions.

Holding my hand to my forehead, I shielded my eyes from the sun. Even with sunglasses on, it was still too bright to see across the field. Ah, September in the South.

"Is that them, over there?" I pointed to a group of about ten kids on a big square marked with a #4 sign, two fields over on the right. "That might be the coach, wearing the blue shirt." His back was to us, but his jersey said "Coach." An excellent tipoff. I *so* had this aunt thing down.

"Yeah, that's my friend Cole." Alexa nodded, then took off in a sprint towards the group, deftly dodging clumps of boys, all Alexa-sized.

"Wait up!" I called, doing my best fast walk across the fields. It was futile; she was already way ahead of me. *I should have worn sneakers. Oh well, at least I'm not wearing heels and I go to the gym.*

When I finally caught up to Alexa, I was a little out of

breath and perspiration beaded on my brow. Flipping my hair over my shoulder, I fanned myself with one hand. I slid in with the group of moms hanging out on the side-lines, just behind the man in the blue Coach shirt. Alexa and all the other kids were in a big cluster, facing the coach.

"Okay, guys, it looks like everyone's here," the coach announced in a loud voice, doing a quick once-over of the Pee Wees.

"What's your name?" He pointed at Alexa.

"Alexa Williams," she said in a soft voice. The other kids chittered away, while Alexa stared down at her sneakers and kicked at a clump of grass.

"Hmmm, I don't see that name on my roster." The coach went down the names on his clipboard. "Oh, here. Alex Williams?"

She nodded up at him with wide blue eyes.

"I'm her aunt." I gave a little wave and stepped forward to clear up any misunderstanding.

The coach turned towards me and my breath caught in my throat.

Coach was drop-dead gorgeous.

He reached his hand out to me and I shook it, noting he had very large, strong hands. He was super tall, probably 6'3", and had deep marine eyes with long, dark lashes. Dark hair, cropped short, and he looked like he'd be ripped.

"Does she go by Alex or Alexa?"

"What?"

"Your niece. Does she prefer Alex or Alexa?" he asked, nodding in her direction.

"Oh. Um, Alex. Or Alexa. I think she likes Alexa." My

voice trailed off as my cheeks burned. *Really, Bree? You don't even know which name your niece prefers?*

"I like Alex," Alexa piped up. "Call me Alex."

Coach grinned over at Alexa, showing off perfectly straight, white teeth. A dentist's dream.

"I'm Ryder, by the way. Ryder McCauliffe." He smiled at me and I noticed he had very cute dimples and a nice square jaw. This man was fine.

"I'm Bree. Bree Hart. Alexa's, er, Alex's aunt," I corrected myself, shoving my hands into my back pockets. *Super awkward.* "I'm gonna just stand over here," I motioned to the group of mingling parents, chatting with each other and ignoring me. "And watch."

"Sounds good, Bree." He grinned at me again as I backed away toward the sideline, torn between wanting to crawl into a hole and die or watch this beautiful man coach Pee Wee football.

Coach Ryder turned towards the Pee Wees. "Does everyone have their mouthguards?" Eleven kids nodded yes, while Alexa shot me a pointed look.

"Oh yes, I have that!" I fumbled in my bag, produced the mouthguard.

Running back out to the field, I handed it to my niece, willing myself not to trip or otherwise further embarrass myself. I felt Ryder's eyes on me. Swiveling back around, I wished fervently for the safety of the sidelines. I was clearly out of my league here.

"Okay, so guys, how many of you have played football before?" Coach Ryder asked the kids. All twelve hands shot up in excitement.

"Great! We're gonna be a great team then. And on my team—your team—we all have to follow a couple rules.

My number one rule is be safe. How do you think we can do that?"

I filed that away; I'd have to tell my sister as soon as we got home. Safety first here at Pee Wee football!

Oh shoot, I never called her to tell her we got to the field. Grabbing my phone, I tapped out a quick text:

> Made it. We're all good. And Coach
> is HOT

I hit send and listened to Ryder talk about rule number two, be kind and show good sportsmanship.

Brooklyn: What's coach's name?

> Bree: Ryder McCauliffe

Brooklyn: THE Ryder McCauliffe?

> Bree: ????

Brooklyn: You know. Former NFL Wide Receiver for the Dallas Cowboys. High school hotshot. Played at UGA, then drafted by Dallas. First round

> Bree: Um, obvi I did NOT know or maybe would have taken more than like 10 secs to get ready

Brooklyn: You're definitely calling things off with Pax, right?

Bree: Yes. I mean, I tried. I *think* we're broken up

Brooklyn: He's single, you know. Wink-wink

Bree: I didn't ask

Brooklyn: You didn't have to. I'm your sister

Bree: Am I that transparent? Geez, I hope I have a better game face than that

Brooklyn: His kid is probably on the team

Bree: Wha-what?!?!

Brooklyn: Yeah, cute kid. Think his name is Charlie. Or something like that

Bree: So you're telling me this hot pro baller is a Single. Dad.?!?!

Brooklyn: Yep. Look around. How many very attractive women are attending football practice right now?

I glanced around and did a quick mental survey. There were several blondes in tight spandex leggings gathered together, another pretty brunette on her phone (snapping a photo or two?), and one intense dad with a clipboard, taking notes.

Bree: Yes, loads

Brooklyn: He's a local celeb. I'm sure
women throw themselves at him. All. Day.
Long.

Bree: I can see why

Inwardly, I groaned. Of course they would. And I'd embarrassed myself already, within the first two minutes of meeting the guy. Mental head smack.

"And our last team rule is to have fun. Because if we do all of those things, we'll be winners! Now I want you guys to put your hands in here, like this," Ryder demonstrated, dropping his hand into the middle of all the kids, "and on the count of three say 'Go Lions! Roar!' Ready? One, two, three!" All the kids yelled out "Go Lions" and did their best roar, which was adorable. Cue heart melt. I glanced around and noticed several of the moms videoing the speech. Oh brother. This guy was a freaking saint.

Ryder had the kids run some drills, so I took the opportunity to find my way to the bleachers and do a quick Google search. A few taps and I had the dude's (Wikipedia) life history:

Age: 32

Height: 6'4" (I shorted him an inch. Shame on me.)

Weight: 220 lbs

Position: Wide receiver

Stats: Football superstar at Peachtree Grove High School, helping lead the team to state victory with 18 touchdowns his senior year. Recruited by University of Georgia (2004-2008), where he played first string Wide Receiver all four years. Team went on to win

Nationals. First round draft pick in 2008. Signed with Dallas, #18, where he continued to play wide receiver position. Five successful seasons as starter for Dallas, including one trip to Super Bowl. Shoulder injury in sixth season left him benched. Retired in 2014.

No mention of personal life, relationship, kid. A few more taps, though, and I had additional dirt.

Ryder McCauliffe and Dallas cheerleader Shayna Bowman tie the knot in lavish multimillion-dollar wedding

Ryder McCauliffe and Dallas cheerleader wife welcome son

Dallas Wide Receiver Ryder McCauliffe and cheerleader wife on the rocks

Dallas cheerleader Shayna McCauliffe files charges of domestic abuse against former pro player-husband Ryder McCauliffe

Former Dallas Wide Receiver McCauliffe calls it quits with cheerleader wife

Sounded like a train wreck. I clicked through the articles, taking in as much info as possible.

There were a few photos of Ryder when he was playing for the team, looking about the same as he did now.

An article about his shoulder injury, sustained during game eight of his sixth season with Dallas. Separated shoulder, requiring multiple surgeries. He sat the bench the rest of the season, then was cut from the team.

Then it looked like his life pretty much fell apart. Domestic abuse charges filed, but he was later cleared of all charges. Divorce looming, nasty custody battle.

From what I read, it seemed like Ryder had full custody and the articles alleged possible substance abuse by Shayna. I zoomed in on every photo of her. She was pretty. Very cheerleader. Chesty. Dark, straight hair, wide smile, curvy in all the right places. Perfect abs. *Just like me,* I thought wryly. Dumb to even compare myself, we were nothing alike. She was taller than me, curvier than me, definitely bustier than me. I had long, blondish hair with a slight wave, her hair was stick straight, and in most photos she had bangs.

It seemed like she was in it for the money. As soon as Ryder got cut from the team, she started the separation proceedings, which led to the divorce. *Bad situation for his kid*, I thought.

Just for fun, I did a quick Google search on Shayna McCauliffe. The same articles popped up, plus her LinkedIn page, describing her as a Dallas Cheerleader/Lifestyle Expert. Interesting plot twist, considering the drug allegations. There was an article about her dating one of the League owners, as well as the Defensive Coordinator. The girl got around, and she definitely had a type. Rich, with athletic being a bonus.

There was only the one mention of their son, Charlie, in the article about his birth. None of the Shayna articles mentioned the child at all and there were zero photos of him. Seemed like Ryder did his best keeping his private life private. I respected that. It was one of my (many) issues with Pax.

"Aunt Bee! Aunt Bee!" Across the field, Alexa jumped up and down, waving me over.

"Coming!" I waved back to her and bounced off the bleachers, taking the steps as quickly as I could. Most of the other moms were already gathered around Ryder, hanging on his every word. I hoped whatever he was saying wasn't critical; I wanted to make sure I got all the information for Brooks. She'd get an email about it, though, right?

Just as I was closing in on our team's huddle, a sharp pain hit me in my left knee. Next thing I knew, I was flat on my back in the soft grass, staring up at the blue sky. *Hmmm, very few clouds today...*

"Are you alright?"

I blinked several times; I wasn't sure if the blurriness was from the sun beaming directly into my eyes or from the blow to the back of my head. Eventually, Ryder's eyes came into focus, tiny wrinkles of concern forming around them. *Cute...*

"Uh, yeah, I think so." I tried to sit up, but Ryder put his hand on my shoulder, gently keeping me still.

"Wait a few seconds. Trust me on this, lots of experience getting tackled." He winked and my cheeks flushed crimson.

"K," I murmured. "Um, what happened? Did I really get tackled?"

"Yeah. A nine-year-old laid you out. Not sure you're gonna make the first-round draft picks this year. You may need a little more work on your game," he chuckled, guiding me up by my elbow.

"How's that feel? Are you dizzy at all?" He gazed deep into my eyes, trying to gauge my concussion risk, I supposed.

"Aunt Bee, are you okay?" Alexa stood by my side, furrows creasing her brow.

"No, not dizzy. I'm fine. I'll be okay, Alexa." I waved my hands to brush off their concern and demonstrate my fineness. I bent my knees to try to stand and involuntarily let out a tiny whimper. "Ouch," I whispered under my breath.

"Let me take a look, I'm a physical therapist by day." He poked and prodded my knee, bending it this way and that. "You're going to need to ice that when you get home. That will minimize the swelling."

"Swelling?" I asked in a panicky voice.

"Yeah. That kid ran straight into your knee." He pointed to the side of my left kneecap. "You'll probably be okay, but it's going to bruise and you could have a microtear. Why don't you come into the clinic tomorrow and I'll take a closer look, reassess the situation?" Ryder tilted his head, waiting for my response.

"I'll be fine." I waved my hand again, brushing off his concern.

"I insist. Plus, I have a knee brace, or at the very least, a wrap to decrease swelling." He touched the side of my knee to demonstrate the wrapping motion and a tingle ran up my leg. That was a good sign, no numbness or loss of feeling. And clearly my libido hadn't sustained any injury.

"Okay, I'll come in," I said.

"Great. I'll give you my card and you can drop in around lunchtime. We're usually pretty slow then."

"Cool. I mean, great, thanks." I blushed, stumbling over my words. Maybe I did have a slight concussion.

Some of the other moms were shooting me dirty looks, like I'd ruined practice, and the kids were getting rowdy since the coach wasn't looking.

"You better get back." I nodded my head towards the group.

"Let me help you up." Deftly, Ryder leaned in and scooped me up, wrapping one of his arms around my waist and putting almost all my bodyweight onto his strong shoulders. The kids cheered; several of the blonde moms rolled their eyes. *So much for good sportsmanship*, I thought.

He gave them a wave with his right hand and together we limped to my rental car, Alexa trotting behind. My close proximity to Ryder helped block out the shooting pain in my knee. He smelled fantastic, crisp and clean, despite having run practice in eighty-five-degree weather. I'd been right about his hands—they were large and strong, supporting me at my waist. His pec muscles were straining underneath his shirt, yet he moved effortlessly through the parking lot, as if I weighed nothing. I tried not to swoon.

"This is it." I nodded at the white Malibu, fumbling in my purse for the keys. I had to lean into him to get to my purse and I fully appreciated his strong, muscled chest against my side. He gripped my waist tighter while I searched, so I wouldn't topple over.

"Here they are." I dangled the keys, unlocked the car.

"Are you alright to drive?" Ryder asked, concern clouding his eyes.

"Yep, perfectly fine," I nodded, stifling a wince. He opened Alex's door first, then mine, easing me down gently into the seat. His face was so close to mine, I saw his five-o-clock shadow. My breath hitched and we locked eyes for a moment. A frisson of heat shimmered down my body as I gazed at the darker navy flecks in his eyes.

"Sure you're okay?"

"Right as rain," I sing-songed in my most cheerful voice, nodding.

In reality, I could barely hear him over the thumping of my racing heartbeat. No, I was definitely *not* okay.

I was crushing hard on Peachtree Grove's most eligible bachelor, Ryder McCauliffe, former pro football player and hot-as-hell single dad.

Read RUSHING INTO LOVE now!

ALSO BY KARA KENDRICK

Brides & Birdies

HOLIDAY NOVELLAS

Christmas in Cayman

Mr. Right Under the Mistletoe

My Charming Holidate

Snowed In With the Scrooge

BILLIONAIRE SERIES

Charming the CEO

Flirt Like a (Fake) Groom

HEART OF A WOUNDED HERO SERIES

Soldier On: Heart of a Wounded Hero

WILD BROTHERS SERIES

Forever Wild

Find them all at www.karakendrick.com

Kara Kendrick writes fun and flirty small-town and sports romance destined to give you all the feels. A reformed English major, she also has a master's in counseling and was an elementary school counselor in her pre-mom life.

She loves the beach, wine, and rock-hard abs, not necessarily in that order. When she's not dreaming up Happily Ever After's, you can find her chasing after her boy-girl twins, working out semi-hardish, or walking her adorable Shiba pups with her husband, who's not too bad himself.

Let's be friends! Sign up for the VIP newsletter and be the first to hear about upcoming releases, promos, and giveaways.

If you enjoyed reading this book, please help spread the word by leaving a review on Amazon, Goodreads, Booktok, Instagram, Bookbub, Facebook Reader Groups, or wherever you talk spicy romance books!

To stay in touch, visit www.karakendrick.com

ACKNOWLEDGMENTS

Deepest gratitude to all the people involved in helping me put this book out into the world:

My alpha readers, Jana and Krysta; Valentine Grinstead and the entire Valentine PR team; Nicole McCurdy at Emerald Edits; Beth Hale, line editor; Emily Wittig, cover designer; Hannah, Ashley, and Anais, beta readers; and my social media team, Cassie and Jackie. And a huge thanks to my ARC team and all the bookstagrammers and bloggers who took a chance on me.

Last, but never least, thank you to my home team—Lance, Luke, and Kinsey. I love you all and am so grateful for the opportunity to pursue my passion. Xoxo.

www.ingramcontent.com/pod-product-compliance
Lightning Source LLC
Chambersburg PA
CBHW071917130726
47909CB00014B/2055